I AM NOT WHO YOU THINK I AM

ALSO BY ERIC RICKSTAD

I AM NOT WHO YOU THINK I AM

ERIC RICKSTAD

BLACK STONE

PUBLISHING

Copyright © 2021 by Eric Rickstad
Published in 2021 by Blackstone Publishing
Cover design by Kathryn Galloway English
Book design by Amy Craig

Printed in the United States of America

First edition: 2021
ISBN 978-1-0940-0033-6
Fiction / Thrillers / Suspense

Version 1

CIP data for this book is available
from the Library of Congress

Blackstone Publishing
31 Mistletoe Rd.
Ashland, OR 97520

www.BlackstonePublishing.com

For my mother
Beth Rickstad
February 1, 1930–May 23, 2020

And in memory of Mark Harril Saunders
1966–2019
Your wisdom and friendship are missed every day.

POLICE DEPARTMENT

To Protect and To Serve

April 15, 2020

Dear Shireburne citizens:

The following manuscript came to our attention by regular U.S. mail from a former Shireburne citizen previously believed to have died in a fire known to many citizens as the Inferno of 1984.

As servants to the town, we faced obstacles, both legal and ethical, before we felt confident we could release it to you, as is our duty; the manuscript being addressed to the town, after all.

After considerable effort to verify authenticity, we now release copies to you. The original is on file at the Town Clerk's Office. (You may ask May Hitchcock at the desk to see it.)

Some citizens who are mentioned in the manuscript, and who are still living, have already seen it in confidence, to help confirm or deny particulars prior to release. Because of the sensitive and sometimes disturbing and private nature of the manuscript, and because of an ongoing investigation, those citizens who saw it early were asked not to divulge to anyone their knowledge of it until we released it. We hope you appreciate our need of such steps and show these citizens, some of whom may be friends or family, understanding.

Attached to the manuscript, which was handwritten but has

been transcribed for readability, were newspaper articles, and two notes. Copies of the notes, which were also handwritten, remain handwritten because of their brevity.

We will provide updates on this matter as they develop.

Serving you,

James Kirkpatrick

James Kirkpatrick
Chief of Police
Shireburne Police Department
Shireburne, Vermont

DEAR TOWN OF SHIREBURNE,

IF YOU REMEMBER ME AT ALL, YOU REMEMBER THE SHY, SLIGHT, DISCOMFITED, AND FATHERLESS SOUL KNOWN TO INHABIT EVERY LITTLE NOTHING TOWN LIKE OURS; THE GHOST BOY SLOUCHED IN THE CORNER AND PEERING OUT WITH ANXIOUS EYES, AFFIXED IN THE FRONT SEAT OF THE SCHOOL BUS TO EVADE HIS TORMENTORS, CLUTCHING HIS CACHE OF POE AND GOREY AND JACKSON AND SHELLEY TO HIS CHEST AS IF CLINGING TO THE SIDE OF A LIFEBOAT THAT'S TAKING ON FAR MORE WATER THAN CAN EVER BE BAILED.

THE QUIET ONE: INVISIBLE AS AN EXPELLED BREATH AND BORN HALFWAY DOWN THE CRACKS THROUGH WHICH HE IS DESTINED TO SLIP.

BUT WHO AMONG YOU REALLY REMEMBERS ME ANYWAY?

AS MUCH AS I'LL WAGER YOU DON'T REMEMBER ME, I'LL WAGER THAT YOU DO REMEMBER THE VANDERS MANSION BURNING TO THE GROUND THAT NIGHT OF THE INFERNO THAT LEFT THE DARK WESTWARD SKY THROBBING AN ORGASMIC ORANGE AND LITTERED ITS ASHES ACROSS TOWN AS AN ANGELIC, BLACK SNOW. I'LL WAGER THAT NIGHT IS AS SEARED INTO YOUR BRAIN AS SURELY AS THE MANSION'S FOUNDATION IS CHARRED INTO THE HILLSIDE THAT OVERLOOKS FORBIDDEN LAKE.

BUT.

BUT, BUT, BUT.

THERE IS ALWAYS A BUT.

WHEN I TELL YOU WHAT I AM ABOUT TO TELL YOU, YOU WILL SUDDENLY, VIVIDLY "REMEMBER" ME:

OH, YES. I REMEMBER HIM. I REMEMBER.

HE RODE MY BUS.

HE SAT BEHIND ME IN CLASS.

HE SENT ME A LOVE NOTE (WHICH I BELITTLED UNTIL HE WILTED IN THE CORNER WITH RED—FACED SHAME).

I ALWAYS HAD HIM PEGGED AS THE TYPE.

BUT YOU COULDN'T HAVE. IF YOU HAD, YOU'D HAVE TOLD SOMEONE. YOU'D HAVE DONE SOMETHING. YOU'D HAVE HELPED ME.

OR STOPPED ME.

FIRST THINGS FIRST

1976

What I need you to understand first is that my father was a good man. He was not that father conjured up in mass-market paperbacks: that mad, cruel, belittling, wife-beating drunkard, dredged up from the basement of Fiction 101 to explain away the wounded protagonist's maligned and fateful existence.

No. My father was a gentle, prim, fastidious man. Emotionally reserved at times, perhaps, though no more so than other men of his stripe who came of age after World War II. He was a barber who operated his business out of a single-chair shop. He wore his hair shorn close as suede nap; his side part as sharp as the edge of his gleaming straight razor. He smelled of hair tonic and talcum powder, and his hands were pale and soft and warm. He rose every Monday through Saturday to eat a breakfast of two eggs, sunny-side up, two slices of toasted Wonder Bread, and three strips of bacon, crisp, washed back with a piping-hot cup of Folgers and a tumbler of cold OJ from concentrate. Finished, he'd dab the corner of his mouth with a paper napkin and give a clear-eyed *thank you, dear* to my mother as he pushed back his chair and set to buffing his Thom McAns until their faux black leather shone like a shellacked beetle shell. He'd grab his steel lunch box, packed with two deviled-ham sandwiches and two dill pickles, venture out to his GMC stepside, and drive to work. He'd appear again at 6:00 p.m., when my mother had some casserole or loaf waiting. This was his routine, his life, Monday through Saturday. He never missed a day. He never once raised his voice or his hand to me or to my sister, and never, ever to my mother. Not that I remember, anyway.

What I do remember of my parents from that time is their affection for each other. It was genuine, gentle, pure, and, at times, for a young boy, embarrassing. Often in the evenings, after supper, my mother would curl up in my father's lap as he relaxed in his easy chair before he settled in to read. She'd rest her head on his shoulder, touch his brow with her fingertips. Many times, too, when my mother was at the kitchen sink, my father would come to stand behind her, wrap his arms around her waist, rest his chin on her shoulder, and the two of them would sway in place to a tune only they heard.

I have pieced together enough to know that what happened on the day of the Incident was not done because he was a bad man. A bad father. It was done because . . . well, we'll get to that. This isn't some magic trick where the secret machinations are kept hidden. No. This is all about the reveal. The truth. And we will get to it. We will.

But first, let me set the scene that may lead you to believe that my father was a bad or troubled man, even while I assure you that he was not. My father was a good man, and he loved me.

Of this, I am almost certain.

FIREWORKS

My stomach felt rotted out from the cotton candy I'd hogged down at the Autumn Carnival the previous evening, and before I knew it, I was puking liquefied sugar on my third-grade classroom's carpet, my guts feeling as scraped out as a Halloween pumpkin.

The nurse called my house, but my mother wasn't there as she ought to have been, so the nurse sent me packing the five blocks home. That's what they did back then: sent you packing.

When I arrived home, my father's pickup truck sat idling in the driveway.

What do you want me to tell you? That as soon as I saw his truck, I sensed a corrosive dread, an implacable horror? I wish I could tell you that is how it was, that I stopped dead with fear, but I can't. There's a blank there. You'd think instead there would be a blank for what came next. But no. I seem to have been born without the DNA for self-preservation.

What I *can* tell you is that his truck idled in the driveway, its driver's door left open as John Denver's "Back Home Again" floated from inside the house, out the open front door, and across the yard. The front door being open should perhaps have triggered foreboding in me as well.

Then I was inside the living room. I don't remember entering the house. Suddenly, I was just *there*. John Denver's singing died, and the record player's needle crackled and spat endlessly in its final groove.

"Dad," I said, or at least, I think I said.

I crept down the hall, the skipping record needle a threadbare heartbeat, heard through a weak ham-radio signal from half a galaxy away: *cssusshh, cssusshh, cssusshh.*

The door to my parents' bedroom stood open. Through it, I eyed him from behind, slouched on the edge of my parents' bed, his back to me.

"Dad," I said.

Something was wrong. Terribly. Irrevocably. I could sense it, smell it, hear it in the sinister silence. Terror sheared through me. My stomach lurched. I felt like I would vomit again, yet nothing remained inside me. My guts heaved anyway, a violent convulsion I thought might rend loose my aorta. The bedroom walls throbbed, and I listed, greasy with sickness, as if I'd stepped from a carnival ride and my body had not yet acclimated to gravity as the world spun on its cockeyed axis.

"Dad," I whispered, my mouth dry as bone dust.

I edged toward his side of the bed.

I saw his feet, dangling above the floor like the feet of a little boy. I knew he was suffering. This fact was as plain as the shotgun propped against his knees and pointing under his chin.

"*Dad,*" I said, and reached out for him.

The shotgun went off.

I shut my eyes and stood disembodied in a soundless, senseless vacuum. Hot blood speckled my lips. I tasted its copper as I stood there with my eyes closed for an eternity, and then stood there for an eternity more. A part of me, that boy, still stands there and will stand there forever. Unmoving. Unfeeling. Unalive. We speak of zombies as the undead, but I discovered in that moment that the true zombies are unalive.

My ears rang from the blast—a high, eardrum-piercing whine, like that of a wet finger traced along the rim of a crystal glass. I peeled my eyelids open, their lashes gummed with blood. I could not look at him. Instead, I looked out the window at our street, where the autumn sun shone golden, and the trees swayed softly in the breeze, oblivious to my ruin.

I wanted to swallow the world whole. Anger boiled in me, and grief swelled like a tsunami out in the middle of the mindless Pacific, invisible to the innocents on shore, yet out there nonetheless, gathering intensity, blind and unfeeling and utterly unstoppable.

I lifted my eyes to the ceiling, to see scarlet fireworks that would have been spectacular had they not been made of gore.

I looked at the floor and saw it: that small square slip of paper, as white as sun-bleached bone, that would be the instrument of my eventual desolation.

"Oh," I said. Or, I think I said. I don't know, to be honest. But that's what I hear in my head all these years later as I write this. After all, I was only eight. What do you recall with certainty from when you were eight? Anything? Anything at all? I might have been howling my throat ragged, for all I know.

Whatever horrors visited me that day, whatever disease was passed that infects my blood no matter the words I write to make sense of it, there is one thing that will trouble me forever about that day: the note.

I picked it up and read those eight words, the *first* evidence that made me believe that not all was as it seemed. I folded the note and slipped it into my pocket. Later, I would secret it away in a box in the rear of my closet, and not look at it again for nearly eight years. Even now, I don't know why I kept it or hid it. I did not understand what it meant. Those eight words were as inscrutable as Sanskrit to me.

But later, after my father had been taken away in a silent ambulance, my mother asked me if there was a note, imploring me to tell the truth, as if she *knew* there was a note, I gazed at her unblinking, and I lied. No. No note.

Some instinct told me this was the right thing to say. The safe thing. Though I'd wish later that I'd said *Yes. Here it is. Take it. Please. Just take the rotten, poisonous thing*, and thrust it into her hand and let her deal with it and been rid of it forever. None of what followed would ever have happened if I'd given her the note, and she'd read those eight words for herself. But I didn't.

And so, here we are.

IN MEMORIAM

My father's closed casket sat balanced atop what I imagined was a solid marble altar concealed beneath a flow of white linen. My mother had not wanted me there, but I'd begged her, ground down her will until she'd succumbed. "Lydia stays with the sitter," she'd said, speaking of my six-year-old sister.

In the viewing room, mourners stood in knots of three and four, stooping to whisper in each other's ears, kissing cheeks, and squeezing each other's hands. Their faces were shattered and eyes empty with sorrow even as another, more potent emotion that I could not describe tightened the corners of their mouths.

I was the sole child present, all but invisible to the adults. When I *was* spied, looks of pity and anguish darkened the faces of the attendees as they forced smiles and whispered what a brave boy I was.

Brave? *Brave?*

The mourners flocked around my mother, mumbled condolences, hugged her, and grazed their lips against her bloodless cheeks.

Mr. Kane, who had been my second-grade classroom teacher, stood at the casket, his palms placed flat on the lid and moving over it, as if searching for a secret seam into which he could force his fingertips. It was as if he wanted to pry open the lid and check for certain that my father's corpse rested inside. Mr. Kane was my father's friend, perhaps his *only* friend, as far as I knew. Sometimes, he came for dinner at our house with his wife. More recently, he came for dinner at our house without his wife. I always felt a dissociation when I saw him in our home. He seemed as out of context there as a frog in a snowstorm. On his visits he did not look or act like the Mr. Kane I knew, and my father called him Henry. The first time he entered our home and said to me, "Wayland, what's shaking?" and roughed up my hair, I had no idea who he was, until my mom said, "Aren't you going to say hello to Mr. Kane?" He would chortle and give me a high five, which he never did in school. At school he was staid in his pleated chinos, his starched collared shirt, his skinny ties, and his oval wire-rimmed eyeglasses. At our house the eyeglasses were gone, and he wore faded, torn jeans, and T-shirts that bore images of exploding zeppelins, Campbell's soup cans, and dancing skeletons. The neat side part in his hair was now untamed curls that reminded me of pencil shavings. Somehow, his disheveled dress and garrulous manner in our home made me feel both embarrassed for him and disappointed in him. It seemed impossible that both versions of Mr. Kane could be real. One had to be phony. Which one, I did not know.

What I did know was that when he visited our house, Mr. Kane made my father laugh as no one else could. I'd seen my father slap him on the back and call him a son of a bitch in a way that I could only infer as a high compliment. My father liked Mr. Kane, and I believed that Mr. Kane liked my father.

At the casket, I stepped closer to Mr. Kane. Squat white candles ringed the coffin, their yellow flames jigging in a draft leaking through the funeral home's ancient windows. A tear dripped from Mr. Kane's nose and extinguished a candle flame with a hiss. A tendril of smoke twisted into the air, followed by a whiff of cinder and paraffin. I wondered whether Mr. Kane was crying for my father or for me, because he had been the first person to show up at our house after my mother found me in the driveway all but comatose, my face painted with blood. Mr. Kane had nearly crashed his Datsun into the fire hydrant before leaping out and ushering me into the privacy of the backyard, where he used the garden hose and his handkerchief to try to wash the blood from my face as my mother dealt with the horror inside our house.

Now, as I stood beside Mr. Kane at the casket, I noted that his dark suit jacket was stretched tight over his soft frame, the fabric straining so much at the gut, shoulder, and elbows that I thought it might burst. His trousers, which were black and did not match his navy-blue jacket in the least, fell an inch short of his loafers, exposing white socks.

As he turned to permit other mourners to pay their respects, Mr. Kane stared at me, his emotionless face contradicting his tears. I assumed that his lack of emotion was due to the same numbness that made every face appear dead under that pallid light.

When he finally registered my presence, Mr. Kane whispered in my ear, his hot breath sour and yeasty, "I'm sorry. For everything." He found his way through the crowd to the exit, not daring to meet my mother's eye.

I skirted around the casket and saw through a gap in the linen that it was not situated atop a marble altar, but perched on a cold, skeletal metal scaffolding that looked so cheap and flimsy, I feared it would collapse if I breathed too hard on it.

As I stood there, worried that the casket might crash down on me, a memory from the previous week crashed down on me instead.

Every third Wednesday I had walked to my father's barbershop for a trim, just before he closed shop at five thirty.

My father preferred to give me a haircut when there were no customers in the place—men from town, whose faces were dimly familiar to me, yet I didn't know their names. Men who bragged about new lawn mowers and the ten bucks they'd won at the Tuesday-night card game. Men who quipped, "Is that stubble on the boy's chin, or chocolate milk?" Or, "Give the boy a slather of aftershave to lure in the lady bees."

"*Enough*," my father would say. "The boy's only eight." And the men would clam up.

Although he never raised his voice, his tone was authoritative. And it was something more too, something that rubbed against the mild man I knew. The way he spoke advised caution. It insinuated a history between my father and the other men—perhaps something that had occurred in the past and established him as the alpha male, not to be defied. In the next instant, however, I would be just as certain that the men simply respected him as the proprietor and as a father.

The Wednesday before the Incident, I had arrived late at the shop, just after closing.

I perched in the Pibbs 9900, a hulking barber chair, all cold chrome, porcelain, and plush crimson leather, awash in the fragrance of talc and tonics that mingled with the rich, ripe scent of the leather. It was a chair straight out of a Gorey illustration, a torture contraption that I felt might fold up on me like a mechanical Venus flytrap and swallow me whole at any second.

The shop was quiet and shadowed that night, with only a lone ceiling light lit to fend off the encroaching dark. *Popular Mechanics*, *Sports Afield*, and *Boys' Life* magazines, and *Tales from the Crypt* comics sat in tidy squared stacks on low tables. The floor was swept immaculate.

In front of the chair hung a wall-length mirror and a shelf of mugs stuffed with badger-hair brushes and straight razors, my father's prized razor with the ivory handle among them. In the mirror I watched the image of my father at my shoulder. He was not wearing his barber's smock. Without it, he seemed robbed of his identity, like a priest stripped of his aura of holiness when he is without his collar. My father snatched a pair of shears from the counter and snicked them in the air above my head. Without pumping the foot lever to position me, dampening my hair, or even clipping a bib to my shirt collar, he set to cutting with a nervous haste. As he snipped away, cupping my chin to angle my head as he saw fit, he seemed pensive and agitated, lost in private thoughts.

The shop door opened. My father's shears nicked my ear. I yelped. Blood trickled from my notched flesh. I pinched the lobe as blood leaked down my fingers and wrist. My father didn't notice. His eyes were locked on the figure in the doorway.

Dead leaves danced around the stranger's feet. I felt a chill from the air that carried the tang of autumnal decay.

The stranger unsnapped the top button at the throat of his long black coat, the collar pulled tight to his neck. The wind vibrated a single errant strand of his long mane of black hair, which was swept back in a wave that appeared poised to crash upon his gleaming forehead. He looked to be older than my father by a good three decades. His facial features were sharp and long and narrow, as if rendered by the same hands that wrought the Easter Island colossi. His eyes were dark and imperious. In one hand he carried a black leather bag. He held my father's gaze without moving or making a sound. They clearly knew each other; my father's eyes betrayed recognition and, I thought, great unease.

The stranger shut the door. Blood tracked along the edge of my jaw and down my neck.

"A word," the stranger said, entirely unaware of, or perhaps just unconcerned with, my presence.

He looked toward the door to my father's small office in the back, a room furnished with a simple metal desk and file cabinet purchased at a school auction. Atop the desk sat various framed photos of our family.

The man had the proprietary air of a tycoon touring the floor of his factory and finding the state of things not up to snuff.

My father tapped his shears against his thigh and went to open the office door. The hinges creaked, and the stranger started across the shop with the erect posture of a military man, his movements so fluid that he seemed almost to glide.

As he passed, I saw just how tall he was. He was the tallest man I had ever seen, looming over my father, who, I knew from my mother's proud mention of it, stood six feet even. The Tall Man stepped into the office behind my father, crowding him. He grasped the doorknob with fingers so long that they made it look as if it were the knob to a dollhouse door. He eased the door shut, sealing my father off from me.

I strained to hear the two men's voices over the pounding of blood in my ears, but the door acted as a baffle, eroding their speech down to an exchange of muted vowel sounds.

I did not like this stranger. I did not like how his presence made my father so servile. I didn't dare go to the door and try to hear them more clearly. The Tall Man frightened me, though I could not say why.

I sat in the barber chair for what seemed days. A fly droned around the shop in fat, lazy loops, its buzz growing as loud as a chainsaw in my ears, until it finally lit on a mug. I waited so long, the blood that ran from my sliced ear along my jaw and neck dried and scabbed.

The voices behind the door fell silent. The silence upset me more than if I'd heard my father crying out.

The fly alighted on the back of my hand. The leather seat grew icy beneath me. I imagined the Tall Man interrogating my father, torturing or strangling him. My heart thumped in my chest. The full moon had risen outside, its light glinting off the rack of shining straight razors and scissors. I strained to hear. The silence echoed. The longer the silence persisted, the more my fears crystallized.

I eased out of the chair so quietly and carefully that the fly remained perched on the back of my hand. I slipped the sharpest and longest pair of shears from a jar, their blades winking silver in a slash of moonlight.

I gripped them tight.

The fly buzzed into the air and spiraled to the floor, to spin on its back.

I put my ear to the door.

I heard a soft scrape. A thud.

I held the shears tighter in my hand, pressed my ear tighter to the door.

The doorknob turned with sudden violence.

I jumped back, my heart jumping with me, and the shears clattered to the floor.

The door started to open. I heard my father say, "You can't make me."

As the door opened fully, the Tall Man walked by me, so utterly oblivious of my existence that for a moment, I thought he passed right through me. His black bag, half unzipped now, seemed not to carry quite the burden it had when he came in. He opened the front door. The wind sliced into the shop, and the Tall Man was gone in the darkness.

I sat in the chair as my father emerged from his office. He ran a comb through his hair. He looked stunned to see me.

He picked up the shears I'd dropped on the floor and came around behind me.

I expected him to say something, do something, but he just clicked the shears and set to trimming my hair.

"Who was that?" I said.

"Who was who?" *Snip.*

"That strange man."

"He's not strange." *Snip.* My father's two fingers felt unsteady as they lifted my chin so his eyes met mine in the mirror. "Who do you love more?" he said. "Your mother? Or me?"

I stared at his reflection in the mirror, not understanding. He had asked the question as if it were a given that I loved one parent more than the other, as if it were something I had pondered, though, of course, no such notion had ever entered my mind.

"I love you . . . both . . . the same," I said.

It was the truth. So why did it feel like the wrong answer? Why did I feel as if I were a game show contestant who chokes under pressure to answer the easiest question while everyone watching shouts, "How can he *not* know the answer?"

I began to tell my father that I loved him the most, to try to calm the fear, the hurt, that I saw in his eyes. But he cupped my chin in his hand and came around to stand before me and assess my haircut. As he did, he stepped on the fly and crushed it.

At the casket now, a woman cleared her throat, and I broke from my reverie of that day at the barbershop.

I thought about the note and the Tall Man's visit and wondered whether one had to do with the other.

AFTER

In the days to follow, my mother trudged back and forth—back and forth, back and forth, and back and forth—across the living room, hauling box after box of my father's belongings out to the curb as I lay on the couch, listless as T. S. Eliot's etherized patient.

My mother seemed hell-bent on ridding the house of every last vestige of my father. In one box I spotted a pair of photographs my father had taken of Lydia and me that summer at the beach. In the photos, Lydia and I knelt beside a sandcastle we'd made, both of us beaming, pink-faced and sweaty and freckled. My father had cherished the two photos and displayed them on his bedside table in frames he'd "commissioned" Lydia and me to make from finger-painted Popsicle sticks.

"Not those, please, not those," I managed to mutter, but my mother drifted on past me without acknowledgment.

When a piece of furniture—my father's reading chair or writing desk or bureau—proved too unwieldy for my mother to manage, two men showed up to haul the pieces away and rode off with them in a truck. Everything my father had owned, except for the few belongings I managed to swipe from the curb and boxes, was soon, like my father himself, gone.

I stayed home from school for a week, or perhaps it was a month. Or months. After tiring of the couch, I sequestered myself in my bedroom and tried to find relief in my illustrated Poe story collection, but I couldn't concentrate or stay awake. Sleep battered me.

My sister Lydia, however, buzzed and chittered. *Dad, dad, dad. daddy, daddy, daddy.* She never slept. It was as if she had sucked all the ebullience out of me and it now erupted as manic energy from a six-year-old body too tiny to contain it. My mother did not ignore my sister's gibberish so much as she seemed not to hear it, as if my sister now spoke in a frequency outside of my mother's auditory range.

My mother never spoke to me about that day, and I never spoke to her about it, or to a shrink or to a priest or to a teacher. Not to my sister, not to anyone except the one friend I would make in eighth grade: Clay. And even to him I did not tell everything.

My mother simply carried on at the scene of the crime with such a stalwart denial of anything amiss that sometimes I wondered whether my father had ever existed. Perhaps, I had even imagined him.

WHAT I KEPT

From the curbside, I rescued a dozen or so of my father's hardcover books. They were thick as bricks and just as hefty, with weighty titles to match: *Darkness Fell Too Soon, No End to It, The Man from Nowhere.* They were so daunting, I could never imagine reading them, yet I wanted them near me because my father had treasured them, and they were likely some of the last books he had ever read. He had often told me, "Books—words—hold power. Not magic. Not wonder. Power. Power to convince you of things, even things that do not exist." Every night at bedtime, he read children's books to Lydia and me. The classics, yes. But more obscure titles too. *How Far to Yesterday?* by Maximilian Sneed. *Come, My Little Ones, I've a Story,* by Dorothy Q. Vale. Often, these stories featured children with peculiar traits. Not ESP or telekinesis or any of the myriad other psychic abilities that were all the rage then. No. The children in my father's obscure tales possessed *physical* anomalies. Perhaps, my father intended for these stories to make me less self-conscious about my malformed pinkies, which were knuckleless stubs of stunted bone and warped flesh, but I doubt it. He never once spoke of my mutant pinkies—or how my fingers, fused at birth, had required surgery to separate them—unless I first mentioned kids teasing me about them. "Tell those bullies you're more evolved," he said. "Pinkies are merely the useless appendixes of the hand. They exist, but for no known purpose." I did not tell my father that defending myself only invited more bullying.

My father read almost every evening in his recliner by the fireplace, occasionally licking a finger to turn a stubborn page. In the weeks leading up to the Incident, although the practice ran counter to his code of respect for books, he had at times penciled notes in the margins, his brow stitched in concentration as if the words were in a foreign language he could not quite decipher.

One evening as my father scratched his pencil across a page, my mother said, "That's a library book you're writing in." Her tone was stiff and impatient—one I had not heard her use with my father.

My father looked up from his book as if waking from a deep sleep. "Oh," he'd said. "Yes."

Finished with his evening reading, my father would place a bookmark between the pages. *Never* did he leave a book open facedown. Never did he fold down the corner of a page. These were unconscionable practices disrespectful both to the books and to their authors. I adopted this practice from him when I inherited his passion for books and stories. I kept as many of his books as I could salvage, in an attempt to remain close to my father in whatever meager way I could.

At times during those first weeks without him, I missed my father with a grief so gutting and debilitating that I yearned to join him. I wanted only to do as he had done, to turn his shotgun on myself as a way to be close to him again, to understand him. Knowing what he had felt at that precise last moment seemed the only way for me to quiet my anguish.

I searched for my father's shotgun but could not find it. Instead, in a packed box at the curb, I found the .22 revolver he had owned since he was a boy and had spoken of passing down to me when I was old enough. I rescued the revolver and hid it in my room.

I wish I never had.

APRIL FOOLS

1984

Only April 1, yet the sun raged in the sky as if Clay and I had been dropped into the hot, humid guts of August.

The two of us lay out on Clay's roof in our boxer shorts, with LP sleeves wrapped in tinfoil, angled to direct the afternoon sun onto our torsos. Our bodies glistened with baby oil as the roof's hot, pebbled shingles branded our flesh.

"Stop being a pussy and you'll start *getting* some pussy," Clay said.

He was so cavalier, so crass about girls and sex. It's easy to be that way when you're the varsity hockey captain, six foot two, 210 pounds, with a physique suitable for immortalizing in marble. It's not so easy when you're as scrawny as a ditch weed, have the complexion of an orange rind, the athleticism of dirt, and malformed pinkies.

"I'm not a pussy," I said.

"If you say so." He punched my arm. Hard. I willed myself to act as if it didn't hurt, didn't matter—something I'd mastered. When Clay saw my eyes watering, he punched me again. Harder. I bit the inside of my cheek rather than reveal my pain.

Clay plucked a joint from behind his ear. I took out a box of matches I kept in my pocket along with my jackknife, for emergencies, but Clay waved me off. He sparked his joint with the Zippo I had stolen from the local IGA and given to him for his birthday several months earlier.

He sipped at the joint and held it out.

I declined. I didn't like smoking pot. It turned my mind to mud and made me paranoid and twitchy. Clay tucked the joint back in his mouth and reached for the transistor radio he had saved up for and bought himself for his birthday. It was the only birthday gift he'd received, other than the Zippo from me. He dialed the radio to 106.7, the Wizard. Squeezed in between "When the Levee Breaks" and "Feel Like Making Love" was "Sexual Healing."

"I'd hate to be that guy," Clay said. "A black kid in the fifties, your last name is 'Gaye' *and* you sing this fey shit? You *know* he got the shit kicked out of him."

"I like him," I said.

"Of course *you* do. He probably gets all the ass he wants, though. Even as an old dude. Some chicks dig that sensitive rap. You should use your sensitive side to get some. You know?"

"No," I said. I didn't know.

Clay got whatever girl he wanted. It was easy for him. I detested how he used girls and tossed them aside like empty candy-bar wrappers. I hated it even more that most of the girls didn't seem to know they were being used, and some of them knew it and didn't care. Some reveled in it. Sought it out. Not just the ones everyone knew to be like that, but the so-called *good girls* too. They seemed to take the same pride in having been used by the star athlete as they had taken in wearing their Brownie badges, just a few years ago. I didn't understand any of it.

Clay propped himself up on his elbows. "Damn, you're tan. All I get is freckles. I'm jealous."

"Yeah. You. Jealous."

"See, man. Don't be a pussy. A man takes a compliment. Confidence—that's the key to getting some, and—"

Getting *some* was not a concern of mine. What I wanted was something else. Something more. Not love, exactly. But romance. Mystery. Ardor. What I wanted was for Juliette Lancaume, who made me glow every time we crossed paths in the school hallway and made my mouth go dry just by sitting in the same biology and history classes, to know how she made me feel. And when I confessed it to her, I wanted her to glow too.

Nazareth's "Hair of the Dog" kicked in on the radio.

Clay and I twisted our voices to match that of the front man, singing nasty and mean. We didn't know all the lyrics, so we mumbled approximations with bravado. What mattered was capturing the spirit of the song. And that we did. Up on that roof, the coarse shingles embossing our flesh, the sun clobbering us, and our certain immortality humming in our veins, we sang, knowing we'd live forever.

From down on the deck below, a voice raged, "Get off my roof!" It was Ike, Clay's father.

"Shit," Clay said, and sat up. He snuffed out the joint and shut off the radio. "Shit."

"Get off my roof," Ike railed. "You'll tear the shingles. You want to pay for that shit?"

"*His* roof," Clay whispered. "My mom pays the mortgage."

"What'd you say?" Ike barked. "Look at you two. Oiled-up pussies."

Ike glared at me, a lug-nut finger jutting at me as if to punch a hole right through my heart. "*You* know better." He swung his finger at Clay. "*He* might not know better, but you do. You've *got* a brain. Use it. Smoking that crap. Ruining people's property. Get down."

"We're *trying*." Clay fumbled to gather his radio as we scooted down to the roof's edge, above the deck.

Clay eased backward over the edge, his new radio clutched in one hand.

Ike grabbed Clay's ankles and yanked. Clay yowled as his naked stomach was dragged across the metal flashing and over the ragged lip.

He came down in a heap on the deck. The radio clattered. The back popped off, and the batteries flew out.

Clay lay there clutching his bleeding abdomen.

Ike kicked the radio.

"Quit it," Clay said. "*Quit it!*"

Ike kicked the radio again and stormed inside.

I eased down onto the deck, to a world leached of color and sound.

Clay cradled the radio, fiddling with the cracked knobs, but it remained mute. "I just bought this thing," he said. His abs were raked and bleeding.

"You okay?" I asked.

"I'll live."

But not forever. I knew that as surely as I knew that when I got home, the house would be empty. My mom would be waitressing at the Wagon Wheel, where she pulled double shifts five days a week. And Lydia, who was now a fifteen-year-old—and whose prescription for post-abortion Erythromycin I'd found in the bathroom trash two months earlier— would be off with her twenty-year-old boyfriend, Dipshit.

"I'm going to kill him, before he kills me," Clay said.

"You're not going to kill him," I said. "And he's not going to kill you. He's your father."

"I know who the fuck he is. You don't have to tell me who the fuck he is."

"I gotta split."

"Stay. He'll calm down."

"I got shit to do."

"You fucking liar."

I walked down the stairs to the lawn.

"Pussy!" Clay yelled. "Let me borrow your revolver. I'll just kill the fucker right now."

Up the street I saw a young boy of perhaps eight, whose face I did not recognize and whose name I did not know. He was in his yard, playing catch with his father. The two of them threw the baseball back and forth, the father tossing it softly, underhand, so the boy could catch it easily and not get bashed in the face if he missed the catch. The father saw me and waved. "Hello, Wayland!" he said. I didn't know how he knew my name. I didn't know his. I didn't know these people.

"Hey," I said.

I realized I was barefoot in the road in just my underwear, oiled up head to toe. The boy and his father didn't seem to notice my condition. Or maybe they just didn't care.

As I walked on, I could hear the soft *whap* of the baseball as it smacked leather.

Whap . . .

. . . Whap . . .

. . . Whap . . .

"Nice one," the father said.

At the top of our street, I paused. I wished I hadn't left Clay, not because I worried Ike would kill him or he would kill Ike—that would never happen—but because I'd abandoned him.

Far back down the street, the father and son tossed their ball. I could no longer hear the ball hit the glove, or the father's words of encouragement. The man and the boy looked like miniature specimens behind a glass wall that blocked out all sound and emotion.

I was overtaken with an urge to run back to Clay's house, but a breeze picked up and a chill ran through me, and I only wanted to get home, shower off all that oil, and go to sleep. The house would be quiet, at least for a spell.

When I arrived at home, it was peaceful, as I'd known it would be. Yet, somehow, it was too quiet. It felt like that moment just before people jump out for a surprise party. Was it my birthday? Maybe it was and I'd forgotten. I wondered whether I had stepped into the wrong house. I'd done that once, late one night—walked right into that letch Mr. Dietrich's house across the street. I'd left before he woke up. Now, I stood in the entrance of my house and waited in the dead silence for someone to jump out and surprise me for an occasion I could not remember.

No one did.

I took a long, hot shower, lathering up my body with a bar of Lava and scrubbing the oil off me, my skin sensitive from the sun and the abrasive soap. I thought of Juliette Lancaume, with her hair so unfathomably black it seemed to have purple in it—a purple I believed that only I could see, only I could appreciate. I thought of how it lay against the naked skin of her neck, until the water ran cold.

In my room I pulled the curtains tight. My skin was still flaming. I'd had enough of the cruel sun. I lay back in bed and thought of the father and son down the street. It made me think of my father. I had not thought of him in weeks, and guilt over having forgotten him devoured me. "I won't forget again," I whispered. I meant it, as I always did. No one besides me ever thought of him anymore, certainly not my mother and Lydia. He existed in my thoughts alone, and it frightened me that if a time ever came when I no longer thought of him at all, he would truly be gone forever.

I sat up on the edge of the bed and put my feet on the floor.

A peculiar sensation swam over me. I looked down at my feet.

Déjà vu slammed through me. Yet it wasn't quite déjà vu. It seemed more like a memory that remained too weak to swim up from the depths of my mind. I stared at my feet planted on the floor. They seemed of monumental importance, a harbinger I could not comprehend. Whatever it was—memory, trick of the mind, or déjà vu—it sank down into the murk of my brain before too long.

I lay back down on my bed and stared up at the pebbled circles of paint on my ceiling. I liked those swishy, careless circles. For years they'd given me something to study, to focus on. I found hidden designs in them. Patterns. Mystery. My father had caught me staring up at them once and asked what I was gawking at. I told him about the circles, how mysterious I found them. He said that the contractor had the painters put sand in the paint and make those circles to cut corners. It saved them from having to finish-tape the Sheetrock seams. Saved time. And money. "There is no mystery," he said.

The next day, I had come home to find his pickup truck idling in the driveway.

I sat up and tuned my clock radio to 106.7, the Wizard, and stared at those mysterious circles of paint. I sang to "Mississippi Queen" and looked down at my feet on the floor. Again, the memory, or dream, jolted my mind.

My feet. *On the floor.*

What . . . ?

A voice on the radio interrupted the song.

It told me that Marvin Gaye, in broad daylight, in his parents' home that sat out beneath the golden California sun, had been shot dead—by his father.

The phone rang out on the hall table. It rang and rang.

The newsman was going on about Marvin Gaye's birthday being the next day. He would have been forty-five. Ancient, I believed.

The phone rang on.

I rose, my legs feeble. I walked out into the hall and picked up the phone. I looked down at my scrawny, naked virgin's body, the flesh so pale where my boxers had been.

"Hello?" I said, my voice a ghost.

The same news report echoed in the background over the phone. How did something like this happen? How did things go so askew?

"Hey," Clay said.

"Hey," I said.

"Sorry I punched you."

"Yeah."

"I don't know why I do that shit."

"Yeah."

In the background, Ike bellowed about Clay's laziness or his worthlessness or something.

"You think maybe I could come over there?" Clay said.

"Yeah. Sure. Cool."

"Okay. Cool. Cool."

He hung up.

From my bedroom, my radio began to play Marvin Gaye's "What's Going On."

THE SCREAMING WOMAN

A half hour later, I jolted awake to a *thump, thump.* My arm tingled, dead. I swung my feet onto the floor and was again assailed by déjà vu. My feet. Flat on the floor. What did it mean? A vision came to me: my father sitting on the edge of his bed as I walked into the room, his back to me. What . . .

Thump. Thump.

I shuffled into the living room. On the tube, in a rerun, Steve McGarrett spun and squinted over his shoulder at the camera to convey the gravity of the situation.

Clay stood on the steps, clad in jeans and a ragged Pepsi-Cola T-shirt, wearing a pained smile.

"Get your revolver," he said. "Let's kill something."

Often, Clay and I traipsed the woods behind my house, and the Vanders estate beyond them, in search of squirrels and woodchucks to kill. Much is made of boys killing small animals. Society's hive mind buzzes with the concept that these killings are the acts of budding sociopaths, the nascent stage of the serial killer. The theory makes for good campfire lore and movie villains, but the truth is, those small deaths eased our minds and dulled the sharp edge of our anger and pain. They were the emergency release valve that kept us from far darker violence, for a while at least.

"And get some clothes on," Clay said.

Addled from my doze, I'd forgotten I was naked.

The day was dark and cool beneath the shadowed trees as we plodded along in a dreary dream of Hawthorne's making.

We sneaked along a creek, cold water seeping into our canvas sneakers as Clay swung the revolver at ghost birds perched in branches high above. Eventually, we emerged from the trees to wade through goldenrod still dead and brittle from winter. Out there in the estate's open fields, the hot spring air whirred and ticked with the wings of insects, and slender serrated leaves abraded our bare arms and left our skin chafed and streaked with blood. We scrambled up the field's yawning slope.

At the crest of a hill, we hid among budding trees, taking in an expanse of pastoral vista that reached clear to Forbidden Lake and across its five-mile expanse to the Spectral Mountains beyond. Amid the broad sweep of fields and the knolls of mature elm and oak trees stood three monolithic dairy barns. Built of fieldstone, brick, and cedar shakes, they harked back to the gilded age when the estate was supposed to have been an "ornamental farm," according to the visitor pamphlets foisted on me during annual grade-school field trips. The colossal barns exuded grandeur with their open marble courtyards and august stone turrets. According to the pamphlets, each barn was some twenty thousand square feet and together they had once boarded more than a thousand dairy cows. The grand Estate Inn, with its curving veranda, stood vigil over lakeside cliffs of jagged and crumbling shale. The inn had once been the Vanders family mansion, a summer retreat they visited for a few weeks in July. The residence contained thirty-two bedrooms. Twenty-five fireplaces. Six kitchens. A library. A billiard room. An observatory. The standing-seam copper roof of each structure had long ago tarnished to a reptilian green patina.

My father had despised the estate, and a few times when I visited the shop while he had customers, the subject of the estate and the Vanders family arose, complete with rumors of ill-gotten money, corruption, bribes, blackmail, and debauchery at the roots of the family's rotten tree of wealth. In the 1950s and '60s, the family had morphed their own Camelot into a nonprofit organization. "Suddenly, a farm with cows and sheep is a nonprofit and doesn't have to pay a dime in taxes," my father had said more than once. "The wealthiest of the wealthy, skating on our dime." To which a mustachioed customer had once replied as he lit his pipe, "Meanwhile, they all drive fancy *German* cars. They own the whole damned town. Act like royalty. Worse part is, half the people in town *treat* them like royalty, like they've actually *done* something, when they're nothing but grifters who got rich on blood money, then ripped off every farmer in town."

Rumor was that Buell Vanders I, the patriarch, had bought up separate small parcels of prime farmland over the course of a week in 1889, telling each farmer to keep the exclusive private purchase mum. He never mentioned that he was purchasing dozens more parcels from the neighboring farmers, until eventually, he had bought up fifteen thousand acres of the most desirable lakeside real estate in all New England.

Clay and I scanned the work roads for the blue pickup truck that patrolled the estate grounds for trespassers who had not paid the entrance fee at the visitor's gate a mile north.

Ants crawled at my feet, each carrying one pale egg in its mandibles. I tapped my toe on an ant to leave it broken and jerking. Its brethren descended on it, seized its thorax and legs and head in their jaws, and pinched their comrade into pieces that they then carried away to their queen.

"Woodchuck," Clay said.

Down the hill, the furry brown head of a woodchuck peeked up from its burrow.

Clay aimed the revolver.

A butterfly danced on the breeze, and the damp earth gave off the sexual redolence of springtime after the rain.

Clay pulled the trigger.

A tuft of fur floated toward us. We crept up to the rodent, the top of its skull sheared away to expose brain. Blood wet the grass. The wood-chuck's jaws gnashed, blood bubbled from its nose.

Clay turned from it.

"You can't leave it like this," I said.

"I can do anything I want."

I put the heel of my boot on the base of the woodchuck's head and crunched down with all my weight until I felt the skull crack.

"Feel better?" Clay said.

I didn't. I felt lousy. But what was I supposed to do, let the creature suffer?

Through binoculars, we watched visitor cars park in the lot across from the grand mansion and its carriage house. Groups of tourists hiked wooded trails and stopped at informational signs to read about the red oak tree or the cottontail rabbit, then looked around hoping to get a glimpse of the real thing.

Clay aimed the revolver at a family getting out of a station wagon.

"Pow," he said.

"Don't mess around," I said, and closed a hand around the revolver's barrel.

I picked up the binoculars and looked through them toward the creamery parking lot. An elderly couple were stretching and touching their toes as they got out of their Volvo. I lifted the binoculars higher, and my view filled with the carriage house's ivied stonework. I dialed in the widow's watch atop the carriage house and looked through the bank of windows.

"Whoa," I said. I worked the dial to bring it into tighter focus. The sun's heat blowtorched me. Sweat stung my eyes, and the sunlight refracted in the binoculars' lenses, obscuring the image. "What is that?" I said.

"*What?*" Clay said.

"It—"

Clay yanked at my arm. "*Run!*" he yelled.

The blue pickup truck sat idling on the hill fifty feet away. The sun sparkled on its windshield. The truck lurched toward us.

"Run!"

We ran, my mind scorched by the images I'd seen.

NIGHT

Midnight, I lay in bed in my boxers, in the dark, my room so hot and humid my flesh wept sweat. The oily green light of a streetlamp outside pooled in my room like the glow from radioactive sewage.

I pondered the image I'd seen, or thought I'd seen, in the widow's watch.

I'd caught only a glimpse. The back of a naked male figure, just its long, lank torso and shock of white hair visible as it wrapped its arms around a woman from behind her. My view of the woman was mostly obscured by the male figure and by the angle I had, but I could partly see, in a mirror beyond them, that she wore a masquerade mask of pink plumage. It concealed her entire face except her mouth, which was wide open, contorted in a silent roar, whether of ecstasy or agony I could not tell. Perhaps both. She appeared naked, though it was difficult to tell, what with her long tresses, as red as the devil's cape, cascading down and hiding most of her flesh. What little skin of her shoulders and legs I could see was a phantasmal white. The image of the two creatures seemed out of a lurid fever dream, at once grotesque and erotic, bestial yet beautiful.

Outside my window the rumble of a pickup truck invaded the silence of the night as my sister's boyfriend, Dipshit, pulled up at the curb. A heavy metal song thundered from the truck's speakers—the screeching guitar, the throbbing, demonic bass. Dipshit liked everything loud, to match his mouth.

My clock showed 12:07 a.m. I sat on the edge of my bed and swooned as I put my feet on the floor. Again, I was plagued by déjà vu so vivid it nearly made me sick. I drew a deep breath to calm myself and peered out my window, the lamplight turning the truck's candy-apple paint job the color of congealed blood. What was it about my feet on the floor?

The cab light blinked on as my sister cracked the passenger door open. I saw her kissing Dipshit, one of his hands shoved in her spiked purple hair, and the other under her shirt.

She offered her neck to him.

I closed my eyes and wondered where Juliette Lancaume was right then. Probably at home. Asleep. Where else? She would never come home at midnight in a pickup truck driven by a twenty-year-old loser. She had parents who were awake and aware, a father who was alive, a mother who was not oblivious from exhaustion like my mom who wouldn't be home from her waitressing shift for another hour.

I wondered what Juliette's bedroom looked like. Smelled like. I wondered what it was like to be home asleep in a quiet, air-conditioned home, on a soft, comfortable bed made up with freshly laundered sheets, both parents home, both parents *alive*, no pickup truck rumbling outside and no shit-ass music blaring, and a dog curled up beside you. Juliette had some sort of hunting dog she worshipped. A spaniel or a setter, one of those feathery pups. Rusty was its name.

I knew all this because I knew Juliette's route and the time of day she walked Rusty, and once in a while, not so often that I drew her attention, I'd bike over to her end of town, where the nice houses were, and spot her, and I'd watch her without her seeing me, watch how good she was to that dog. She would kneel and pat its head and scruff its chin and say, "Rusty, Rusty, Rusty, such a goo-ood boy," and feed it a biscuit, kiss its wet nose and slobbery mouth full-on with her lips, and continue their walk together. Friends.

We had a dog, a beagle mutt named Molly, old now, who came to us just after the Incident. She'd wandered out of the woods behind the house and adopted us, so long ago I could not remember my life without her. My mom objected to our keeping her at the time. We couldn't afford a dog, but Lydia and I had pressed until we exhausted our mother. I was the only one who walked Molly anymore. Otherwise, we just let her out to pee and crap in the yard and tied her with a rope to the dead tree out front, where she ran in mad circles, baying and lunging at the few rare solicitors who happened by. At her rope's end, she had worn a moat in the lawn around her, tramped the grass dead and reduced the ground to packed dirt that turned to muck in the rain.

My mom could never afford Molly's rabies shots or her tags or to get her fixed. When Molly was in heat, as she was on this night, we put her in the cellar so she wouldn't get the male dogs after her. There was no light in the cellar, and I felt bad for her down in the damp, musty darkness. She would crap and pee and drip her menstrual blood on the concrete floor. I'd clean her crap with a trowel, and her pee and blood with a mop as best I could, holding my nose against the caustic bleach and menstrual tang, gagging while she watched me from the corner, panting, shivering, huddled in a ball as if she were as ashamed as I was for her sorry state.

A few years before, when she was in heat, Molly got out of the house at night, and a monstrous Rottweiler got after her, and she was bawling out on the front lawn as if she were lit on fire. I ran outside with my Wiffle bat, and I beat on the Rottweiler's head, but that beast kept right after her. Molly's haunches were squeezed under that Rottweiler as he took her, strings of saliva flying from jaws as I thrashed away with the Wiffle bat and wailed at my inability to protect my dog. I felt sick. I had left the screen door open. It was my fault Molly had gotten out and was attacked. I'd wished I had the revolver. I would have shot the beast in the skull, but Clay had borrowed the gun to plink at cans, so I was left to beat the creature on the head with a toy of thin, hollow plastic.

Mr. Dietrich ran out and grabbed the bat from my hands.

"You crazy?" he said. "That dog'll kill you."

"Let him!" I cried, "Let him, let him, let him!"

Mr. Dietrich led me to his porch, where we waited for the violation to end. Molly keened. That Rottweiler was three times her size and locked on to her like a vise, and there wasn't a thing I could do. My father would have stopped it.

The Rottweiler finally dismounted and swaggered off, all rippling muscle and swinging balls. I swore that if I ever saw it again, I'd crush the back of its skull with my wooden bat or shoot it between its evil eyes, but I never saw it again.

I thought about Molly now, down in our dark basement. Outside, my sister laughed and tumbled out of the truck as Dipshit hit the gas with her door still open. The door swung and struck Lydia. She fell to the ground, hysterical with laughter. Drunk. Dipshit's truck rocked as he punched the brakes, and the passenger door slammed shut. Then the truck roared off down the street.

My sister swayed toward the house.

I waited in the hallway. I needed to say something. Do something. I was her older brother; it was my responsibility to warn her. Help her. I needed to tell her she shouldn't see Dipshit anymore. *Couldn't* see him. Tell her she was better than this. She was better than he was. *We* were better. I needed to tell her I loved her. I couldn't remember how long it had been since I'd told her that. Years.

Lydia staggered through the kitchen door and looked at me, her mascara smeared like war paint on her cheeks.

"What are *you* doing up?" she said. "Why are your boxers on backward?"

I looked down. She was right. My boxers were on backward.

When I looked up, Lydia was tottering into her bedroom. The door shut, and the lock clicked. Music pumped—the same spastic guitar scales and suicidal rants that had howled from Dipshit's truck, so loud that the floor shook beneath the soles of my bare feet.

My bare feet.

Déjà vu hammered and bewildered me.

I stood listening to the roar of music, thinking of Lydia's post-abortion prescription, of the mom we hardly ever saw, and the father we didn't have, and I knew I was wrong. We weren't better than *this*. We were exactly as the evidence suggested.

No, a voice said. *You* are *better*.

I opened the cellar door. The stench of Molly's feces and piss gagged me. "Girl," I whispered.

I heard the *click-clack* of Molly's unclipped nails on the concrete as she trudged out of the darkness to the bottom of the stairs and wagged her tail in the pale light from the kitchen.

"Come on up," I said. "It's all right. Come on up, girl."

She waddled up, fat and lazy from eating table scraps. I was glad to see she was no longer in heat, that blood no longer dripped from her hind end to dot the linoleum as she waddled into the kitchen.

"It's okay," I said.

We didn't have dog biscuits, so I grabbed an open bag of stale Hydrox, led her to my bedroom, and told her to hop up on my bed. She whined, tail swishing, her old legs unable to make the jump.

I eased her onto the bed near my pillow. She reeked so badly that I had to breathe through my mouth. I cuddled up to her, and she licked at my face and made small contented grunts as I fed her cookies until the bag was empty.

She snuggled up closer and let out a deep, long sigh.

"I know," I said, "I know," and finally I fell asleep with my dog in my arms, as I imagined how Juliette might sleep with her own dog. As close to normal as I would ever get.

PEEPING TOM

I awoke at dawn to a silent house. The jagged angle of sunlight in my room was all wrong. I felt drugged as Molly pressed against me, her sour breath steaming my face. My mind fizzed with thoughts of the woman in the widow's-watch window.

I moaned and slung my legs over the side of the bed, feet on the floor.

And it slammed me again. The waking nightmare.

Dangling legs.

I sat still at the edge of the bed, waiting for the memory to crystallize.

My mind had to be remembering wrong. Because . . .

In my shock eight years earlier, when I entered my father's bedroom, the importance of the detail had not registered.

Now it eviscerated me.

My father sat on the edge of the bed, his back to me. Legs dangling. Suffering little boy. "Dad," I'd said, and reached out for him. I never saw his face.

I rushed out of my room and careened down the hall.

My mom was home. I heard her shower running in the bathroom, heard her coughing, hacking wetly from breathing cigarette smoke at the restaurant.

Mondays were her only day and night off from work all week,

yet she was always up and showering earlier on her day off than on workdays. Despite her exhaustion from working nearly seventy hours a week, she woke by six on Mondays. During school vacations she would spend the morning with me before burning up the rest of her free afternoon grocery shopping and running errands in service to Lydia and me. The only times all week that she took even a couple of hours for herself were Monday and Friday nights. She bowled in a women's league and would come home late, relaxed and renewed, it seemed, almost happy as she picked at her takeout dinner on the couch and watched a movie on VHS.

Lydia made herself scarce on Mondays, and I figured she had already left the house that morning or else would stay in her room until my mother and I left. Normally, I welcomed the time with my mother. I enjoyed her company, and I saw in her eyes how much pleasure it gave her to spend part of her day off with me, however fleeting and banal the interaction, playing a few hands of crazy eights or laughing at game shows on television. Before the Incident my mother had stayed home to care for the house and her family. The one break from her routine she'd granted herself was watching a soap opera she had become obsessed with.

That morning I would derail our ritual.

I put my ear to the bathroom door. Convinced that my mother would be in there a while, I sneaked into her bedroom. I hadn't entered it in years. It frightened and saddened me. All the furniture from the day of the Incident was gone. In place of my father's nightstand stood a folding TV dinner tray. In place of my father's stack of bedside books and the two photos of Lydia and me at the beach, displayed in our Popsicle-stick frames, sat opened jars of night creams, a toenail clipper, and a bowl with a sludge of sour milk and mushed cereal caked to it. I stared at the bed. Had I ever seen the bed itself carried out from the house? I had no memory of it. It seemed I would have recalled it.

I sat on the bed's edge.

It was the same bed. I was sure.

My father had been six feet tall, three inches taller than I was.

Yet my feet were planted flat on the floor.

My father's feet had dangled a couple of inches *above* the floor. This was impossible—unless the man who shot himself that day was not my father.

I looked out the window at the same tree I'd seen sway in the breeze that day. The tree was dead now, leafless, and hollow with rot.

THE NOTE

My mind was an empty, cracked parking lot with a few stray weeds of thought wilting in the baking sun of a new reality.

I slouched back to my room, where Molly whined on the bed.

The note. It was secreted away in the back of my closet, folded up and tucked in the middle of a mason jar crammed with pennies. I dug around behind my clothes and abandoned toys and found the jar. Molly whined beside me. I spilled the pennies out, half expecting to find no note, doubt having made every memory of that long-ago day suspect.

Yet it was there. Folded tight, as if to keep the words from escaping. I unfolded it and read those eight words for the first time in eight years.

I AM NOT WHO YOU THINK I AM

Printed on the back of the note, in the same hand, were the initials "SFL." I hadn't noticed them on the day of the Incident; I'd simply folded up the note and hidden it away. I didn't know anyone with those initials.

For the first time, I wondered whether my father had written the note. I'd never questioned it, because I'd never doubted that it was him in the room. Had SFL written the note? Was SFL sitting on the edge of the bed that day? Had I only *believed* it was my father sitting on the bed, because his truck was in the driveway, and the room was my parents', and I was feverish and weak with a roiling gut, and he had shot himself before I could see his face?

I needed to find a sample of my father's handwriting, to compare it to the note. I had no idea where I might find one. My mother had scrubbed every trace of my father's existence from our lives. Why, exactly, had she done this? I wondered for the thousandth time. Except that this time, I wondered with a sense of suspicion instead of confusion. Why would anyone, any *wife*, purge every last reminder of a husband from her home only days after his death?

If the man on the bed was not my father, who was he? And why had he killed himself in my parents' bedroom? And what happened to my father? *Something* must have happened to him. If he *had* written the note, what did he mean? If he was not who we thought he was, who was he?

I tucked the note into my Velcro wallet. I needed to tell someone about it and about the dangling legs. Lydia would only mock me. And what could I tell my mother? That I'd lied to her and kept the note all these years? Never told her about it or given it to her when she begged to know whether there had been a note?

I called Clay's house. No one picked up. I read the note again.

I AM NOT WHO YOU THINK I AM

Was I supposed to just hand it over to my mom now, eight years later, and ask whether it was my father's handwriting? If I'd shown my mom the note that day and she had seen that the handwriting wasn't my father's, perhaps she would have had questions, sensed he was alive and that the dead man with no face on her bedroom floor was not him. Perhaps the cops would have investigated. Looked for my father. Maybe found him, alive. I had never quite believed that my father would do what he did that day, right in front of me, because it was beyond him. Because he loved me. Yet something awful *had* befallen him. He would not have disappeared and never contacted us, me, again. What possible reason could he have to do such a thing? No one had looked for him, because I had thought it was him that day, and I'd kept the note a secret.

I couldn't tell my mother about my lie. Not yet. Not until I knew whether the note was written by my father.

I needed a sample of his handwriting. Out in the hallway, I listened at the bathroom door. The shower ran. I tapped on the door.

My mother shouted, "Just a few more minutes."

Back in my mother's bedroom, I eased open her bureau drawers. Using a pencil to move aside fraying and sagging underthings, I looked for old love letters from my father. I didn't need to read them. Didn't want to. Just hunting for a note to compare the script was violation enough. All I needed was a comparison. Evidence.

I fished through my mom's J. C. Penney blouses and her sweaters decorated with snowflakes and reindeer, her elastic-waist jeans and ratty sweatpants. I found nothing.

In the bottom dresser drawer, I found scattered pocket change, knotted strings of rosary beads, old school photos of my sister and me, and a cache of envelopes that at first lit a wild hope in me. However, the envelopes contained only past-due payment demands from the electric, oil, and water companies, and the Shireburne Trust Bank's mortgage department.

I put my head out in the hall and listened. The shower was still running.

I searched shoe boxes in my mother's closet, unearthed old thread bobbins, torn Butterick patterns, packs of shoelaces, stray bulbs for Christmas tree lights, and prescription bottles crammed with buttons and wheat pennies.

Under my mother's bed, a stuffed black trash bag smelled of sweaty socks and mothballs. I found no sample of my father's writing, no evidence he had ever even lived. Though I'd watched my mother rid the house of my father's belongings, a part of me had always believed she must have kept a few of his effects for a private trove of memories. I'd been wrong.

My mother coughed in the bathroom.

I dodged back out into the hall.

Behind the bathroom door came the *hwuuuush* of my mother's hair dryer.

I leaned against the hallway wall, steeling myself for my new reality.

TO TOWN

In the kitchen I scribbled on a notepad:

1. FIND A WRITING SAMPLE
2.

2 . . . 2 . . . ? What was 2?
I had no idea.
I called Clay's house. No answer.
Where could I find my father's handwriting?
An idea sprouted. Maybe the library had the story of my father's death in its microfilm archives. Maybe I could ferret through the reels until I landed on a small but critical clue that did not jibe with what everyone thought about that day. It was worth a try. I whistled to Molly. "Come on, girl," I said.

Molly and I hurried across the street to the railroad tracks behind the neighborhood. We walked along the tracks between old farmland and the LaPlatte River, a ditch of slow, dirty water that oozed past Shireburne Lumber & Gravel's high wooden fence, from behind which came the groan of logging trucks and the shouts of men.

I liked how the tracks were tucked away unseen, hidden in the heart of town. I liked how the steel rails got so hot in the summer that when I poured Coke on them, the soda sizzled and turned to black tar.

In the shade beneath the low-hanging branches of apple trees behind the library, I left Molly where she'd keep cool. "Be good," I said, and kissed her muzzle.

The library was housed in an 1817 Greek Revival brick building, painted yellow, with front columns and marble steps. It stood on a small green at the center of town, facing the only traffic light. Stately as the structure appeared, it could not conceal its neglected state—the peeling paint and cracked windowpanes, the hornets' nests in the crevices of the arched entrance.

The town meeting house had once stood here, but that structure burned to the ground under suspicious circumstances. It is believed that the place was torched by a remnant Algonquin population that made its way westward when the native Mohican tribe dwindled. Others claimed it was the descendants of the Mohicans who lit the place, in revenge for a traitorous massacre of their forefathers—a massacre in which babies had been beheaded and women and men burned alive.

I passed beneath the stone archway and stepped into the library. The dark slate entrance floor sucked up much of the light that filtered through the leaded windows high above me. Dust corkscrewed in the fusty vestibule. The library was my sanctuary, the place where I submerged myself in the depths of books, swept into an alternate reality that protected me from the one I lived in.

The library crackled with silence and smelled of stale binding glue and fresh magazine ink. An alcove beyond the circulation desk housed the card catalog—drawers of dark, ancient wood dressed with brass pulls. The cards, even the newest ones, were yellowed with age. The stubborn drawers mewled as I pulled them open on their crooked tracks. Still, I preferred these to the new, lifeless, cheap, metal ones at the school library.

Many days, after school, not wanting to go home to an empty house, I had spent hours lost in the cards themselves, amid their lexicon and their peculiar coded series of numbers and abbreviations, abrupt descriptions, and staccato punctuation. I would trail my fingertips along their surfaces, feeling the indentations left by typewriter keys that had smacked each letter into the stout card stock. The letters were often a wee bit cockeyed, as if whoever typed them had had their elbow nudged by a puckish fellow typist who wanted their attention, perhaps to tell a joke amid the boredom of entering ciphers. I pictured a monolithic office, a sea of desks fixed in strict rows and columns, each occupied by a lone typewriter over which hunched a lone typist dressed in a white smock, joining in the concert of typewriter keys click-clacking away monotonously, ceaselessly, straight out of Kafka's *The Trial*.

While flipping through the cards, I grew entranced by their sheer numbers, each one the first cryptic clue to the mystery of the book it described. Ink smudged my thumb as, card by card, I was drawn deeper into the file by such titles as *The Cross My Brother Carried* and *Here to the End*, and authors such as Xander Freznaz and Georgietta Peeves.

Now, I nodded at the old woman at the circulation desk, who looked at me judgingly over her cat-eye glasses before shoving her nose back into a Danielle Steele hardcover.

The periodicals section was devoid of patrons except for one old gent who dozed in an armchair, a newspaper spread open on his lap. I wondered where he lived, whether he even had a place to live, and why he was always asleep in that chair every time I visited the library. He was a fixture of the place. What sad event had befallen him to reduce him to this? Perhaps he was retired, or just tired.

I set off for the microfilm machines. They were in a cozy, bright room whose leaded windows were aglow with sunlight. Comfortable cushioned chairs stood at each cubicle. The walls were festooned with colorful Muppet posters.

The microfilm reels were organized by date in deep, wide drawers. I pulled film for the regional newspapers for each of the ten days after the Incident.

For two hours I sought a news story about what happened at my house that day. A man killing himself by shotgun in front of his young son seemed worthy of a story.

All I found was an obituary: a few spare lines about a loving father and husband. Barber. Bowler. Angler. Community man. Died unexpectedly.

As I stared at the brief, dispassionate obituary, ire edged out my grief. My father's supposed death was not worthy of a story. I did not know then that, unless the deceased person was famous, the press didn't cover suicides. They were kept private.

How was I ever going to prove that my father was not the man who had shot himself? How would I find out what happened to him? Where could I find a sample of his handwriting?

A voice behind my chair startled me.

I froze.

I knew the voice.

I'd dreamed of it.

Juliette Lancaume.

I saw her reflection in the screen of the microfilm machine. I did not dare turn to face her, as much as I wanted to, for fear that she would disappear.

"Is it?" she said.

Is it what? What had she asked me?

Perhaps she was speaking to someone just outside the room. She couldn't be speaking to me. She didn't even know I existed.

"Is it?" Her hand touched my shoulder, her fingers warm through my thin T-shirt. The air seemed deprived of its oxygen by the scent of Bonne Bell lipstick and Breck shampoo.

"Something wrong?" Juliette said.

I had still made no move to turn and face her. How had she come to close the vast abyss between us down to mere inches? How had events conspired to bring her life to mine? Never once outside biology or history class had I been so close to her, as if a force field had been set up between us to keep my pining at bay.

Juliette took her hand away, and cold reality snapped back to me like a rubber band stretched from a thumb until it breaks and lashes your face.

Her reflection in my microfilm screen went away.

"Wait," I rasped.

And turned.

Juliette stood there tapping her orange Dr. Scholl's sandal on the floor, fingertips of one hand hooked in the rear pocket of the Lee jeans she had cinched with a length of twine threaded through the belt loops and tied in front in a big bow. Her other hand played with the frayed hem of her tie-dyed T-shirt, a psychedelic sherbet swirl. The air around her pale face shimmered, and the hint of purple shadow on her eyelids seemed the dust of a rare moth's wings. Her nose, I saw up close, had the subtlest bend at the end, as if she'd wriggled it when it was itchy, and it had stuck that way.

"Well, is it?" she asked again, her voice a song on a breeze.

"Is it what?"

"Your dog under the apple tree?"

"Oh, Molly. Yeah. Yeah. She's my dog."

"I hope you don't mind I tied my dog up next to her so they could have company. Plus, it's the only spot in the shade."

"Right. Sure. Right. She loves company."

"Great." Juliette started to sit at the microfilm machine behind me, her back to me.

I stopped her. "What made you think she was my dog?" I asked.

"I've seen you two around."

She'd seen me? Around?

"Where?" My voice cracked. I feared she'd caught me watching her and Rusty when I biked to her neighborhood to catch a glimpse of her.

"Just around, walking. She's cute. And we have biology and history together—you and I, of course, not Molly."

"Of course," I croaked.

Juliette leaned over beside me and glanced at the screen on my machine. "What are you looking at? Stuff for our Vietnam War papers? Brushing up before school starts again?"

"No," I said.

"What class then?"

"It's not for a class."

She bumped her hip against my chair's arm. "What are you doing in *here* if it's not for schoolwork?"

"It's sort of personal," I said.

"Oh." Her inquisitiveness flagged, and again she started to sit in her chair.

"I'm investigating a mystery," I said.

"*Really?*" she said, her voice bright, eyes aglimmer. "What kind?"

"The death of my father," I managed to say.

Her eyes darkened, and a reflective expression came over her face. "What do you mean?"

"My father died, a long time ago."

She didn't say a word, just stood there with her head tilted like a bird listening for danger. I didn't know what she knew about me. There had been rumors about my father after it happened, but Juliette hadn't lived here; she'd moved to Shireburne my freshman year. March 3. I didn't know whether she even knew that my father was dead or had heard how he died. Five minutes ago I hadn't even known she was aware I existed.

"What's the mystery of it?" she said, her interest piqued.

"I came here to look up old newspaper accounts of his death, hoping to find a clue."

"A clue to what?"

I didn't know what to say. Here she was, captivated by my mystery. I wanted to keep it that way. So I told her the truth. I told her about the Incident as I believed it had happened: the truck, walking into the house, going into my parents' bedroom, and what I found in there, what I saw in there. Who I saw. Or, who I believed I saw. I told her about the dangling legs, and how I'd found the note but never shown it to anyone.

Juliette dragged a chair over and sat beside me, her head bowed so she looked at me sidelong from under a wisp of hair. She looked solemn and did not speak for a long time.

In an exhalation of breath, she said, "That's . . . awful."

I regretted telling her. My tale was too macabre to elicit anything but pity, and I'd rather have remained invisible to her than be the object of her pity.

Juliette shook her head slowly, as if to help her mind sift and settle the information I'd given her into a neat and organized story she could grasp.

"What did the note say?" she asked.

"I am not who you think I am."

She sat silent, thinking.

"I've always thought *he* had written it," I said, "that it was some kind of . . . "

She nodded. "How can you investigate now? It's been forever. And you're not a cop or anything." I was relieved to hear her voice lower with pathos instead of rise in pity. "What more is there to know?"

"Everything," I replied. "It wasn't him. It wasn't my father."

"But you just said he . . . the shotgun . . . "

"He was taller than I am now by three inches, yet when I sit on the edge of that bed, I can place my feet flat on the floor."

Her eyes clouded with doubt.

"I can show you," I said, too fast. "I can show you the bed. I can show you the note."

"I believe you," she said, in a tone that made me feel certain she did *not*, in fact, believe me. A hot ember of anger flared in my chest. I did not need her humoring me.

"It's impossible that it was my father," I said.

"But his truck was in the driveway, and it happened in your parents' bedroom."

"I know."

She went down the list. The same list I had gone over and over in my head. And I gave her the same nonanswers I kept giving myself:

Q: How could my mother not know it wasn't my father?

A: Because his face was—I think, it must have been just . . . gone. And his truck was in the driveway, and she was distraught. And I had told her it was him, because I'd seen it. I'd believed it was him. Why would she want to take a close look herself at . . . that?

Q: Wouldn't the police need to ID him?

A: Why would they, if his own son witnessed it and had already identified him?

Q: If it wasn't your father, where is your father now?

A: I don't know. But I'm going to find out. Find out what they
      did to him.

"*They?*" Her eyes clouded again. Not with doubt, with concern.

I'd no idea where my words had come from. I had not been aware I
was thinking them. "He wouldn't just *leave* me. Us. And never contact
us again. Something . . . There was a man at my dad's barbershop a week
before, and he terrified me. And . . . "

Juliette's silence unnerved me.

"I need to get a sample of his handwriting," I said. "To compare to
the note. Whoever wrote it *was* confessing to hiding something important
about themselves. That's a clue. If my father wrote it, what did he mean?
If he's not who we think he is, who is he? He was adopted, I know that."

"Maybe that's what it was about."

"He never hid the fact. It wasn't a secret." My father had never cared
that he was adopted, was never curious about his birth parents. His
adoption was just a boring fact, like his hair being brown, and he spoke of
his adoptive parents as his real and only parents.

"Maybe . . . " I continued. "Maybe my father wrote the note, and it
drove the man on the bed to do what he did. Or maybe the man on the
bed wrote it, and it was meant for my father or—"

"Or your mother," Juliette said.

I hadn't considered this, didn't *want* to consider what it meant to
have a man kill himself in my parents' bedroom and leave a note for my
mother. I thought about the very first question my mother asked me that
day: *Did he leave a note?* She hadn't asked how I was or what happened.
Not at first. Not that I recall, anyway. But the first thing I *remember* is
her asking about a note. I wondered now whether she had asked because
she expected there to be one. Had she suspected that the Incident would
happen? Had she *known* it would?

"Or maybe your mom wrote it," Juliette suggested.

"No," I said, but the truth was I'd been so focused on my father—or
the man on the bed—being the one to write the note, that my mother
had never entered my mind. Had she written it? I hadn't seen my mother's

handwriting in years. I had no occasion to see it and did not remember it. Before the Incident my mother had given me a birthday card each year, but she would sign "Love, Mom" with an exaggerated, fanciful, celebratory cursive, all swirls and exclamation points and underlines—not a sample I could use to compare to the note. She hadn't given me a birthday card since the Incident. I still gave her birthday cards every year, though I did so with an undercurrent of sorrow and guilt. Her birthday came just a day before my father's birthday, and it always made me think of him and miss him. My mother never left me notes about where she might be or when she would be back, because she was always at work and always came straight home unless it was bowling night. She wrote a grocery list, I supposed, but I'd never seen it. I had no idea what my mother's printed handwriting looked like, and it suddenly seemed very odd to me that I didn't, that perhaps it was deliberate.

"Show me the note," Juliette said.

I had the note tucked safely in my pocket. "It's at my house," I said, lying in the hope that she'd want to follow me there, in the hope that I might prolong our time together. Lying just as I had lied to my mother when she asked me whether there was a note. One more lie on my road to ruin.

MYSTERY OF MYSTERIES

Molly and Rusty lazed in the shade of the apple trees as Juliette knelt beside them, rubbing their bellies and cooing. Juliette untied Rusty and let him weave through her legs a few times. Her girl's sky-blue ten-speed Schwinn Varsity leaned against the tree, its chrome spokes sparkling in the sunlight that shone through the bare branches. A loud yellow smiley face sticker was emblazoned across the handlebar post. From a brown paper lunch bag stuffed in the bike's wicker basket, Juliette took two dog treats. She fed one each to Rusty and Molly. "Come on, boy, we're hoofing it from here," she said. "We're on an adventure." She looked at me. "Ready?" I was ready, and hoped my mom was already off running her errands.

We took the sidewalk back to my house, exposed in the brightness of the world instead of hidden in the shade along the railroad tracks. With each step I rued my decision to bring Juliette to my house, dreaded having her lay eyes on its rooms of drawn shades and gloom, dishes barnacled with crusted food and heaped on the counter and in the sink, bales of soiled laundry, the stench of Molly's menstruation, and the burned, greasy odor of the TV dinners Lydia and I heated in the toaster oven.

We came to my driveway, where weeds wrestled up through cracked asphalt stained with the fluids that leaked from my mom's Pontiac, which, thankfully, was not parked out front. The yard was scabbed with hard soil and clumps of dog shit.

"What's wrong?" Juliette said as I stared at my forlorn home.

"Wait out here," I told her.

"I want to go in. I want to see where it happened. I don't mean it like that. That sounds disrespectful. Just . . . " Her eyes sparked, or maybe it was just the light, or I'm remembering wrong. "I want to know every-thing. To help you, I need to see everything."

Juliette unleashed Rusty, and he ran about the yard snatching up sticks in his mouth. Molly joined in the play, and though she was no match for Rusty's enthusiasm, I'd not seen her so animated in years.

I took a deep breath and led Juliette to the front door, looking straight ahead, not daring to glance at our yard, hoping Juliette wouldn't look if I didn't.

The house stank worse than I remembered, and I swear I heard Juliette suck in a breath at the odor.

"This way," I said.

I hurried down the hall, reaching in my front pocket to take out the note.

In my room milky sunlight bled in at the edges of my pulled shade as I kicked my grayed K-Mart underwear on the floor toward my bed. With my back to Juliette, I yanked the nightstand drawer open, palmed the note in my hand, and pretended to take it from the drawer.

"Got it." I turned to Juliette. She was leaning in the doorway, arms wrapped around herself. Her eyes flitted about my room.

"Sorry," I said. "Our place is—"

"A shithole," she said.

I would have died of humiliation, but Juliette's smile and shrug of knowing acceptance lifted the dark clouds of my disgrace.

"Don't sweat it," she said. "My dad's *so* fussy, out in our yard on his knees rooting up weeds with his little special forked garden instruments, spraying poison on every tiny blade that isn't his beloved pure strain of precious emerald grass. But my *mom. Slll-ob.* If not for my dad hiring a cleaning lady, your house would be sterile as a NASA lab compared to ours. My mom's car is exhibit A. Shitstorm central. *And* it smells worse than your room, even more . . . " She scrunched her nose. " . . . funky."

I ought to have been mortified, but I wasn't. Her words made me feel at ease with the wreckage of my life.

"Let me see the note," she said.

For eight years I had never even touched the note. Relinquishing it, even for a moment, even to Juliette, seemed a betrayal of my father, whether or not I believed he had written it.

I handed her the note, our fingertips touching.

Juliette cleared her throat as if she were going to read it aloud. She didn't. Instead, she pushed a hand down in the pocket of her jeans and fished out a pair of purple-framed reading glasses. She propped the glasses on her nose and read the note, squinting despite her glasses.

She handed the note back to me and tucked the glasses back in her pocket.

"I am not who you think I am," she said. "You're right, we need to find a sample of your dad's writing. If he wrote the note, maybe it was because he felt so bad that he actually did want to do something awful to himself—hated himself, or something." She flipped the note over. "Who is this SFL? Maybe they wrote it?"

"I don't know. But it wasn't my dad on the bed. Come see."

For the second time that day, and only the second time in eight years, I entered my parents' bedroom.

The room was in as much disarray as my own, with bras and underwear blooming from a laundry basket at the foot of the bed. The sight of it made me blush.

I shoved the underthings aside and sat on the edge of my mother's bed and put my feet flat on the floor as Juliette entered the room and stood with her hip cocked, her chin cupped in a nest of fingers as she studied my evidence.

"See?" I said.

Juliette paced in front of me. She chewed on the tips of her hair.

"Maybe he was sitting back farther," she said, calculating my position. Her Dr. Scholl's left slight depressions in the shag carpet.

I slid back on the bed. The position was clearly an unnatural and uncomfortable way to sit.

"No one sits like this," I said. "We sit with our knees bent at the edge, not sticking out awkwardly. And the legs can't be dangling over the edge if the knees aren't hinged."

"Maybe you're remembering it wrong. Maybe his feet *were* on the floor."

"I'm *not* remembering it wrong," I snapped. "I know what the hell I saw."

Juliette flinched and stepped back. As she did, I felt as if I were falling from a cliff with her standing at the top and with no way for me to get back to her. Each passing second the distance between us grew. Blood pulsed behind my eyes; my breathing came shallow and sharp.

"I was there," I rasped, trying to calm my voice. "I was *here*. I saw it."

"And you believed it was your father you saw right up until this morning, so . . . "

"But I've always *known* deep down he would never do that. The dangling legs are enough to convince me now. I still want a handwriting sample, to help corroborate it, but I've searched everywhere I can think of."

"Maybe your mom has a stash somewhere, or a safe-deposit box."

"She didn't keep anything of his."

"She must have kept something."

"She didn't keep a thing. Not one thing."

"That's . . . really weird."

I know, I thought. The more I considered what my mother had done, the more suspicious it became.

"Ask her," Juliette said. "Ask her what stuff she kept and where it is. She had to have saved *something*. Old birthday or Christmas cards, documents, love letters, whatever."

"I *can't* ask her."

"Why not?" Juliette fished a pack of grape Bubble Yum from her pocket, unwrapped a cube, and popped it in her mouth.

"I've never asked her about that stuff," I said. "Why would I ask now? She'd think it was suspicious."

"*Suspicious?* The *note* is suspicious. Legs not reaching the floor—*that's* suspicious. Your mom keeping nothing, dumping *all* your dad's stuff— that's not just suspicious. That's—"

"—Crazy," I said.

"Tell her you're older now. You're curious. And what about an old photo album? You could look to see if your dad scribbled anything on the back of any of the photos. Names or dates."

"Gone."

"Photo albums? Of all of you? Wouldn't she want them for herself at least?"

"I don't *know*," I said.

"There has to be something, somewhere."

"I can't think in here."

We sat out on the steps, our dogs dozing at our feet. I'd made strawberry ice-cream cones for us. The ice cream was furred with freezer burn and had a taste of tin, but if Juliette minded the taste, she gave no indication. She spit her gum into a nearby bush and nipped away at the ice cream like a bird.

"Just ask your mom," she said.

"I can't tell her I've had a note all this time that she asked for eight years ago. That I suddenly don't think my father was in the room that day. That someone else is . . . " For the first time, the thought entered my mind. " . . . buried in his grave. And he was, what? Murdered?"

There. I had released the word to the universe as a magician releases a bird from his cupped hands. I'd thought I would feel my spirits buoyed when I finally spoke the truth that had been incubating inside me: that someone had done something to my father after, or perhaps before, another man shot himself in my parents' bedroom. Instead, I felt angry and frightened.

Juliette popped the last bit of sugar cone in her mouth and wiped melted ice cream from her lip with the back of her hand.

"What about public records?" Juliette said. "Your birth certificate? A house deed? Something your dad signed that would be at the town clerk's office."

"Genius!" I said.

I looked down the street. I feared my sister would come home with Dipshit any second and they'd humiliate me in front of Juliette. I stood. "Let's go to the town clerk now. My sister will be home soon. I don't want to be here."

Juliette grabbed her bike and we walked down the driveway. "What's with that creep who picks her up at school in that truck?" Juliette said.

"How do you that's my sister?"

"Why wouldn't I? Is it a secret? Why would she ever hang out with him?"

As much as I loathed Dipshit, it stung me to hear Juliette speak about Lydia in a way that mirrored my own thoughts.

"My sister's . . . lonely," I said.

Juliette and I were at the end of my driveway when I saw Clay. Shirtless, the ripped muscularity of his physique bared, his white T-shirt stuffed in the back pocket of his faded Levi's, he sauntered toward us with the powerful yet agile movements of the born athlete.

Juliette fingered a piece of hair from her eyes.

Clay smiled, his mop of unruly hair tousled just so. His eyes worked over Juliette's body unabashed. "*Mi amigo*," he said to me, now ignoring Juliette as if he'd never seen her. "Can I borrow your pistol? The old man's bitching about a woodchuck in the yard and wants it fucking dead."

"It's in the house," I said.

"Sweet. Go grab it." He eyed Juliette.

"We're in a hurry," I said. "We've got something important to—"

"We've got time," Juliette said.

"I know *I* do." Clay smiled.

"Actually, we don't have time," I said. "We've got a lot to do at the town clerk."

"Town clerk," Clay said. "You two getting hitched by a justice of the peace?"

Juliette's eyes shifted from Clay to me, back to Clay.

"You want the revolver, you get it," I said.

"I don't know where it is," Clay said.

"Where it *always* is. You know where. You want it, you go grab it."

"Chill, man. Easy. I'll let you two lovebirds get back to whatever's so important at the *town clerk's*." He powered toward the house without another glance at Juliette.

"Should we wait?" Juliette asked.

"He'll manage. He's a big boy," I said.

"He is," Juliette said.

Juliette and I climbed the steps of the town clerk's office just as a woman in a denim skirt and a flowery blouse was locking up the place.

"Damn it," I exclaimed, "Damn it all."

The woman flinched. "We're just closing for lunch. We open again at two."

"Who takes a two-hour lunch?" I snapped.

"We open again at two," she reiterated, and walked down the steps past us.

"If Clay hadn't held us up on purpose, we—"

"He didn't do it on purpose," Juliette said.

"You don't know him. He—"

"We would've only had a minute or two whether he showed up or not. I should head home, anyway. I usually feed Rusty lunch by now."

I glanced at Rusty. He didn't look hungry. Juliette started down the stairs. With each step she took, I felt as if I were being slowly erased. At the bottom of the steps, Juliette turned and looked up at me. "I'll see you back here at two, though, right?"

"Two? Yeah. Right, of course."

"Two sharp. We need to get to the bottom of all this."

"Yes," I said. "We do."

I watched as Juliette raced away on her ten-speed, Rusty trotting along beside her.

I traipsed back and forth along the railroad tracks, unable to calm down.

At 1:30 I returned to the town clerk's office and loitered at the top of steps.

The clerk returned at two o'clock and afforded me a grudging smile as she unlocked the door. I waited for Juliette, my eyes fixed on the corner of Main Street where I expected her to appear. The beat of blood in my head kept the torturous metronomic passage of time. I waited until 2:40.

Dejected, I entered the town clerk's office alone. The woman who had unlocked the door looked up from her desk. Her smile sat crooked, and one eye, smaller than the other, twitched behind the lens of her glasses as if she had a grain of sand irritating it.

"Yes?" she asked me.

"I'd like to see the public records," I said.

She eyed me warily. "Whatever for?"

"A school report."

She ventured around the desk with a huff, a clutch of keys in her hand, and led me down a corridor whose wall boasted photos of the town's historic floods and blizzards, and of the fire that burned down the old Palladium theater in the 1950s.

File cabinets crammed the neglected annex where the woman brought me. They were so close together, I had to walk behind her down the narrow aisles.

The woman pointed to each section as she rattled off, "Birth and death certificates, row A. Deeds, row B. Divorce filings and criminal records, restraining orders, and the like, row C. Marriage licenses, row D. All arranged by date. The door locks behind you as you exit, so you may wish to stay in here until you find what you're after. Otherwise, I'll have to let you back in each time. If you need to make copies, I can do that for you for five cents each. We've got one of the new Xerox machines. No more carbon paper, thank God. I hate that purple ink."

As I started down row A, the woman yelped. I turned to see what was wrong.

"Excuse me!" she exclaimed as Juliette pushed past her.

"Sorry," Juliette said breathily. "Problems on the home front." She unslung a backpack from her shoulder, arching an eyebrow at the tight quarters. Her black hair was now shoved recklessly behind an orange headband, and a yellow happy face decorated the front of a fresh white T-shirt that fell to just above brown corduroy pants that replaced her jeans. In place of her Dr. Scholl's were flip-flops with a plastic daisy blooming between the big and second toes. Despite her sunny attire, she looked fatigued, with pink-rimmed eyes. I wondered whether she'd fallen sleep or had been crying.

"Problems?" I said.

"*Parents*. You know how it is."

I didn't know how it was. Not at all.

"My dad stopped in from work unexpected, and—never mind." She flapped a hand in the air as if absently waving off a mosquito. "Find anything?"

"I haven't started."

"Divide and conquer," she suggested. "You take birth and death? I take property and land deeds, look for the deed to your house?"

I told her my parents probably bought the house in the late sixties, after they'd moved here from Maine.

It did not take me long to find my sister's and my birth certificates. To my disappointment, only unhelpful cursive signatures were on these records.

"Got it," Juliette announced.

I hurried over to her as she showed me a deed for our house. My heart lurched at the sight of more signatures that had no relation to the printed script of the note.

"My father owned a barber shop. The deed should be here," I said, though I expected the same result: a signature that would mean nothing to my pursuit. Our pursuit.

As I searched for the barbershop deed, Juliette wandered away.

I thumbed through the range of file dates from well before to well after where I surmised the deed should be. I found nothing. After another ten minutes, I lucked upon it. The description and address of the property were correct, but my father's name was not on it. His signature was not on it. My father was the proprietor of his barbershop's business, but he was not, as I'd always imagined, the owner of the property. He was a tenant. I felt embarrassed for my father, and ashamed that I would think less of him for not owning the shop. On the deed, in place of his name, was scrawled a signature to go with the typed name: Buell Vanders III.

The grandson of the patriarch of the Vanders family. It angered me that my father paid rent to the Vanders. Did the royal family own the whole damned town?

I thought about the stranger, the Tall Man, who had come into the shop that night long ago, and how he had behaved as if he owned the shop. He wasn't anyone from the Vanders family that I knew. The members of the family were depicted in the estate's tourist pamphlets, and I'd never seen his face. "You can't make me," my father had said to the Tall Man, just a week before the Incident. Make him what?

Juliette came over. She placed a hand on my shoulder, but I was distracted and scarcely noted what would have elated me just moments earlier. "Anything?" she said.

"We need a sample of printed letters, not worthless signatures," I said.

"We'll find it. We just have to think. Hard."

"I need to get out of here."

Outside on the steps, Juliette sat beside me, knees clutched under her chin.

We sat there, thinking hard. Where would I find my father's writing?

A checkbook? Holiday or birthday cards? Old business ledgers for the barbershop?

Love letters to my mom? Postcards?

Postcards.

I remembered that my father had gone to some sort of annual barbers' convention or trade show or something, in Boston or in Concord, New Hampshire. He'd brought souvenirs home for Lydia and me. Miniature felt Red Sox pennants. Saltwater taffy. Yet he always sent a postcard, too, and the joke had been that he always got home before the postcard arrived. My mom would ask why he bothered. He'd say he did it because he missed us, postcards were fun, and you never know what might happen when you go away. My mother had called him morbid. The postcards would bear his writing. Though I had no memory of it, he would likely have printed the address for legibility. A postcard would tell the tale, if I could find one. They were long gone, as far as I knew.

Except . . .

I stood up and sprang down the steps, shouting back to Juliette, "Let's go."

By the time I reached my driveway, I was panting. Juliette rode her bike up beside me, her upper lip glistening with sweat.

In my room I knelt at the back of my closet and dragged out several milk crates in which my father's books were stacked. I'd never read them, but I thought right then that when this was over, I would finally sit down and read them all, one after another.

"My father used postcards for bookmarks sometimes," I said.

Juliette knelt beside me as I snatched a book from the nearest crate: *Lost Among the Trees*. I flipped through it in search of a postcard. I found nothing.

The next book, *Remember Me*, sported a plastic slipcover. I picked it up and thumbed the sticker at its spine: FIC EDW. A library book, eight years overdue.

I fanned the pages, Juliette at my shoulder. No postcard fell out.

"Stop!" Juliette shouted and poked her finger at a page.

An underlined sentence read:

She didn't have a choice.

Next to the sentence was one word, hand printed:

UNTRUE.

"*That's a library book you're writing in*," my mother had said to my father one of those last evenings before the Incident.

I took out the note from my pocket.

I AM NOT WHO YOU THINK I AM

"They match," Juliette said at my shoulder. "Your dad wrote the note. It was him on the edge of the bed."

"No. It *wasn't*," I said. "It wasn't. Just because he wrote the note doesn't mean it was him on the bed. I know it. I feel it."

"You can't go by feelings. It's his handwriting. You have to go by evidence."

"The evidence is that the man on the bed was shorter than my father, by several inches. That's evidence. Physical evidence."

I stared at the note in my hand and the word written in the book open on my lap. I compared them. Identical. No doubt.

My father was not who I thought he was.

So who was he?

And to whom was the note written?

My father could not have known I'd come home sick that day and find him. The note was never intended for me. Had it been intended for my mother? She should have been home. She was *always* home at that time. Always. That was when she watched her soap opera. She ironed while she watched. She scheduled her errands around the show. My father must have expected her to be home. He must have been surprised when she wasn't. Where *had* she been? I thought about my father's truck idling in the driveway, its door flung open.

"He was in a hurry," I said. "His truck was *idling*, the door flung open."

"So?" Juliette said.

"That's *evidence*. Who is in a hurry to run inside and do *that*? And he must have expected my mother to be home. She was always home that time of day. Was he going to do that knowing she was home? Do that in front of her?"

Juliette sat cross-legged on the floor beside me. "I hate to say it, but . . . he did that in front of you."

"*He* didn't. God damn it. It wasn't him!"

Juliette recoiled at my outburst. After a moment she said, "You think he ran into the house because there was something important inside that he had to do?"

"Or had to *stop*," I said.

"Stop what? A stranger from shooting himself on your parents' bed? Then why didn't he stop him? Where was your dad when you got there, if that wasn't him on the bed? His truck was outside, so, where was he?"

"Maybe he heard me come in and fled out the back, and then . . . something happened."

"Like what?"

"I don't know," I said. "How should I know? Maybe you're right. Maybe he did care so little about me, he'd do that in front of me. Just blast his brains all over me. Maybe he was that awful. Does that make you happy?" I threw the book across the room. It slammed my nightstand so hard that my bedside lamp fell to the floor and broke.

Juliette rubbed her palms over the thighs of her corduroy pants, making the ribbing appear darker, then stood up. "I should get home."

"I didn't mean to get so mad."

She shrugged. I would have preferred a slap across the face to that shrug of indifference.

"Stay. Please, stay," I pleaded, hearing the fragility in my own voice.

"It's late anyway. And I told my mom I was going to hang out at Shelly Crawford's and would be home by now."

"Why'd you tell your mom you were going to Shelly's?"

"She doesn't have to know where I am at all times, especially when it's with some guy."

Some guy.

"And what am I going to tell her?" Juliette said. "I'm looking into your dad's suicide or . . . worse? She already thinks I have a screw loose. She'd stop me. Or at least *try* to stop me. She can't *actually* stop me from doing what I want. No one can."

"I'll walk you home."

"She's home," Juliette said. "She's always home. I don't need her hounding me about some boy walking me home."

Some boy.

"Maybe we can sneak out and meet after dinner," Juliette said as she stood at my bedroom doorway. "The library at seven? It's open till eight."

"You'll be there?"

"I swear." She rapped on the doorjamb with a knuckle as she turned to leave. She stopped and looked back at me. "You know, there *is* another reason why your dad might have left the truck running and its door open, besides being in a hurry to get inside the house."

"What?"

"He didn't plan on being inside the house for long."

I stood in the kitchen, scarfing a bowl of nuked SpaghettiOs for a late dinner, the book *Remember Me* open on the countertop. My fingertips traced where my father's pencil had left indentations like those stamped by typewriter keys on the library's catalog cards.

I felt adrift, like a balloon escaped from a child's grasp and floating alone in the sky, tossed about by random winds, drifting higher and farther from Earth, from myself and the world I thought I knew, with no way back down until I popped from the pressure and crumpled back to the ground, shapeless and spent.

I flipped through *Remember Me* and came to a page, deep in the book, with another underlined sentence: <u>Some secrets must be shared, the cost of keeping them too high.</u>

In the margin beside it was a note printed in my father's hand:

SHE SHOULD HAVE KEPT IT SECRET ANYWAY

I was rereading the sentence when Lydia burst in through the front door, startling me. Dipshit stomped in behind her, smoking a cigarette, his foam-and-mesh trucker ball cap tugged on backward and crooked. He'd never been in our house while I was home. His presence revolted me.

"Why the sour puss, sport?" he teased, and slapped me on the back of the head so hard, I bit my tongue. "Lose your puppy?"

"You can't smoke in here," I said, tasting blood.

Dipshit tucked the cigarette in the corner of his mouth and picked up the opened can of SpaghettiOs. He crammed two fingers down inside the can and came up with an orange glop, which he shoved into his mouth.

"Pig," Lydia giggled, and elbowed his chest.

Dipshit squeezed her rear end. "You love it." He blew a smoke ring in her face.

"You. Can't. Smoke. In. Here," I repeated.

"What's with your spaz brother?" Dipshit asked Lydia, before blowing a chain of smoke rings up at the ceiling.

"Come on." Lydia pulled him down the hall into her bedroom, and the door closed with a *clack*.

I stood there, trembling with hatred and impotence, until I had to flee the house and the repugnant sounds coming from behind my sister's bedroom door.

I waited for Juliette on the library steps until 7:40 p.m. I reasoned that she might be late, despite her assurance she'd be there at seven. Maybe she'd had another problem with her parents. When she hadn't shown by the time the library closed at 8:00 p.m., I walked down Main Street in the direction of her house, past Whipple Pharmacy, the Grotto Arcade, and Midnight Video. I waited at the corner, searching for her. The only open place was the Main Street Diner two blocks down, its neon sign fritzing in the dark. The sidewalks and streets stood empty, and a breeze blew, turning my flesh cold as I wandered for hours, a specter making its nightly rounds of a ghost town.

I kept sensing that I was being watched, judged, and mocked—by whom, I could not say. But the feeling of eyes on me was as physical a sensation as the pang of humiliation in my gut at being stood up after driving Juliette away with my temper. The tip of my tongue was swollen and sore where I'd bitten it when Dipshit cuffed the back of my head.

I trudged home, meandering through the blackness of backyards, my way lit by the stars and moon. Dogs barked. Floodlights blinked on. A voice shouted, "Who's there!"

When I arrived home, the windows of my house were dark. Dipshit and his truck were long gone. Lydia was gone too—with him, I supposed. I didn't want to go inside the house. I stood in the middle of the street with no place to go.

I thought about going to Juliette's house, rapping on her bedroom window. I didn't know which window was hers, but I figured I could peek in each one until I found it. And then what? Say, "Where were you?

What did I do to make you not want to meet me? I'm sorry I got mad and snapped at you . . . "? I imagined that in the intervening hours, she had started to think about what we were up to, about my theories, about my anger at Clay—my anger at most everything, even her—and had determined that I was sad and desperate.

I gazed at the moon for answers, stared into the woods behind my house. I thought about the screaming woman in the widow's watch. The lure of seeing her again and discovering more about her proved more powerful than the consequences of getting caught. I started off in the direction of the woods behind my house when a single headlight beam lit me up. My mom's J2000 bore down on me. The horn blared as the car swerved around me and shuddered to a stop in our driveway. After my mother turned it off, the engine chugged for a few breaths, bucked, and died. I could scarcely believe how long the day had felt. It seemed that weeks had passed since I spoke with my mother through the bathroom door just that morning.

"Wayland," my mom said, alarm in her voice as she got out and shut the car door. In the quiet night, I could hear rust flakes falling from the Pontiac's front fender. "What are you doing in the road? I almost killed you."

"Just . . . coming home," I lied.

She unclipped her earrings and tucked them in the pocket of her jean skirt. Her fright after almost running me down subsiding, she exhaled and relaxed. Smiled. Her night of bowling had left her in bright spirits, even if those spirits would be dimmed by morning.

"Coming home from where?" she asked me without any real concern for where I'd been, more out of obligation or idle curiosity. Not that she didn't care about my safety, she did when there was anything for her to be genuinely concerned about, but my being out on a vacation night didn't meet the threshold.

"The library."

"This late? Were they out of books?" She eyed my empty hands. I always returned from the library with a backpack crammed full of books.

"I was just on the steps, hanging out."

"Alone?" She eyed me the way a store clerk eyes a suspected shoplifter. "Have you eaten?"

"Not really."

"Hungry?"

"Nah," I said, although I was famished.

My mother frowned as her mood plunged from joy to melancholy. I had no idea then what could have caused it. I see now it was, in part, me: her only son, skinny and fretful and all but friendless. My tattered sneakers and shirt and jeans, Goodwill bargains, all a size too small yet needing to make it through one more spring and summer; my shaggy hair overdue for a cut my father had once performed with punctual ceremony every three weeks; my face and hands grubby—not in the way of a boy who has had fun being adventurous outside all day, but in the way of one who's been soiled by life—a grayness to the skin that cannot be scrubbed away. A boy who was clearly ravenous after not eating all day out of worry, yet pretended he wasn't hungry, because he did not want to bring attention to the fact that the refrigerator and cupboards were all but empty and that he hadn't communicated with his mother except through a closed bathroom door for going on a week now—not out of any attempt to avoid her, but due to the nature and need of their existence.

How did a mother carry that weight of concern for her children when her obligation to provide for them consumed so much of her waking life that it meant neglect in most other aspects, in time and attention, and made the children and the parent strangers to one another in the same home? How did my mother carry this weight? I admired and respected her even then without realizing I did, and without possessing even the vaguest notion of the sacrifices she made.

My mom reached an arm through the driver's window and grabbed a take-out bag from Knock 'Em Down Bowling Lanes. She smiled. "I brought your favorite: fried chicken."

Fried chicken, from the lanes especially, wasn't my favorite anymore. It hadn't been for a couple of years. Fried food turned my stomach sloppy, but I didn't say anything. I tried to smile. "Great," I said, nearly overwhelmed with an urge to hug my mother the way I had so easily and unabashedly hugged her when I was six or eight, or even ten, but had not done in more than five years without feeling a conspicuous discomfort and sense of loss.

Inside, I pushed aside piles of junk mail and dirty dishes on the counter while my mom patted the cold chicken with a paper towel to absorb the grease. After arranging the pieces on paper plates, she sat on a stool on the kitchen side of the bar, slipped her shoes off, and rubbed her ankles. Her hair was down, as she preferred it on her night out, and now she pinned it up in a bun.

Slouched, elbows planted on the counter, she picked the breading from a piece of chicken with her chipped fingernails and popped the fried skin in her mouth. She caught me staring and smiled. "What?" she asked, straightening her posture.

"Nothing."

I glanced at the chicken, its once-crispy coating damp with cooled grease. The meat would be cold and rubbery.

"I got you the dark pieces you like," my mom said. She cracked open a can of my sister's warm Tab sitting on the counter and took a drink, then covered her mouth with her fist to stifle a burp. "This stuff's horrible," she said, setting down the can. "God knows what's in it."

We sat eating and not saying anything, avoiding each other's eyes. I forced down the dark, fatty chicken meat to avoid disappointing my mom.

She wiped her greasy fingers on a paper towel and said, "So what have you been up to?"

Perhaps it was the events of the day that piqued my suspicion, but I detected in my mom's question more than just cursory interest.

"Nothing," I said.

"Really?" She nibbled at her piece of chicken.

"You know."

"If I knew, I wouldn't ask," she said. "Just sitting alone on the library steps doesn't sound like much fun on a vacation night. Did you do anything fun today? You took off so early without saying and never came back for our morning together. It must have been something important. Or fun."

"Just stuff." My skin felt too warm.

She sipped her Tab and winced, got up and dumped the soda down the drain, and poured a glass of tap water for herself. She sat again.

"I have to ask," she said.

My heartbeat slowed.

"What were you doing in my bedroom this morning?"

My face warmed. If I tried to deny that I'd been in her room, my voice would betray me.

"Just . . . looking for something," I said.

"For what?"

"Why do you think dad killed himself?" I blurted. I hadn't planned to say it. The words escaped from me of their own accord.

My mother's face seemed to undergo sudden rigor mortis; the muscles locked in a grimace.

She slid her water glass back and forth between her hands, gripping it so tightly, I feared it would shatter and slice her hands.

She placed her hand on mine. "Let's just have a nice dinner."

"This isn't a nice dinner," I said, and slid my hand out from under hers.

"You love this chicken. It's your favorite."

I lifted up a congealed and pathetic drumstick. "It's gristle and grease. It makes me sick. It's made me sick for years."

My mother's face caved as my own rancor cracked me wide open.

"I didn't know," she said.

"Tell me why you think he killed himself."

"What's gotten into you . . . ?"

"Into me? I *saw* it. I was *eight*. I *saw* it. And you did *nothing* to help me. Nothing but clear out every last sign of him. Then you kept us here, in this place, where I have to go past that bedroom. Every. Single. Day. See it all over again, every single day. Dozens of times a day."

My mother looked at me as if I'd stabbed her in the chest.

"Where . . . ?" she whispered, eyes downcast. "Where were we supposed to go? What was I supposed to do?"

"What are you hiding?"

"*Hiding?*" She looked at me, blinking, terrified. "I'm not *hiding* anything."

"I'm not asking why you think he did it. I'm not asking you what you think his motive was. I'm asking why you think it was even him who did it, him who was there that day at all. Because it wasn't him. It was someone else."

My mother's elbow jerked and knocked her water glass off the counter. The glass shattered on the floor. "I don't even know what to . . . " my mother began, but her voice tapered off and an opaque film glazed her eyes, as if she were lost in a daydream.

She stood up and yelped in pain. She'd stepped in the shards of broken glass with her bare feet. Blood leaked onto the linoleum. She didn't seem to notice.

"You're cut," I said. "You're bleeding."

"What happened today?" she said, ignoring my words and her bleeding feet. "Why are you doing this?"

"I don't know who it was," I said. "But that man was not my father."

"You need to *stop* this. It's unnatural. It's harmful."

"Harmful to *who*?"

"You need to stop. Let it go."

"You mean like you did? Toss out every single scrap of him, throw it all out at the curb to be hauled off to the dump, and just forget him?"

"I haven't *forgotten* him. You have no idea what I've been through."

"You tossed *everything* he owned. His favorite books. His favorite chair. His favorite photographs of me and Lydia. Entire photo albums of us as a family. I'd think you'd at least want to keep those for yourself. How could you just toss out all his stuff?"

"I . . . I don't need *stuff.* And your father—he was more than just your father, you know. He was my husband. More than just my husband. He was . . . We had a life together long before we were even married, just us two, and no one—"

"Your bed. Is it the same bed you and Dad had?"

"What?" My mother glanced toward her bedroom door down the hall.

"Is your bed now the same bed as it was then?"

"Of course it is."

"I knew it," I said. "Whoever it was, his feet didn't reach the floor.

They were dangling, and even *my* feet reach the floor, and I'm shorter than he was, so it wasn't him."

"What are you saying?" Fear shone in her eyes.

"The bed is the same. But the man's feet didn't reach the floor, and if it was Dad, they would have. Easily."

My mother's lips moved, but no sound came. "I thought you meant the bed frame," she said finally. "It's the same. I got rid of the mattress and box spring. I got new ones. I had to. The old ones were . . . soiled. The old mattress must have sat up higher."

"It would have had to sit up *way* higher. It would have had to be a big, expensive mattress, which we probably couldn't afford even then. And that's not what you meant before you had to think about it. You said the bed is the same."

"I should have gotten you help," she whispered. "Whatever else happened, whatever else I did or didn't do, I should have at least done that. I'm ashamed I didn't. But with everything else that went on . . . it took all I had just to keep *breathing*. There was so much to get straight, so much to do and to think about, to consider." Her wet eyes gleamed. "And then the days went by. They go by *so* fast. And I can't hang on to a single moment, and—especially with your sister. Especially her. I screwed up. Screwed *her* up. You too. Royally. I keep screwing up. You were a good boy. You *are* a good boy. None of it was your fault. You should never ever blame yourself or feel it was your fault, or—"

"My fault? Why would I ever think it was my fault?"

"No . . . I—it wasn't. Of course, it wasn't. I just don't know what guilt you might—"

"Guilt? I walked in on him. I didn't *do* anything." A thought struck me that left my flesh ice cold. "You think I could have stopped him, should have stopped him, don't you? Is that what everyone thinks? I was there, so I should have stopped it? That I . . . I was eight. I was—"

"No. God, no. Please, don't ever think that. I never thought that. That's not what I mean. I . . . We never talked about what happened," she said. "I know. This is not how I . . . He's gone. It was him. You were *there*. You saw it. You saw *him*."

"I never saw his face."

"Oh, honey," she sobbed. "Wayland, it was him. If I could prove it to you, I would. God, I wish I could. You can't keep thinking these things." She reached out to touch my cheek.

I slapped her hand away.

"Why weren't you *here* that day?" I needed to know. "At home. You were always home that time of day."

My mother's face paled. "Not always."

"Yes. Always. You watched that soap opera. You joked about being addicted to it. You never missed it. You *always* watched it."

"Not always. Not that day."

"Why not? Where were you?"

"I don't remember. Just . . . out."

"Of all days, you don't remember where you were on that one? Just '*out*'?"

"In town."

"Doing what?"

"It doesn't matter now."

I stepped close to her. Close enough to see her pupils dilate with fear. I was the scrawny skin-and-bones pussy, but I was still five inches taller than my mom. Twenty-five pounds heavier. Compared to her, I was strong. "It matters. To me," I said. "You tell me what you were doing, or . . . " Blood pounded in my head so hard, I thought I'd pass out.

My mother took a step backward. "I was supposed to meet someone."

"Who?"

"I told you it doesn't *matter*," she said again, her voice quavering.

"It matters to me!" I shouted, crowding her.

She backed away. "I never ended up meeting him."

"*Him?*"

"Please, don't think—"

"Think what? *Him?*" She was lying. I knew. She'd met him.

"It doesn't matter," she repeated.

"Tell me." Hot blood boiled in my veins. I was going to black out. "You tell me right now, or—"

"Stop! I won't talk about this anymore!" she shouted and smacked her palm on the counter so hard it startled me. "I'm your *mother*. I don't have to do anything you tell me." A shadow passed over her eyes. "What were you doing in my bedroom this morning? What aren't you telling me? You need to tell me the truth. Tell me everything."

"I was looking for pictures of Dad. But I didn't find even a scrap that he ever existed, because you threw it all away." If she could lie to my face, I could lie to hers.

NOW YOU SEE HER,
NOW YOU . . .

I slammed my bedroom door behind me, picked up *Remember Me*, and threw it across the room. I grabbed each of my father's books, ripping out pages and flinging them around my room until I collapsed amid the debris, spent and sobbing.

Molly shivered in the corner, frightened.

Sitting there, I realized I'd never read any of my father's books, because I feared that reading the same words he had, on the same pages, might overwhelm me and suck me down a drain of despair.

I dragged a book, *Gone All This Time*, toward me. It was not a library book, but one my father had owned. I flipped through its pages and found no notes, no underlined sections. I picked up another book he had owned and did the same. I found nothing inside the covers except the words the author had written. I picked up one titled *A Forest So Deep.* Its pages, too, were free of marks.

As I set the book down, a slip of paper peeked out from under the back inside flap of the dust jacket. I lifted it and saw the edges of more slips. I peeled the dust jacket off the book. Several pieces of paper lay hidden beneath it. I laid them flat on my bed and read them.

It took me a moment to figure out what they were. The papers on top were adoption papers. They showed my father's name and gave his adoptive parents' names as Betty and Grant Maynard of Henryville, Maine, where my father had grown up. My father's birth mother's name was given as Silva Francesca Vanders. Birth father: N/A.

Silva. Francesca. Vanders.

I got up and locked my bedroom door, then sat back down among the strewn books, adoption papers in my hand.

Vanders. I knew that surname, of course. Everyone in town knew it. It was the most revered and reviled name in town. Except I'd never heard of a daughter or granddaughter, or *any* woman or girl, named Silva Francesca Vanders. I knew of no woman with the name Silva who had married into the family. There was a Gvenn Vanders, an elderly, widowed matriarch who'd survived her husband Buell II. She didn't have a daughter, Silva or any other, as far as I knew, and I was sure I would know. Her son, Buell III, prided himself on regular announcements of his social and charitable galas in the weekly *Shireburne Gazette,* replete with photographs of tuxedoed men and gowned women bedecked in pearls. I'd never once heard or seen mention of a Silva Vanders in any of these, and never read about her in the estate's pamphlets.

Perhaps, the surname was just coincidence. It was a rare name, but other families of no relation surely went by it too.

Why had my father had his own adoption papers? Adoption records were confidential and, except in special legal cases, never shared with the adopted child. My father had never mentioned or shown any interest in his biological parents—at least, not to me. Yet, he had his papers, hidden away. How had he gotten hold of them? Had he stolen them? Had someone given them to him?

The second paper hidden under the book jacket was my father's birth certificate.

It named my father's adoptive parents and gave his place of birth as Shireburne Medical Center.

Shireburne. I'd always thought he'd been born in Maine, where he'd grown up.

I took the note from my pocket.

I AM NOT WHO YOU THINK I AM

I looked at the initials on the back. *SFL.*

A third paper had been tucked under the dust jacket. A single page. A document.

I jolted upright and stared at the paper, my brain rendered numb by the two names typed a bit crookedly in the official space provided. *Plaintiff: Laura Maynard.* My mother. *Defendant: Roland Maynard.* My father.

"What is this?" I whispered to Molly, though the document's intent was typed at the top, squarely in the center. I knew also that the larger question I was asking—*why?*—could not possibly be answered by anyone except my mother.

The document was dated two weeks before the Incident.

"This is a mistake," I said, though I knew that it wasn't. Molly wheezed, cuddled close. "I would have sensed something was wrong," I said, my voice strained, rising. "I'm not *stupid*."

Molly cowered away.

I'd been only eight years old at the time the document was partially filled out, but surely, I'd have sensed the discord that would lead to this, no matter how my parents tried to hide it from Lydia and me. Wouldn't I have? Now, I wasn't so sure. I thought again about my mother not saving a single scrap from my father's life. I thought about her not being at home the day of the Incident. I thought about her mentioning the "him" she'd met in town that day.

Only one other part had been filled out: a section halfway down in which were typed two names, Lydia's and mine. Next to our names, our birth dates were typed. No other part of the document had been filled out. The check boxes for reasons for the filing of the document were left unchecked. The descriptions for each box distressed me.

There were no signatures at the bottom.

I scrutinized the treacherous page again. If I'd been staring at divorce papers, I would have been less dismayed and confused. But a Complaint for Annulment . . . ?

This made no sense at all.

I wanted to ask my mother about it, but I didn't trust her. I didn't need more lies, but I did need to investigate further and share the weight of these discoveries with someone else—Juliette, perhaps. But she had stood me up and clearly wanted no part of this anymore, and I doubted she could make any more sense of this than I could.

I lay back on the bed and stared at the ceiling, trying to piece it all together but getting nowhere. I must've fallen asleep because I awoke in the morning with a start. Molly was whimpering beside me and panting hard—too hard—her breathing labored, her eyes milky as she gazed at me and licked my cheek. I hugged her. "Good girl," I whispered in her ear as I rubbed her head. "Sweet girl."

With trembling hands I folded the documents along their creases and slipped them into the hip pocket of my jeans. I unlocked my bedroom door and peeked into the hall.

"Wayland," my mother said from the kitchen at the sound of my door opening. "Wayland, I want to—"

I shut the door and locked it and climbed out my window. I dashed across the yard and the street, not stopping until I reached the railroad tracks.

Down in the recesses of Town Records, I searched the files for this Silva Francesca Vanders's birth certificate. If she was from Shireburne, too, born here, she had to be the daughter of the matriarch, and her birth certificate would be filed in her hometown, my hometown. I imagined that whoever my father's birth mother was, she'd been young when she gave birth to him and gave him up as a baby. Calculating backward eighteen years from my father's birth date, I searched every birth certificate for the name Silva Francesca Vanders.

I searched the year 1927, eighteen years before my father's birth. Then 1928, 1929.

Nothing.

I searched the year 1930. *There.* There she was.

Born August 14, 1930, at 3:34 p.m.

She'd been just fifteen years old at my father's birth. Fourteen when she became pregnant.

Her birth father and mother were listed as: Buell Vanders II and Gvenn Vanders. She *was* of the prestigious Vanders family.

It struck me to search for the original copy of my father's birth certificate. Perhaps, the copy he'd hidden in the book was fake or forged, though it looked real enough to me. All the information was correct as far as I knew: the birth date and the names of his adoptive parents, the only grandparents I knew on his side.

I rifled through certificates in the drawer marked with the year and month of my father's birth, scanning the certificates of other children born that month. And, finally, Roland. Roland Kenneth Maynard. My father.

I compared it to the copy. It was identical.

I sat on the floor and tried to let the fact settle in my bones. I was related to the Vanders. I *was* a Vanders.

Did any of the Vanders know that my father had ended up back in the town of his birth after marrying my mother and moving here from Maine? Did he even know he was born in Shireburne? Did any of the Vanders know he was in the hometown of his birth mother? Had Silva known? If my father didn't know she was his birth mother, he couldn't know that she lived in the same town where he moved to and was starting his own family. Not until he'd seen the adoption papers. I wondered again, how had he come by them? Had he discovered them in his adopted parents' belongings when they passed away? Had he told my mother his birth mother was Silva Vanders? Since the Incident, my mother had lived and worked so hard in the shadow of the estate, forever a breath away from squalor, and this woman had never helped her. Adoption or not, blood was blood. If the Vanders family—my family—had known, they had let my mother, let *us*, suffer anyway.

Silva Vanders. Why and how had I never heard of her in our small town, never seen her face on the society page? I'd never heard her name or read of it in the pamphlets about the estate and the family. This was the daughter of the matriarch of the most prominent family in town. Her brother Buell III was the most prominent man in town, yet it was as if Silva never existed.

Perhaps she had died. Perhaps she left town after her teen birth, was shipped off. Banished. Or perhaps she'd moved away of her own accord or gotten married and taken on a new surname and still lived right here in town, maybe even on the estate.

I wondered who might know, who might help me, yet keep my inquiry private. I could not ask my mother, not yet. There was only one adult I knew who might shed even a glimmer of light on the matter.

In the intervening years, I'd crossed Mr. Kane's path only rarely, and in the past several years I hadn't seen him at all. Shortly after my father's memorial, it was rumored that Mr. Kane had fallen gravely ill. The gossip among the kids was that he had contracted an odd disease by accidentally eating a worm in an apple grown in South America. He never returned to school, though he did work at the Stop-N-Go for a while, pumping gas. I wasn't sure what he did after that. I was a kid; I paid no attention to trivial matters such as careers and income. I wondered now about Mr. Kane crying at my father's memorial. "I'm sorry for everything," he'd said.

Mr. Kane had lived in a spiffy bungalow hemmed by manicured hedges on a quiet side avenue off Pine Street, very near the school. He'd lived there with his wife. He had moved soon after he grew ill, I'd heard, though I didn't know where. I didn't know for sure whether he still lived in town or was even still alive.

I walked to the phone booth on the corner of Main and Maple and flipped through the book until I found Mr. Kane's number and address. He lived on Lost Swamp Road; a dirt road populated with derelict camps from the 1940's on the outskirts of town that dwindled to a dead end at Lost Swamp.

I considered calling Mr. Kane but decided to visit him instead.

Lost Swamp Road was a trek, but if I hurried, I could be there in a half hour.

I cut through the woods behind the lumberyard, hoping to shed minutes off the trek while also keeping out of sight. I felt again as if eyes were on me, as if someone, somewhere, knew exactly what I was up to at every turn, and could read my mind.

Sunlight cascaded down through the tree limbs, the woods tremulous with shifting shade and light, leaving me a bit unsteady on my feet as rocks and roots seemed determined to impede my progress.

Several times I stopped at one or another of the many stout old trees in the woods and peered back behind me to see only the trees and ferns quaking in the wind, even while the sensation of being followed persisted.

Finally, coming to the dirt road I'd hoped to find, I burst out of the woods, darted across the road, and tucked myself into the trees on the other side. The fetid stench of the Lost Swamp seemed to cling to my skin. Ahead through the trees, beneath a pale, ethereal fog emanating from the dark water, I could just make out the swamp itself, vast and oozing and scabbed over with decaying algae. From the swamp rose dead, skeletal trees with massive stick nests of blue herons perched in the branches. The herons stood still as wood carvings at the edge of their nests, their tall, bony silhouettes reminiscent of pterodactyls.

I hiked in the direction of Mr. Kane's address, paralleling a strip of wooded land wedged between the road and the swamp. Once, I heard a branch snap and looked behind me, but saw nothing among the mossed shadows. Up ahead, a rutted trail emerged among the ferns, and I hoofed along it until it brought me to a creek spanned by an old wooden ladder laid down from one bank to the other as a makeshift footbridge. The trees had changed from old oaks and maples to dark hemlocks and cedar. On an ancient hemlock at the far end of the footbridge was stapled a hand-painted sign: PRIVATE PROPERTY. KEEP OUT.

Beyond it, down the thread of trail, a cabin stood. I could just make out its rusted tin roof and dark, grimy windows. I wondered whether this could possibly be where Mr. Kane lived. If so, surely the sign on the tree was meant for hunters that Mr. Kane did not want traipsing around the property with rifles and shotguns. Surely, he wouldn't be angry to see one of his old students, the son of his good friend from years ago.

I crossed the creek on the ladder and approached the cabin by the meager trail among the rocks and ferns.

Set back in those dark, dank woods, the cabin appeared almost black, and as I came upon it and saw it more fully, I realized that its vertical wood siding was indeed black with mildew and wet, forever damp amid the suffocating cedar and hemlock trees that edged the swamp. I could not fathom that Mr. Kane resided in such a woeful dwelling. I expected I would soon be on my way to the next place along Lost Swamp Road.

The wooden door was cancerous with lichen and splintered with woodpecker holes. I knocked, the sound a dead thump on wood ravaged by rot.

Mosquitoes clustered around my head and bit the soft flesh behind my ears. Blackflies chewed my bony ankles. I knocked again.

From behind the door, a quailing voice said, "Who's there?"

"Wayland," I said.

"*Who?*"

"Wayland."

I heard a hacking wet cough behind the door.

"I was your student," I shouted.

"I don't—"

"Wayland Maynard," I stressed. "My father, Roland, was your friend."

Silence.

A woodpecker flitted down from the cedars and perched on the gable above my head, then flittered back into the swamp.

I heard a metal clack on the other side of the door.

The door creaked open.

A mosquito bit my cheek. I slapped at it too late.

A man I did not recognize stood before me. This was not Mr. Kane. This man was stooped and gaunt. Except for the clown fuzz that ringed his scalp, he was bald. He stood in shabby, grayed pajamas and bare feet with yellowed toenails in dire need of clipping.

I was about to apologize that I had the wrong place, when the man cleared his throat, set his watery eyes on me, and said, "I hardly recognized you. You've changed." He coughed. "As have we all, I suppose." His morose smile revealed a missing lower tooth. He clasped his hands behind his back and studied me as if he suspected me of devious motives.

He did not welcome me inside.

"What is it?" he asked.

"My father."

His eyes seemed to soften. "Of course."

"I'd like to talk to you about some things," I managed.

I had the sense that Mr. Kane wanted to look behind himself, that in his cabin with him was someone or something he did not want me to see. Perhaps that was why he lived out on the edge of the swamp now: he had something to hide.

Or perhaps something to fear.

"I doubt I'll be able to help," Mr. Kane said.

He had the breath of someone who had slept with his mouth open all night and awakened with a furred tongue pasted to his palate.

"I need to know what he was like the days before what happened," I said. "And . . . I've learned some things and don't know who to ask. Not my mom, not after . . . There's a lot going on. A lot I found out that doesn't make sense, and—"

"Let's take it one step at a time."

"I thought since you were my dad's friend—"

"We were not friends," he said. His statement caught me off guard—not just the words, but also the coldness with which he spoke them.

He glanced at the path in the woods behind me. "Come inside, then," he said as if it had been my choice to remain on his step, feeding the mosquitoes.

I entered. Mr. Kane glanced about at the woods and shut the door with haste.

The cabin was one room—at least, from what I could tell in the murk that shrouded the place as the door shut. Through the filmed and flyspecked windowpanes, muddied light fell on a ratty, old low-slung couch that hunkered in the shadows like a wounded animal.

The cabin had a funk about it, that of documents left to molder in damp cardboard boxes.

"Please, sit." Mr. Kane touched my shoulder and then sat in the middle of the couch, flipping his hand toward a fuzzy black armchair across from him.

I sat.

"So," he said, rubbing his knobbed knees with pink, chapped hands.

I could not hold back, and before I knew it, I'd told him about the note, the handwriting, the dangling legs, the adoption document, and how I knew that the man that day was not my father.

He nodded but did not look me in the eye. His look seemed focused on the door behind me, as if he expected a knock on it at any moment. "Troubling," he said, and coughed.

"Tell me what my father was like in the weeks before. You were his friend; you must have noticed something."

"I wasn't his friend," he insisted. "I thought I made that clear."

"You bowled with him. You came to our house for dinner, with Mrs. Kane and by yourself." I wondered what had happened to Mrs. Kane.

Mr. Kane sighed. "Men are not friends in the same way boys are friends."

However he chose to define an adult friendship, Mr. Kane and my father had been friends. I was sure of it. I'd seen them together.

"It was an awful thing," Mr. Kane said. "Very upsetting. Very troubling. The whole of it."

"You cried at the memorial," I said. "Why did you cry if you weren't friends?"

His eyes darkened. "It was tragic. Pointless. But we weren't friends. Men don't share secrets like boys do. As a boy becomes a man, he shares less about what's inside him. Men do things together. Bowl. Fish. Share a beer. Talk bullshit. But it's not like when we are boys. Our openness, our freedom, closes down. Out of survival and . . . self-respect." He stood up and swiped at the sweat on his forehead with the back of his hand as he stepped over to a small kitchen counter cluttered with generic black-and-white labeled cans of soup, beans, and veggies. "I don't know what to tell you," he said as he picked up a can of beans.

"Tell me what my father was like in the days before."

"It was a long time ago. I've forgotten."

"You must remember *something*. Think—"

"I'm sorry," Mr. Kane said, and he sounded it. He sounded as sorry as anyone I'd ever heard utter the words.

"What do you know about a man in a dark coat?" I asked.

Mr. Kane peeled the label from the can of beans and let the shredded paper float to the floor.

I recounted the Tall Man's visit to the barbershop.

"I don't know him," Mr. Kane said. "I'm sorry I can't be of help. I understand why you're troubled. I empathize. But having such troubled thoughts is dangerous. Mentally, emotionally. I can't know the impact that seeing such a dreadful thing would have on a young boy. But denial is a strong—"

"I am *not* in denial. I need to know what my dad was like the week before it happened. Because he did *not* do it. It has something to do with his adoption, with his real mother. His birth mother. I need to know about her too."

Mr. Kane's left hand trembled. He clasped it in his right hand to calm it.

"There are things in the adult world that kids need never know," he said.

"I'm not a kid anymore."

"Your dad loved your mom. And she loved him." He scratched at his unshaven throat. "And she loves you and your sister. Take comfort in that."

Comfort?

"What happened?" I demanded. "It makes no sense."

"These things never do, especially to those on the outside who don't know everything." He licked at the spittle bubbling at the corner of his mouth.

"Did you see or hear anything that made you think he'd do that?" I said.

"There are trials in every marriage . . . " He worked his jaw as if his ears were popping from a rapid change in elevation. "Forgive me, I'm tired. Very tired."

"What do you know about Silva Francesca Vanders?"

Mr. Kane stiffened as if bracing himself before stepping naked into an icy pond. "Why would you want to know about her?" His manner convinced me his puzzlement was genuine.

"I just do." I wanted to see what Mr. Kane might offer in the way of details before telling him that Silva Vanders was my father's birth mother.

"Why?" Mr. Kane said.

"It has to do with my father."

"How could it, after what she suffered years before?"

"Suffered?"

"She tried to kill herself," Mr. Kane said. "Or perhaps it was just a gruesome accident, or . . . No one knows for sure. Or *I* don't, anyway. Someone must. Someone always does. If it *was* a suicide attempt, it was a horrific way to go about it. Not that *any* way of going about it . . . " His face flushed. "My apologies. What little I know from loose lips, she was . . . odd. What used to be called melancholic, I heard. Delusional. Paranoid. The family, the brother, turned the top floor of the mansion into a ward to cure her, or at least make her presentable, respectable. Respectability, or the appearance of it, goes a long way with a clan like that."

"Mansion?"

"Forget it," he said. "It's just a rumor from sixteen or seventeen years ago. I shouldn't traffic in such lurid hearsay. I got caught up in the moment. Gossip is a disease that rots you from the inside out. And memory and time are slippery fish." His pale eyes seemed haunted. "All I heard were watered-down fourth-hand rumors. I wasn't *in the know*. I was young. I was a teacher. A nobody. My ex-wife will attest. Forget I said anything." He tried a smile, but his wan face collapsed in the effort.

"This happened sixteen or seventeen years ago?" I said. "Which? What year?"

"Really, it doesn't—"

"*What year?*"

"Maybe sixty-eight."

Year of my birth. "What day?"

"I couldn't say. Spring? . . . March? April?"

March was the month of my birth.

"What *day?*"

"I'm not even sure it was spring."

"What happened? Why do you say what she did was so *gruesome?*"

"She doesn't have anything to do with your father," he said, his voice flat.

I was no longer sure Mr. Kane's mystification over my inquiry was sincere. I sensed he was baiting me, that he knew that Silva Vanders was my father's birth mother and wanted me to admit it. He took a step toward me. "Why do you want to know so much about her? How do you even know about her?"

"I was just curious," I said, suddenly and inexplicably afraid. "I'll let you rest."

"You're not just curious," he said. "Why are you lying to me?" He took another step and reached a hand out for me, perhaps to grab me. I dodged his grasp and opened the front door.

"Wait!" he shouted as I stepped out into the dreary woods. "If you need help, I'll . . . I'll give it to you. I just . . . "

But I was gone.

FOOLPROOF

I crashed through the trees and never slowed once on the long trek back toward town, as the tale Mr. Kane had told me turned over in my mind. Suicide. Delusion. Paranoia. A ward on the top floor of the Vanders mansion. How much was true, and how much was lore? Were such mental ailments and tendencies passed along in families? Had my father suffered them? I'd seen no sign of it. *But.* There's always a but. I'd been eight. Had my father, after all, shot himself? Right in front of me? No. It could not have been—physically could not have been—him.

I lost my way in the woods, and when I finally emerged, I found myself at the entrance of the town graveyard. I stopped at its rusted wrought iron gates.

The sun was gone now behind the first clouds to appear during that spring vacation. A drizzle fell, and fog threaded among the headstones of the forgotten.

The hinges cried as I pushed the gate open and skulked into the cemetery. Gravel crunched beneath my sneakers.

It had been years since I'd visited my father's grave. Being there had never made me feel closer to my father; instead, it had made me feel forgotten. A grave was no place to connect with a spirit, a soul, or whatever aura or entity the dead leave behind, if any. A grave was a site of sad finality, and I'd never felt my father's presence at his. What spirit would choose to loiter at the site of its putrefying remains, anyway, when that spirit, if one believed in them, could be anywhere at all?

In the low-lying section of the graveyard, I passed modest headstones, a great many of them adorned with faded miniature American flags or arrangements of faded plastic flowers.

On a clear day, the crest of the gentle hill at the center of the cemetery would have presented me with a dramatic view of the Vanders estate and Forbidden Lake in the distance beyond. Now, in the fog, that view was obscured as I passed among monuments and sepulchres of immense granite blocks that stood watch over the moneyed dead—weeping angels and miniature obelisks and pillared mansions with ornate carved epitaphs to those adored in lifetimes past.

I made my way down the other side of the hill, to the farthest-back reaches of the cemetery, where my father's grave was marked by a plain, thin rectangular slab of granite, laid flat among weeds withered from winter. The stone was carved only with my father's name and the dates of his birth and supposed death.

The cemetery was so quiet, I felt as if the headstones were listening to my thoughts.

In all my earlier visits, I had felt a hollow, dull anguish, and when I thought too long about the remains of my father, his corpse, mere feet below me, desiccated and confined for eternity in an airless wooden box that also would crumble to dust, I felt repulsed. Now I knew why I had never sensed my father's presence at this grave. Because he was not in it.

And I would prove it.

I dug around in my pocket, past my box of matches to get at my jack-knife. I levered out its largest blade. I jabbed the blade into the ground. It sank about two inches before meeting any resistance.

The unseasonal warmth of the past few days had thawed the earth enough that before too long, the ground at my feet would yield to the hard blade of a shovel.

At home I walked up the driveway and stared at the garage door. My father had kept an old army-issue foxhole shovel in there long ago. I'd been captivated by it. The way it folded up on itself in such a stealthy manner made me imagine clandestine uses for it, such as digging hidden escape tunnels from one hideout to another. Its pointed steel blade was hard and sharp. My father explained the tool's purpose for soldiers in war. He told me the shovel's sharp blade wasn't just for digging, but for soldiers to use as a weapon should it ever come to that. I didn't know whether the shovel was still in the garage, but my plan required one—and a crowbar.

Inside the garage I searched through the clutter and found an old squared garden spade I'd used long ago to dig up earthworms for fishing with my father. After a brief search, I located the foxhole shovel among the rakes and hoes leaning along the side of the garage. I picked it up and touched my thumb to the blade. It was as sharp as ever. Lethal. It could crack a skull open with one whack. I packed the shovel, a crowbar, and a flashlight into a backpack and hid it all in the rear of the garage.

I could not set about digging up my father's supposed grave in the daylight, and I wanted to learn more about Silva and the "gruesome" happenings at the mansion.

I had an urge to see Juliette, to visit her house, find her bedroom window, and knock on it. I resisted. If she didn't want to see me, I wasn't going to bother her and further degrade myself.

I visited the library alone. The librarian peeked over at me from where she was aligning books on a cart, gave a tight smile, and returned to her task.

I strode past the periodicals where the old man dozed in his chair, mumbling and twitching in his slumber.

At the long steel cabinets that housed the microfilm, I found a drawer marked "SHIREBURNE GAZETTE, 1968 January 1–December 31." The drawer squeaked as I drew it open. I searched through the dated boxes and selected one marked "Feb. 12–March 31, '68."

I stationed myself at the farthest microfilm machine. A harsh bare light jumped onto the screen, the silhouettes of dust and errant hairs jittering in the screen's lower corners.

I threaded the microfilm and hit the *forward* button. The film raced under the glass slide, tugged along by the reel opposite. Black and white images of the *Gazette*, cockeyed and a bit blurred, sprang onto the screen. I backed the zoom off, and the images focused.

I assumed that whatever *Gazette* issues covered Silva Vanders's story, it would be front-page news, even if it didn't mention attempted suicide. I knew enough about suicide now to know that it was kept secret. Still, I moved forward through the town newspaper, one page at a time, with meticulous scrutiny. I found nothing through the first ten days of March. I came to March 11, 1968. My birthday.

Somehow, I knew that her tale would be in that issue. Except that it wasn't. The article ran in the March 13 issue. Two days after my birth.

THE SHIREBURNE GAZETTE

FIRE IN VANDERS ESTATE MANSION NEARLY
CLAIMS LIFE OF SILVA VANDERS

Prominent Shireburne citizen Silva Vanders, 38, nearly died in an apparent accident yesterday afternoon in her family home on the historic Vanders estate. Her brother, Buell Vanders III, and members of the house staff say Miss Vanders was not well at the time and was undergoing treatment at home for chronic illnesses that have plagued her since childhood. She was wearing a highly flammable nightgown when, as Buell Vanders III said, "She must have come in contact with candles she put in the room to give her a measure of calm." The gown burst into flames and stuck to her body.

A staff member told the *Gazette* she heard a sound "like a wolf baying. I was on the stair landing on the third floor, where her room is, when I heard it behind the door. I didn't think it was her at first, because I didn't think the sound was human. I wondered if it was the TV or coming from outside through her bedroom window. Then, the sound didn't even seem animal. It sounded like . . . a demon. Then I smelled it. Smoke. It wasn't smoke from wood burning in the fireplace or candles going out. It was an awful, horrendous smell, like burning grease."

The staff member ran to the door to find it locked. "The door was never locked. So I panicked, started screaming. For help and to her. I knew now that she was inside. And I knew it was her making that . . . *sound*."

Miss Vanders's brother, who was in the library next door, broke down the door.

"By the time I got into the room, I thought it was too late to save her."

According to the staff member, Miss Vanders was engulfed in flames and careening about the room, catching curtains and wall tapestry on fire, all the time making that high-pitched, ungodly wail.

Whether Miss Vanders intended to or not, it is reported that her wild movements took her to a window, which smashed as her body pitched out into the air, to fall three stories to the ground below.

Her brother ran outside and used a garden hose to douse his sister while the staff member used a fire extinguisher to put out the blazing curtains and tapestries.

"My sister," Mr. Vanders said, "has, sadly, suffered a great deal already in her life. If she survives, I can only hope she can have a semblance of normalcy from here out."

No investigation is under way, and police chief Steele Dubrul suspects no foul play in the incident.

I stared at a photo taken from a great distance, probably with a telephoto lens, that depicted, on the back side of the mansion, a wisp of smoke rising from an immense lawn. I zoomed in, the image pixilating and fuzzing out, but not before I could make out a smoldering heap. The mansion did not look then as it looked in its current incarnation as the inn. The windows were wrong, and the trees too. I imagined it was due to the passage of sixteen years.

I read the article again.

Apparent accident.

Was that word, *apparent*, what fed the rumors of attempted suicide?

It didn't seem like much to go on. The newspaper was simply using journalistic language, wasn't it?

There were no witnesses when she caught fire. The door had been locked.

The door was never locked, the staff woman said. *Why* had the door never been locked? For the safety of Silva? So she wouldn't do this sort of thing? A depressive, a melancholic, locks herself inside what amounts to her personal psych ward, and takes a candle to her bathrobe. It was an agonizing way to go. Just to stand there as flames crept up around your nightgown. And she did it the day after I was born.

I reeled through the next two months of the *Gazette*'s microfilm, one page at a time, and found no follow-up story to Silva's "accident" other than a single paragraph published two days later—a sort of public service announcement:

> The Vanders family thanks the town for its immediate and sincere outpouring of condolences, and also for respecting our privacy at this tragic time. We hope and expect that the people of the town can appreciate our sister's need to heal and recover as much as possible.

No follow-up article appeared.

I thought of the screaming woman I'd seen through the binoculars.

Was she Silva Vanders?

I had the clerk make copies of the *Gazette* article for me. I wanted to show all the evidence I'd found to Juliette, tell her of the plan I had to dig up the grave, to prove, once and for all, that my father was not the man I'd seen on the bed. But I didn't dare go see her yet and risk being turned away. Instead, I decided to confide my findings to my only friend.

YOU PROMISED

Clay's father's truck wasn't in the driveway, so I strode up and rapped on the front door. When Clay didn't answer, I tramped around to the side of the house. Loud music from his bedroom vibrated the windowpanes. Clay kept an overturned plastic bucket beneath the window. He used it as a step to make it easier to sneak in and out of the window anytime of night without his parents knowing. I stood on the bucket and peered in the window. Clay was standing in the middle of his bedroom in boxers and a T-shirt, legs spread as he thrashed an invisible guitar to "Sunshine of Your Love." I knocked on the window, but he continued to plow through his air guitar solo. I reached down and turned on the water spigot and picked up the hose by its pistol nozzle. I eased the window open and sprayed Clay in the back. He wheeled around, face crazed as his hand reflexively snatched my revolver from his bed. I had not seen the gun, but I couldn't miss it now that it was aimed straight at my face. I fell off the bucket, onto my back.

The music stopped.

Clay shoved his head out of his window. "Fuck, what're you doing? Idjit! I could have shot you."

"Get out here," I said. "And bring my gun. I want it back. I got serious shit to tell you."

"You finally score with that—"

"About my *dad*."

I met him on the front steps. He'd thrown on jeans and flip-flops and carried a six-pack of Moosehead bottles.

"Your dad is going to go ape shit if he sees you swiped his beer," I said.

"He hasn't been around for three days. And I'm betting that whatever lunacy you're about to spout will require beer."

"Give me my pistol."

"You're too wound up to have a gun."

"It's *mine*. Give it to me."

"Throw a tantrum. I'm fucking with you." Clay handed me the revolver. I stuck it into my back waistband and covered it with my shirt tail.

As we hoofed it toward the railroad tracks, I blatted about the dangling legs, the adoption papers and birth certificate, Silva Vanders, and the annulment document.

"Slow down," Clay said. "You're like a Gatling gun. My head is going to fucking explode."

We hiked down to the tracks and climbed up on a stack of decaying railroad ties. The acrid reek of creosote stung my nostrils.

Clay fished a bottle of beer from the six-pack and popped the cap with the butt of the lighter I'd given him. He swigged down half the beer and held a bottle out to me.

I waved him off.

"So what are you raving on about?" he said, and belched.

I took a breath and, as calmly as I could, told him again about the dangling legs, the note, and the adoption and annulment papers. About Silva Vanders. I handed him the printout of the *Gazette* article and showed him the note. He read it and stared at me as if my face were disfigured without my knowing it, and he didn't dare tell me how grotesque I looked. I could see that, despite my proof, he didn't believe a word I had told him. "If that crazy woman was your grandmother, I mean, that sucks," he said.

"No," I said. "Your dad breaking your radio sucks. What I just told you is—"

"I know you've always been a bit psycho from what you saw back then, but—"

"I'm not psycho," I said.

He looked at me as he took a swig of beer and set the bottle on the railroad tie beside him. "If you believe the shit you just told me, that's psycho. If your old man wrote that note, that pretty much proves he was the one you saw that day. And dangling legs? That's a reach even compared to all the other wild-assed reasons you've dreamed up. It probably just isn't the same bed now as it was then." He polished off his beer and cracked open another.

"I don't *dream up* reasons."

"I just mean, you've never really come to grips that your dad did it, and—"

"I never understood *why* he would do it. I questioned why he would *want* to do it. *How* he could do such a thing. I never believed it wasn't actually him. Until now."

"If you say so."

"I *do* say so. Look." I shoved the adoption and annulment papers and the photocopied article of Silva's "accident" in front of his face. "She jumps from a window while she's on fire? The day after I'm born? Read this shit." I dropped the papers in his lap.

Clay glanced at them.

"Read them," I said.

Clay started to read the papers while chugging his beer. Eyes working down the page, he set his beer bottle down on the dark, splintered wood. "You're actually saying your dad is this whack job's son?"

"I'm not *saying* it. The documents prove it."

He eyed the papers. "Even if this trippy shit is true, it doesn't prove your dad wasn't the guy you saw. It's messed up that his mother is a loon who tried to burn herself alive. And if she is your relative, be careful. That mental shit runs in families. Maybe that explains what your dad did. It was in his DNA. And the other papers. Annulment. That's, like, worse than divorce, isn't it? It's like their marriage never happened. That's depressing shit." The look on his face was grave. He smiled, tried to shrug off his gloom. "There's a bright side, though: if you're part of *that* family, you got beaucoup bucks coming. Don't forget your broke friend when you're loaded."

I hadn't thought about that. Was an inheritance at issue here? Had my father found out who he was, who his mother was, and approached Silva Vanders about it, made demands of her or the family? Had she denied it? Rejected him? He'd rented the barber shop from his own family. Were they going to evict him and ruin him?

"I don't care about any of that," I said. "All I want is to know what happened to him."

"No offense, but your dad's in his grave. I mean, the papers all look real, and the article is *sur*real. But—"

"They *are* real. And he didn't own the shop. The Vanders did. We saw the originals."

"We?" Clay raised an eyebrow. "Ah. You told *her*. That explains why you want to believe it so bad. So you can keep her close. Good play. Here I thought she'd be into the sensitive shtick, but maybe she has a dark side and is into the freaky stuff."

"That's not why I believe it," I said.

"Maybe I'll share my own crazy story with her to get her to—"

"You stay the hell away from her," I said and shivered with disgust and jealousy. I loathed his smug smile, the glee in his eyes.

"Don't get pissy," he said. "She's all yours. I'll let you have her. For now."

"Fuck you," I spat, and stood up so fast I nearly fell off the stack of ties.

"Easy. I'm messing with you. Sit down, spaz."

I didn't want to sit down. Clay didn't take me or my plight seriously. He didn't believe in anything real. To him, everything was a ploy to get what you wanted.

"Don't mess with me about her," I warned.

"Okay. All right. Truce. I'd never do that—not to you, anyway."

I was suddenly exhausted. All I wanted was to crawl home and flop into bed and draw the covers up over my head. Shut out the world and lie down in darkness. After a long stretch of silence, I said, "She's lost interest in me anyway." I regretted it as soon as the words left my mouth and braced myself for more mocking.

"What happened?" Clay asked. He remained silent, awaiting my response. His concern seemed genuine, yet I wondered if it was just another act to get me to calm down and not "spaz."

"She stood me up," I confessed. "We were supposed to meet at the library."

"Maybe her parents were on her ass, or some girlfriend drama came up. Believe me, with chicks, the drama never ends. Call her or go see her and ask what gives."

"I can't just show up or call out of the blue."

"The fuck you can't. You *have* to. If you don't, I'll do it for you. I'll—"

"*No.* Don't fuck this up for me."

"*Fix it*, you mean. You're the one fucking it all up with your pansy behavior."

"I'll find out myself. If she isn't blowing me off, I have a foolproof plan she might dig, to prove it wasn't my dad."

"What plan?"

"You'll just think I'm fucked up."

"That's established. What plan?"

"Never mind."

"You can't say you have a *foolproof* plan, then not tell me what it is."

"I can," I said. "I am."

"Asshole." He punched me so hard, square in the sternum, his fist felt like a sledgehammer. I tumbled backward off the railroad ties. My ribs struck the steel track. Pain splintered through me. The revolver clacked on the ballast stones. When I tried to gulp down a breath, it felt as if I were breathing glass shards.

Clay climbed down and offered me a hand.

"Get the fuck away from me!" I screamed.

"I didn't hit you that fucking hard," he said. "Don't be such a candy-ass." He smirked and held out his hand to help me up.

I snatched the revolver and pointed it at the center of his face.

"*Whoa!*" he said, recoiling. "What the fuck? Don't point that thing at me."

"I'll point it at you," I said. "I'll fucking point it at you." I got to my feet, grinding my teeth against the pain, and thrust the muzzle right in Clay's face. I cocked the hammer. "Don't ever fucking hit me again," I said through clenched teeth. "Not *ever* again. You fucking hear me?"

"Okay, okay, okay. Jesus H. What gives? Just stop pointing the fucking gun at my face. Are you fucking crazy? Maybe you *are* related to that psychopath bitch on the estate."

"Shut up," I barked. I slipped my finger onto the trigger.

"Okay, okay. Just put it *down*."

I lowered the revolver to my side.

Clay planted his palms on his knees and exhaled, panting. "You're an asshole," he wheezed.

"*I'm* an asshole? You mock me. Punch me. You don't take my life seriously. Joke about taking my girl—"

"She's not your girl. Not yet. And she won't ever be if you keep fucking it up. You're a fuckup where that's concerned. You gotta—"

"And you're a fucking liar." I brought the revolver up again, pointed it at his forehead.

"Jesus Christ," he thrust his palms up in front of his face. "Cut the shit."

"You promised you'd never punch me again," I kept the revolver on him.

"I—"

"You *promised*. I'm sick of bullshit. Of lies. All I get is fucking lies and bullshit. From everyone. Everyone is so full of shit."

"I shouldn't have hit you. Okay? *Okay?* But you shouldn't wave a fucking gun in my face, either. I'll help you, if you want. Help you figure out what's what with this dad stuff, I swear. I believe you, okay? I'll help you investigate, or help you with—"

"I don't need your fucking help," I gripped the revolver tighter, the muzzle aimed right between his eyes. "I don't want it."

"Don't be like that," Clay said. "Stop pointing it at me. Please. Jesus. Let me help."

I lowered the revolver and stalked away with it gripped tight in my hand, hammer cocked, ready to fire with the slightest pressure from my finger.

Clay yelled after me, but I never looked back.

IN THE TREES

I hoofed it down the tracks and ducked into the woods behind the old Methodist church. The late-afternoon clouds had parted to let the sunlight kaleidoscope through the budding spring branches of the poplars and silver maples. The ground here was wet and soft, the summery warmth of this April week forcing winter to relax its grip.

I ventured out of the woods onto Main Street, between Marsh Tavern and the Grotto Arcade. I didn't want to head home. I wanted to go to the estate. I wondered whether the woman I'd seen through the widow's watch windows days earlier was Silva. I was curious about what I might learn if I were to creep closer to the place in the dark of night. An ancient tree grew close to the widow's watch. If I could climb it, I might be able to look inside a window.

I headed into the woods that isolated the estate from the town. Tree frogs hiccuped and nighthawks screeched as large, unseen creatures crashed through the underbrush. Mud sucked at my sneakers. Several times, I lost my way in the maze of branches.

I stumbled out into the field and climbed the hill, where I waited until nightfall.

The clouds had parted, and the moon cast the open landscape in silver hues, as if I'd stepped into an old gel print negative. I worked my way up to the crest of the hill until I saw, far below me, a glimmer of light leaking from the widow's watch beside the mansion. Two of the mansion's impressive third-story windows glowed with golden light. There seemed to be something off about the place, something wrong, compared to the photo from the newspaper story about Silva. Perhaps it was just that the trees were now taller and there were more of them, more new outbuildings around it than there had been when the photo was taken.

I sneaked down the hill and darted across the dark road toward the mansion.

A white van approached from the north on a gravel side road. I ducked into the trees beside the carriage barn and wedged myself beneath the stairs that led up the side of the building to the widow's watch above.

The van sputtered to a stop out of sight, in front of the carriage barn. A door shut. Another. A male voice barked an order. The van's side door slid open with a rasp of metal on metal. "Come," a male voice said. Another male voice, which sounded familiar though I could not quite place it, said, "All right, all right." The two men ventured into sight but remained dark silhouettes in the pewter moonlight.

I heard an animal vocalization of some kind. It came again, a voice slurred, unable to enunciate, perhaps drunk or drugged. Yet it was clearly human and clearly female.

As I watched through the trees and between the stair treads, three figures ghosted out from the shadows and onto the stairway.

Above me, a light flicked on outside the door to the widow's watch. Beneath the stairs, my face was mere inches away from three pairs of strangers' shoes as they made their way upward. A woman's high heels, tall and delicate as champagne flute stems, seemed to float up the steps, flanked by two pairs of ominous black boots. I imagined the woman with her arms slung around the shoulders of two sturdy men, her heels just grazing the treads as she ascended.

The woman groaned and mumbled approximations of words, mostly vowel sounds.

Long after the door closed and the light winked out, I remained crouched in the dark. I caught a whiff of peppermint, a balm of some sort.

I crouched under the stairs until my thighs quaked and burned. I had no way to know whether the woman I'd seen was the screaming woman.

A peculiar electric-blue glow, like that radiated by some of the deepest-dwelling fish in the sea, lit the windows high above me. I climbed up into the tree beside me and squatted on a limb near the side window of the widow's watch.

Screened as it was by the trees, the window did not have a shade and was propped open with a book wedged between sash and sill. A sound from inside came through the open window. A woman sobbing. Or moaning. The sound of ecstasy or else stifled pain.

With every effort to keep silent, I climbed higher in the tree until, through the window, I saw a pedestal sink with gold fixtures, and a cabinet with a can of shaving cream and an expensive-looking silver razor on it.

I could just make out the round white porcelain edge of a tub with brass claw feet. The bathroom door was open, leading into a room of wood floors that shone under lights as harshly bright as those in an operating room. In my restricted view of the room beyond, I could see a zebra skin on the floor, the tongue like a ribbon of dried black tar leaking from the dead creature's sad open mouth. Against the far wall, an enormous bed was topped with a comforter as purple as a ripe plum. On the bedside table sat a prescription pill bottle.

I inched closer. The branch I sat on bowed beneath me.

A figure appeared in the mirror on the bedroom's far wall. It took me a moment to discern the image of a woman. She stood at an angle to the mirror, yet even at that distance her pale bare back appeared marbled with knotted pink and purpled flesh. Her head and neck were bent so far forward, she appeared headless between her broken-bird's-wing shoulders.

Suddenly, almost violently, she flipped her head backward with a jerk, and her red hair tumbled down her back. Then she limped from view.

I edged farther out on the branch. It bowed more, creaking under my weight.

I heard a sharp cry that reminded me of the time I heard a rabbit being killed by a fox.

The sound seemed to trip a cascade of brilliant blue flashes that spat white-hot sparks at the window. The barrage of light startled me. *Flash-bulbs*, I thought just as the branch gave with a loud crack.

I crashed down through the branches. A limb caught my side, my ribs taking the hit as they had on the railroad tracks. I cried out as a firework display of pain lit me up and I hit the ground with a hard thud.

I lay there stunned. From the window came another cry, as if a woman were being impaled. The sounds carved images of a Bosch painting into my brain. More lights flashed from the window; then, the world fell black and silent.

I felt wetness at my side and put my fingers under my T-shirt to touch my ribs. My hand came back out slick with blood.

The door at the top of the stairs squeaked in the dark, and the silhouette of a man stepped out onto the shadowed porch.

I scrambled to the tree and pressed my back tight against the trunk. Above me, an orange ember pulsed in the dark.

A man spat over the rail, his spittle misting my face.

I turned away and caught a branch in my face. My shout rang out like a gunshot in the silence.

"Someone's out here!" the man barked.

I sprang from under the tree and darted across the road in the dark.

"Hey!" the man yelled.

Footsteps pounded down the stairs behind me.

I tripped and fell and was staggering to my feet when a hand clutched my neck. I squirmed, but the hand dragged me backward. Thrashing and kicking, I reached for the revolver. I jerked free of the fingers and stumbled uphill into the dark.

"Halt!" the voice echoed in the hills.

A different voice yelled, "Stop him!"

I scrambled up the hill, the revolver clasped in my hand.

At the crest my ankle plunged into a hole and seemed to snap in half. I fell, yowling. Below me, two flashlight beams shone like sinister eyes in the darkness.

"Up there!" a voice cried.

I held the revolver in a trembling hand, pointing it down the hill toward the men as I forced my other hand down in the hole and tried to work my ankle free. Flashlight beams sliced the dark, closing in on me. My ankle was stuck. Any second the flashlight beams would illuminate my face, so that even if I escaped, I would be identified.

Using my free foot for leverage, I shoved myself backward with all the force I could muster. The flesh seemed to peel off the bone as my foot popped out of the hole. A light shone on my face. I waved the revolver wildly and rolled away to careen and tumble down the other side of the hill.

At the bottom I looked up to see the lights on the hilltop. I got to my feet and nearly collapsed from the pain in my ankle and ribs. I pushed into the dark trees and flailed through the woods until I finally made it home.

THE MAN OUTSIDE

I burst through the door, locked it behind me, then collapsed to the floor, panting.

Frenzied thoughts volleyed in my mind. Had they seen my face? Would they track me to the house? What would they do to me if they found me? What would they do to my mother?

The door rattled in its frame. The knob turned.

I inched backward.

The doorknob twisted.

I pulled myself upright and aimed the revolver at the door, cocked the hammer.

A fist banged on the wood so hard, the sound vibrated in my jaw.

"Open up!" yelled a voice. "C'mon, open up!"

Lydia.

Lowering the gun, I hopped over and unlocked the door.

Lydia bull rushed in, knocking me against the wall. She stared at me balancing on one leg, revolver in my hand.

"Shut the door!" I shouted. "Lock it."

"What'd you do, get hit by a truck? You're bleeding all over."

I looked down. My shirt was soaked with blood and mud.

"I fell," I said.

"From what, the Empire State Building?"

"Shut the door. Lock it."

She sighed, exasperated, and bumped the door shut with her hip.

"Lock it," I said.

"Jeesh. What are you on, angel dust?" She locked the door and eased past me to lean defiantly against the breakfast bar. "You look seriously wigged out. What's wrong with you?"

"Nothing."

"Yeah, clearly. Nothing."

"I don't want to talk about it."

"No skin off my butt." She plucked a piece of the soggy fried chicken from the fridge and gobbled it down without taking a breath. "This stuff's pretty good," she said. "What's with the gun?"

"Nothing."

"Whatever you say."

Lydia and I had not always been so alien to each other. There had been a time when we created our own language while playing with the stray Lincoln Logs, Tinkertoys, and Legos our mom had bought at garage sales. We'd while away afternoons building elaborate towns and making up stories for the yard sale Fisher-Price people who inhabited them. The characters always faced mortal peril—were stuck on precarious ledges, trapped in burning buildings, or buried under avalanches. We let them perish, taking delight in their demise.

"If someone comes here looking for me, asking if I was out tonight, you need to tell them I was here. All night. With you."

"Neither of us was here."

"Just *tell* them we were here together."

"Did you shoot someone?"

"No. Of course not. Tell them we were playing Risk or something."

"Risk? Do we even own Risk?"

"Or watching the tube or eating cereal—anything. Just tell them I was here, with you."

"Tell me what you did, and I'll think about it."

"I didn't *do* anything."

"Well," Lydia said, "whatever you *didn't* do, you look like you paid for it. You look like dog food." She sauntered into her room and shut the door.

I peeled back the curtain on the front door's window and peeked outside. I saw no one lurking, though in the darkness anyone could have been hiding anywhere. As I let the curtain fall back in place, I caught movement along the edge of the driveway, but pulling it back again, I saw only a white plastic trash bag drifting on the wind.

I limped down the hall and into the bathroom. I took my time as I showered. I was sore and stiff, and my ankle throbbed. Afterward, I rinsed my muddied, bloodied clothes off in the tub, scrubbing out as much of the filth as I could. I sat on the toilet seat and looked at my ankle. It was puffed up and tender. I washed a couple of aspirin down with a cup of water and put on jeans and a T-shirt. I stuffed my soiled clothes into the washing machine and dumped in twice as much detergent powder as I ever saw my mom use. I poured in a large chug of bleach too. I dozed on the floor, against the machine, and woke with a start when the wash cycle stopped. I put the clothes in the dryer.

On my way to the kitchen to get some cereal, a voice startled me. "Why are you doing laundry?" my mother said from the couch, where she sat in her bathrobe.

"You're home?" I said.

"It's late," she said. "Of course I'm home."

She stood and assessed me.

"Why are you doing laundry?" she asked me again.

"I got my clothes muddy."

"You've gotten clothes muddy a thousand times before and never washed them. Especially late at night."

I shrugged.

A knock came at the front door. I froze.

"Can you get that?" my mother asked, clutching her bathrobe at her throat, but I was already rapping on my sister's bedroom door.

I looked back to see my mother. She checked her face and hair in the toaster's mirrored metal side and scuffed to the door in her slippers as another knock sounded.

"Hey," I said through my sister's door. "Get out here. I need your help."

I heard the front door open as I limped to my mom's bedroom and peeked out the window. Whoever was on the steps stood too close to the door for me to see them from my angle.

I crept back down the hall, the revolver tucked in the waistband of my jeans, its hammer cold against my spine. I stood in the living room behind my mom as she opened the front door a crack, blocking me from seeing the visitor. My mother glanced back at me, opened the door just enough to slip out onto the steps, and shut it behind her.

I limped to the door and pressed my ear to it. I could hear the rise and dip of my mother's voice but could not make out any words. The other voice was a man's. Grave in tone. I could make out that much.

I hurried back to my sister's room. "Come out here," I hissed. "You need to do what we talked about." My sister did not respond.

I shuffled to my room and peeled back my curtain at the window. Molly whined behind me. I saw nothing out on the dark porch at first but then discerned movement in the shadows. My mother. She stepped off the porch to stand in the walkway, worrying the belt to her bathrobe. She stared across the street.

I looked out to see a man stride away from the house and get into a black car parked across the street. I couldn't see his face, but the sight of his frame made my heart crash in my chest.

The car drove off, too far away for me to read its plates.

I went out to the kitchen.

My mother remained outside for a long time before she came back inside the house.

She entered the kitchen and looked at me as if she didn't know me.

"Who was that?" I asked.

"No one you know."

"How do you know?"

"I know," my mother said.

"What did he want?"

"Nothing that concerns you."

"Who was he? What's his name?"

"It doesn't *concern* you," my mother said.

"I thought I heard him mention me."

"He didn't."

"Why didn't you invite him in?"

"The way this house looks? I'm going to invite someone like *him* in?"

"Someone like who?"

"Never mind."

"Like what?"

"Respectable."

"*Respectable?* So we're not respectable?"

"Wayland, quit hounding her," Lydia said behind me.

I turned in surprise to see my sister standing there.

"He's been a nuisance all night," she said, "watching the tube but getting up to click through the stations every two seconds, picking up a book to read, sighing and setting it down and picking up another. All night long. I finally told him to take a shower and wash his clothes if he couldn't stop fidgeting. He stank."

"You were here tonight?" my mom said.

Lydia and I nodded in unison.

"Both of you?" She sounded confused, suspicious. "Together?"

"*Together?*" Lydia said. "God, no. I was gabbing on the phone and doing my nails." She held up her fingers, wiggled them, each nail the bright purple of a pomegranate seed. "Wayland was being his annoying, depressed self. That's hardly hangin' out *together*." She sauntered back to her room and shut the door behind her.

I stared at my mother.

"What do you know about Silva Vanders?" I blurted out, seizing on the moment to catch her flat-footed. What did she know about my father's mother? Anything at all?

At my mention of Silva, my mother winced as if she'd bitten her cheek. "Never heard of her," she said.

I didn't mention the proof I had, the birth certificate. The adoption papers. I wanted to gauge my mother's reactions first.

"She burned in a terrible . . . accident, out on the estate, years ago," I said.

"Oh. Her."

"Yes, her. What do you know about her?"

"Nothing. Except that horrible accident you mentioned."

"You don't know anything else about her?" I prodded.

My mom shrugged. She took a seat at the kitchen table. From the laundry basket sitting on the floor, she picked up a pair of my sister's cutoff jeans, which were so short that half the pocket liners showed. My mother frowned and set the shorts aside. "Is that blood?" she asked of a stain on the front of the T-shirt I had changed into earlier. A cut on my chin from the fall through the tree branches had started to bleed again.

"I got cut on some picker bushes earlier today."

"If that's blood, your shirt's ruined."

"It's just a crummy used T-shirt," I said.

"You need it to last. You need to be more careful with your things and with yourself."

"Tell me more about Silva Vanders."

"I don't *know* more." My mother picked up a balled sock and wedged her hand into it as if to turn it right side out, wearing it like a sock puppet.

"It happened the day after I was born," I continued. "Her . . . accident."

My mother rested her socked hand on the table.

"That explains why I don't know details," she said. "I was a bit busy recovering from bringing you into the world. I was in the hospital for three days with you. They really drugged me for your delivery and recovery, compared to your sister. I heard nurses mumbling about a fire, probably through the fog of medication. Never really thought about it—or her— since." She smiled, but there was no joy in it.

"Do you know who she *is*?"

My mother peeled the sock off her hand the wrong way, so it was still inside out. She dropped it in the basket. "I don't know what you mean."

"Did Dad know her?"

"Why would he know her?"

"Did he know who she is?"

"You worry me, Wayland," my mother said.

I wanted to ask her more, but I believed I could see in her eyes that she didn't know that Silva Vanders was my father's birth mother, and I did not want to be the one to tell her. My mother's life was one withdrawn from social circles and community, from friends. I could not recall, other than her bowling nights, the last time she had done something with a friend, gone to a movie or to a book club or a bridge game, had someone over to visit, or gone to their house to visit, as normal parents did. Even single parents.

As I saw it, her life of isolation was brought on by the necessity of keeping the three of us from ending up living in the Pontiac. Her bony fingers were raw and pink, and her eyes extinguished of any flicker of exuberance that once lit them. I never thought about my mother's toil, a mundane, exhausting routine every day, with never a pause in its monotony and drudgery. I never thought of what it took to rise in the still-dark night while I luxuriated in sleep, under my warm covers. I never once thought about the will it took for her to resist the sleep her body and mind and soul must have begged her for each gray dawn. How easy it would have been for her simply to surrender one morning and remain in bed, slip back into sleep, neglect her responsibilities to her children, and give herself what she needed. I never thought of what it took to face the same day she had faced yesterday and would face again tomorrow, never thought of the long, tedious hours on her feet, waiting on others, putting everyone else's demands before her own, with no encouragement from another soul to keep her going—just herself and her obligation to my sister and me. What a triumph of commitment, of love. Yet I'd never thought once about it. And I didn't think about it in that moment, either, as we sat in the kitchen together.

Instead, I thought about how my mother must be hiding something from me. I wondered what secrets she kept hoarded in her heart, walled off from me, from everyone. I wondered what had possessed her to haul every single one of my father's belongings to the curb, to be trucked to the dump. It hurt me to know she had done it. It seemed so selfish, so wicked. I looked at her with disdain and distrust as she got up from her chair. Her knees popped and her back cracked, and she scooped up my sister's cutoff jeans shorts and tossed them in the trash can.

I started back toward my bedroom, checking that the revolver was tucked under the back of my shirt.

"Why are you limping?" my mother said. I didn't answer her as I headed to my room and shut the door, thinking about the man I'd seen outside our house a half hour earlier. I hadn't seen his face. But his movements had been fluid. And he was tall. Taller than any man I'd ever seen, except one. I'd bet my life on it.

HOTSHOT JOCK

The next morning I stayed in my bedroom and pondered what to do next. Part of me did not dare leave the house after what had happened the night before. My ankle ached too. It had ballooned overnight, and it hurt so much with each step, I could barely walk.

I needed to do something, dig deeper into who Silva was and what I had seen at the estate. Yet, part of me feared learning more, and the rest of me was too fatigued from fear and suspicion to do anything more than lie about my room with Molly. The next few days, I didn't leave the house. I stayed inside and iced my wrecked ankle, the revolver within reach at all times as I braced for the knock on the door, or the ring of the phone, the return of the Tall Man or someone else from the estate. I did not call Clay. I hoped Juliette might call me, but the phone never rang. When I was not obsessed with trying to make sense of what had happened over the past few days, I nuzzled with Molly on the bed and drifted in and out of sleep, in and out of reality and dreams.

On Friday I pleaded with Lydia to get off the phone so I could use it and started to dial Juliette's house. I didn't follow through. Instead, wanting to include her in what I'd discovered, and determined to overcome my fear of facing her and the prospect of outright, face-to-face rejection, I marched down the sidewalk toward her house. At the least, I'd find out why she stood me up, and be able to start licking my wounds.

I walked down River Street and onto Oak. Juliette's street. Her house stood just out of sight around a curve in the road. I kept to the opposite side of the street, walking along the edges of lawns, in the shadows of the oak trees for which the street was named.

A garbage truck trundled past me, stopped, and backed into the driveway just ahead. The garbage collector who was hanging on, outside the passenger door, leaped off and trotted up the driveway as he tugged thick leather gloves onto his hands. Walking backward, he directed the driver to back the truck up to the garage door, shouting "Good, good!" As I passed the end of the driveway, the garbage men threw open the garage door and dragged the metal cans from inside the garage, the lids clanging as they struck the driveway.

The soured-cabbage reek from the truck churned my stomach. I picked up the pace.

As Juliette's house came into view, I stepped off the curb, onto the lawn of a Cape house, and stood behind a lilac bush, screened by its wild snarl of branches.

I looked out at Juliette's house. I imagined her inside watching TV as she ate a bowl of cereal and sat cross-legged on a couch, gabbing on the phone with a girlfriend, the phone cord spiraled around her wrist. I wondered how she would receive me when my knock disrupted her leisure.

I stepped out into the street and crossed to the curb at the end of the driveway. The man hanging on the side of the garbage truck gave me a two-fingered salute as the truck bucked to a crawl in front of the next house.

Juliette's white-clapboard Federal-style house stood atop a gentle slope of lawn, its short, even grass already green and unblemished by a single twig or leaf from winter. The driveway's asphalt shone so black and fresh, I expected steam to rise from it.

Out there at the curb, I felt exposed and vulnerable, a soldier caught in no-man's-land. Juliette could be looking out at me right then, deciding whether she would bother to answer the door. Perhaps she'd already made up her mind.

I walked up the driveway, my heart beating wildly.

Behind me, the shrill *beep-beep-beep* of the garbage truck reversing seemed to sound the alarm at my presence.

I advanced up the concrete walk toward Juliette's porch. I was about to knock on the door when a Saab approached from down the street and swung into the driveway. I felt trapped. It was one thing to knock on the door and face my fate with me on one side of the doorway and Juliette on the other; it was quite another thing to be caught out in the open like this, as if in the midst of committing a crime.

Straining to smile, I braced myself to greet Juliette.

A man in a rumpled blue suit and an untucked white shirt climbed out of the car and raked his hand through his thinning hair, scratching at his scalp. I expected Juliette to get out on the Saab's passenger side or out the back. She didn't. The man leaned against the car, took a pack of cigarettes from his shirt pocket, and tapped it against his palm. He shook a cigarette free, stuck it between his lips, and lit it with a lighter from his coat pocket.

He started toward the house, then stopped when he looked up at me standing on his porch, staring at him.

"Juliette's out. With her mother, I imagine." He eyed the front door behind me, and I stepped aside.

He pushed past me. The drifting cigarette smoke made me sneeze.

"When she comes home, could you tell her Wayland stopped by?" I said.

"I'm not her secretary. If she wants to call or see you, I'm sure she'll let you know. When will you boys learn not to come by unless she's expressly invited you and I've signed off on it? Yesterday that hotshot jock, now you." He went inside the house, closing the door behind him.

I stood rooted on the stoop. *Hotshot jock.*

I don't know how long I stood there, numbed by the words, until feeling returned to my legs and I managed to wander down the drive.

I looked back from the street to see a window curtain jiggle on the second floor. Or perhaps it was my imagination.

I walked the streets in a daze, afraid I would run into Juliette on the sidewalk. I didn't and was glad. I didn't know what I would have said or done. *Hotshot jock.* It could have been any jock from school, I tried to convince myself, without success.

I wondered whether Juliette had been home all along, watching me from the upstairs window. Her father had acted as if she'd mentioned me to him, maybe even instructed him to warn me off if I showed.

VACATION IS OVER

Spring vacation ended, and the fleeting false-summer weather it had brought succumbed to the season of dark clouds and cold rain and raw wind that chilled my marrow as the world returned to the normal state of things.

School resumed, and I felt a change in the air that had to do with more than the weather. I doubted that I could just walk up to Juliette in the hallway and pick up where we'd left off. The days that had passed since she stood me up on the library steps might as well have been a thousand years.

Nonetheless, that first morning back, I found myself drawn toward Juliette's locker, unable to stop my legs from bringing me closer to her. Despite what humiliation might await me, I was eager to give her a full accounting of the progress she had missed and share my plans for the cemetery.

I threaded my way through the student mob and spotted Juliette up ahead, one shoulder leaning against her locker, her back to me. I was about to shout out above the heads of the throng, but saw she was speaking to the guy next to her. Clay. My eyes had been so fixed on Juliette, I hadn't noticed him straightaway. He leaned against the neighboring locker, thumbs hooked in his jean belt loops, biceps bulging in his Deep Purple T-shirt, a triumphant glee in his eyes as if he'd just won the state hockey championship single-handedly. He smiled, and Juliette's melodic laugh floated over the raucous banter of the other students that crushed around me. I stopped dead. Blood roared in my ears. My cheeks grew hot.

Juliette twined her long hair around her slim index finger as Clay whispered in her ear and grinned, looked down at her, into her eyes. Juliette's laugh sucked the oxygen from my lungs. Clay unleaned himself from the locker, took Juliette's hand, and held her palm against his cheek. He laughed, winked at her, and strode away. Juliette watched him go.

"Hey, dickweed, move it," a kid said as he and a gang of his fellow seniors plowed past me, shoving me aside to get to their lockers.

I staggered backward. When I looked toward Juliette again, she had turned toward me, but she was now engaged with several girlfriends who circled around her, their books and Trapper Keepers clutched to their chests, heads leaned in, and hands cupped at their mouths. The girls erupted into laughter, and Juliette slapped at one of them as they all glanced in the direction Clay had gone.

The bell rang, and teachers appeared at classroom doorways to herd us students into class. Moans and grunts of resignation followed as the kids dispersed and shuffled along.

My classroom was back down the hall behind me, the other direction from Juliette.

I watched as Juliette's girlfriends strolled away from her.

Juliette opened her locker to retrieve her books. When she slammed the door and turned to go, she saw me watching her and gave a start. She smiled.

I hurried down the hall, away from her.

In Earth Science I sat up front, distracted and tense, feeling betrayed. My chair was too stiff, my desk too hard and cold. The scratch and chirp of Mrs. Harris's chalk on the blackboard made my teeth ache. I tried to rid my thoughts of Clay at Juliette's locker. Juliette's laugh. As the moment replayed itself in my mind, I pounded my fist on my desk so hard that my pencil went flying and my notebook fell with a slap on the floor.

"Problem, Mr. Maynard?" Mrs. Harris said.

Laughter erupted.

"Enough," Mrs. Harris said. "Wayland, pick up your things, and please refrain from abusing your desk."

More laughter.

Eyes down, I crept out of my seat to pick up my pencil and notebook and slithered back into my chair.

"*Freak*," a voice whispered behind me. "*Fucking freak*."

I pushed the tip of my pencil into the web of flesh between my thumb and forefinger until I bled.

I entered biology class early, before everyone else, and perched on a stool, my back to the door, at the lab table closest to the teacher's desk—the one that was never occupied, to avoid having to see Juliette.

As students filed in, I heard Juliette's voice amid the chitter of her girlfriends. I fiddled with the microscope as the classroom filled up. When Mr. Bouchard set his bag on the desk, he gave me a skeptical look. "You need a partner," he said. "If no one sits with you, you'll need to find a table to share." He took a sandwich wrapped in waxed paper from his bag. It reeked of tuna fish. "Anyone wish to join Wayland at the table of exile?" he asked the class. "He doesn't bite, that I know of."

Sniggering rose from the back of the room, and someone barked, "But he does stink of BO."

A finger tapped my shoulder. Juliette sat in the stool beside me. "Hey," she said.

I fidgeted with my microscope's coarse-adjustment knob. I couldn't look at her and not feel acute humiliation—and something else too. Rage. Not at her, but at Clay. I felt pity for her, for falling for the same tricks Clay used on any girl in his orbit.

"*Hey*," she said again, and bumped her knee against mine as Mr. Bouchard began his spiel on paramecia and other ciliates.

I peered into the microscope's ocular, dialed the knob.

"Hey," Juliette said again. She elbowed me right in my sore ribs. I winced and inched my chair away from her. "What gives?" she said.

"Nothing." I flicked on the microscope's light to stare at squiggling dust beneath the slide.

"You ignored me in the hall. Then, just walked off."

"You were busy."

"My girlfriends don't bite. You can come say hi."

Did she really think she could pretend I hadn't seen her with Clay? Did she really expect me to gag on what tiny shred of self-respect I still had and mention it, mention I'd seen them together? I could see in her eyes that she knew I'd seen her with Clay.

A loud slap brought my head up from the microscope. Mr. Bouchard was staring at us. He'd smacked his notebook on the desk. "If you love-birds don't mind . . . " he said to a round of snorts and laughter.

Juliette and I barely spoke during the rest of class, but between bouts of peeking in on the short, happy lives of paramecia, and doodling approximations of them in our lab books, Juliette scribbled a note in the margins of her biology book and slid the book to me.

What gives?

I wrote back, NOTHING.

Where have you been hiding? I didn't hear from you the rest of break. How come you never called to update me?

YOU STOOD ME UP.

Sorry. Parents. Gaaawd. I thought you'd call and reschedule. What'd I miss? Tell me.

WHY DIDN'T YOU CALL ME?

I felt like an idiot for standing you up. I was afraid you'd hang up, but hoped you'd call or stop by.

I thought of telling her I had stopped by, but either she knew I had, and would deny it, or her father never told her. Either way, it didn't matter. Not anymore.

Mr. Bouchard strolled up and tapped his pencil on our table as he walked toward the back of the room, where a girl thrust her hand into the air as if hailing a cab.

Tell me.

I MESSED UP MY ANKLE AND STAYED AT HOME THE LAST FEW DAYS. BUT I FOUND OUT SOME STRANGE STUFF BEFORE THAT.

"Meet at the library right after school?" she whispered. "Fill me in, in person. I'll be there. I swear."

I doubted it and doubted I even cared anymore.

Despite all that, I found myself saying, "Okay."

Juliette showed up at the library ten minutes early.

She bounded up the library steps two at a time and sat beside me.

"So. What's so strange?" she asked.

I told her about the adoption papers, about Silva Vanders possibly being my grandmother, and about how she burned and jumped out a window, maybe on purpose.

"Suicide can run in families, I think," she said.

I bristled at hearing a response so similar to Clay's. I wondered whether they'd spoken about me together, *discussed* me. This, more than anything, stung as the ultimate betrayal.

I told her about sneaking over to the mansion and carriage house, about the two men in the van and the drunk or drugged woman. I told her about being chased. My heart wasn't in it, though. I told her of my adventures in a rote manner, just the facts. Yet even while I did this, my face grew hot and my armpits damp. And I didn't dare meet her eyes, didn't want to meet them. I kept hearing her father saying, "*hotshot jock*," and kept seeing her and Clay at her locker, her hand in his, her palm against his cheek. Her laugh and the way she playfully elbowed him. His wink. My guts coiled. My veins sang with anger.

"That sounds . . . depraved," Juliette said. "What is going on over there?"

"And," I continued, "the mansion doesn't look the same as in the photo. It looks off. Maybe it's just that it's been sixteen years, and it looks different as an inn, and there are more trees and stuff. But—"

"Maybe the photo in the paper is of the other mansion. Maybe it happened in that one."

"*Other* mansion?"

The old man I'd seen sleeping in the library periodicals section staggered out of the library, startling us. He stopped short at the sight of us sitting on the steps, blinked as if to assure himself that we really existed. Then he lurched back inside.

"Poor man," Juliette said. "I wonder what his story is?"

I didn't care about the old man's story. I cared about *my* story. "What's this about another mansion?" I pressed.

"There's a second mansion," Juliette said. "When we first moved here, my father could not wait to visit the estate, the mansion, and all that stuff."

"Your dad doesn't seem like the kind of guy who'd be into that sort of thing," I said. "He seems pretty straitlaced, the tie and the suit and—"

"When have you ever met my dad?"

I couldn't think of a lie fast enough, so I confessed: "I stopped by your house, and he was there."

"Stopped *by*? When?"

"During break. A few days after you stood me up."

"When? What time?"

"Late afternoon. Your dad said you were out with your mom."

"What was he doing home at that time of day?" she murmured to herself. "Why didn't you tell me you stopped by?"

"I gave him my name. I thought he'd tell you."

"My dad? Tell *me* anything? He's in his own world."

"He did seem it. And he didn't seem like a guy who'd be into old mansions."

"He calls it *history*, but I think he just liked to see how rich people live. He's always wanted to be rich. *Wealthy*. Still talks about all his schemes, his *ship coming in* before his *ticket gets punched*. And when we first moved here, he went to see the mansion near the carriage house where you saw the weird stuff. But he took a wrong dirt road, I guess, and ended up at a different mansion, like, right on the lake, on a huge cliff. One not for visitors. Behind an old gate. He got out of his car to take pictures anyway, but he got kicked out right away. Two guys in a truck pulled up and told him he couldn't be there. Said it was private property."

"What kind of truck?"

"Beats me."

"Was it blue?"

"I doubt my dad mentioned the color."

"We need to find this other mansion. The van I saw—it came south on a dirt road between the trees, from the direction of the lake. We need to get inside that place."

"Why?"

"Because it's where it happened. Where Silva tried to burn herself alive and—"

"But why would you want to be in a place where something like that happened?"

"To find a clue. I mean, she's my father's mom. She's got to be. And she burned herself the day after I was born, and maybe threw herself from a window. Don't you think that's weird?"

"*Too* weird."

"Right. So, let's go."

"I don't know. I'd—"

Rather hang out with Clay, I thought. Why didn't she say it and spare me, get it over with? Instead, I said: "Hang out with your girlfriends. I get it. Sneaking into an old abandoned mansion is creepy stuff. Illegal too. Trespassing."

"I can handle it."

Other than checking out the mansion, there was only one other thing we could do at that point. "I have another plan that will prove for certain whether it was my father that day. It's a ton riskier than the mansion and way creepier."

I sensed she was on the verge of the confession about her and Clay that I'd wanted to just moments before, to end my torment. Now, with the admission seeming imminent, I didn't want to hear it. I wanted to deny it, pretend it had never happened, if it meant that nothing changed between us. "We do the mansion first, then execute my other plan, together," I said.

"What's the plan?" She put a hand on my knee. "Tell me."

"First, the mansion," I said. "In or out?"

"In."

CONDEMNED

Concealed in a snarl of dead sumac branches atop a hill, Juliette and I kept vigil over the brooding stone mansion below us. Even from so far away, it seemed to heave up, out of the earth, its immensity and grandeur daunting despite its decrepitude. The facade was scarcely visible beneath a cloak of ivy and leprous, scabby lichen. Its enormous windows and entrance were strangled with vines. The windows had to be ten feet high, and each story at least fourteen.

No fewer than a dozen chimneys thrust up from the single-seam copper roof, green from weather and age. At the center of the roofline stood a gruesome weather vane, its copper green as mold—a colossal, fearsome-looking raptor with a malevolent hooked beak wide open in an eternal shriek. If an avian creature of its kind had ever inhabited earth, it must have been during the age of dinosaurs. It would easily have hurtled through the sky and slaughtered a pterodactyl with a single swipe of its murderous lacerating talons.

Through my binoculars I spied a wrought iron gate at the entrance of a long, snaking drive of crushed stone. Overgrown with weeds, the drive disappeared into the woods behind the mansion. Riveted to the center of the gate, above a knot of rusted chain, was a metal sign bleeding rust, its bold red letters warning, CONDEMNED! KEEP OUT!

I was certain the place held clues, evidence, within its walls.

We sat there watching. Nothing moved. No one approached or left.

"Let's get out of here," Juliette said.

"We just got here."

"Maybe we could—"

"Go do what you want," I said. "With whoever you want. I'm going down there."

I crept down the hill toward the mansion. I could hear Juliette following behind me.

Nearing the gate, I examined its lock and chain. The key slot at the bottom of the padlock was too caked with rust to receive a key. Rust had also long since fused the chain to the gate. No one had come or gone by this entrance in decades.

"We're not going to find anything," Juliette said.

I ignored her and ducked into a stubborn choke of scrub that surrounded the property. I came to a tree that grew high near the fence. I climbed it. Straddling a branch, I scooted out on it until I hung over the other side and dropped to the ground.

I stared at Juliette through the bars, as if she were a specimen in a zoo, or perhaps she was observing me, locked up in a penitentiary. She easily climbed the tree, shimmied along the branch, and dropped to the ground beside me.

What had once likely been a vast expanse of emerald grass that I imagined played host to posh celebrations, games of bocce and badminton, and perhaps even polo had long been taken over by rapacious nettles, goldenrod, and blackberry canes.

I pushed my way through the unholy thickets, holding branches so they wouldn't slap Juliette's face, keeping low even though no other houses or humans were anywhere in sight.

Thorns scratched my hands and face. Vines tried to ensnare me. The vegetation now seemed to be more a defense against intruders than a green lawn gone to seed, wittingly allowed to grow thick to discourage the curious. After much struggle Juliette and I poked our heads up above the suffocating overgrowth. The field seemed, through some aberrant sorcery, to have lengthened, and despite our efforts, the mansion seemed farther away instead of closer.

We pushed on.

Finally, we reached the looming south end of the mansion. I tried to peer into the windows, which I now saw were not ten feet tall, but perhaps as much as twenty, and were set too high up—from the south end, at least—for me or anyone else to get a peek inside. I reached up, yet the sills remained a full arm's length beyond my reach.

We tracked along the wall, toward the back. Behind the manor, between it and the lake, the field grew even more rampant and wild, except for the long driveway that led into the trees, its crushed marble stones so white they glowed in the pewter-gray day. The stones were packed tight, as if a roller had recently pressed them down. Not one weed sprouted between them.

"Someone uses this driveway," I said.

We stepped onto the drive and walked until we were about fifty feet from the mansion. I craned my neck to see up to the third-story windows, which mirrored the silver-gray sky, causing them to shimmer like mercury. In my mind I conjured the image from the *Shireburne Gazette*. The center window. It *had* to be the one Silva Vanders had fallen, or jumped, from while engulfed in flames.

A wind kicked up, and I could hear the muted crash of waves on the lakeshore behind me. Wanting a better vantage point, we followed the drive back toward the lake, through the lofty trees. I thought the drive might bring us to a stony beach. Instead, we came to the precipice of a shale cliff that plummeted straight down to a shoreline of jagged rocks some two hundred feet below. The height dizzied me as pieces of weathered rock crumbled beneath my feet and fell away. My heart pounded as Juliette clutched my arm. No one would survive a fall, or a push, from that ledge. They would be smashed like an egg on the rocks below.

As we came back out of the woods, Juliette said, "Over here," trotting along the drive.

I followed her to a carport at the north end, where the drive looped back on itself in a circular sweep. At this side entrance, a stately door hewn of a single wide plank of handsomely grained wood hung on black iron hinges and bore a circular knocker that might once have served for hitching horses. Two narrow vertical windows bracketing the door were made of old glass, honeycombed with air bubbles and so thick it was opaque. The door and both windows were all clear of weeds and vines.

A depression in the gravel drive in front of the door caught my eye. Not one depression, but two. Parallel tire tracks left by a heavy vehicle. A truck, perhaps, operated by a caretaker.

"From the other side, you'd swear the place was abandoned," Juliette said.

I tried the doorknob. Locked. The windows appeared too solid to break with a kick of my sneaker. It didn't matter. I wasn't going to enter by force and risk alerting a caretaker or whoever might be inside. I put my face to a window but couldn't see through the dense glass.

We cut around the back in hopes of locating a bulkhead or an unlocked door. In places, wild saplings grew so thick, we had to pry our way through them and stay close to the back walls. My foot snagged on a vine, and I pitched forward onto the end of a blunt stake, which, had it possessed a sharp point, would have skewered me. Even though it was blunt, it hurt. Juliette knelt to free my foot of the vine. "What's this?" she said.

Not a vine, but a croquet wicket. The stick I had fallen into was a croquet stake. Its bands of color had been bleached by time. No doubt, the rest of the wickets and the other stake—perhaps even the croquet balls and mallets—lay abandoned out there amid the goldenrod and nettles and blackberry cane.

I yanked the stake out of the ground in anger and threw it. I heard the sharp, bright sound of glass breaking.

I waded through the vegetation toward where the stake had flown.

It had shattered a small, solitary cellar window.

The window looked like a tight squeeze for me to wriggle through to get inside the basement. I grabbed the stake again and, quietly as I could, tapped out the shards of glass that protruded like shark's teeth from the window sash.

I lay on my belly and eased my head through the tight cellar window, my shoulders raking each side of the sash as I squeezed in. A putrid odor of damp and rot overwhelmed me as I looked into blackness as deep as the inside of a closed coffin. There was no telling how far the drop was down to the cellar floor.

I pulled my head out and turned around feet-first into the window.

"Careful," Juliette cautioned as I shimmied backward.

I gasped as a protruding nail I'd missed tore my jeans and gouged my thigh. Warm blood trickled down my leg. I adjusted the revolver in my back waistband, to keep it from falling out.

"Careful," Juliette said again.

I lowered myself farther, backing into the cellar, with no idea what lay below me in the darkness. My feet dangled as I felt around with them for anything solid. They found only air. I lowered myself until only the last joint of my fingers clutched the sill above me, my body hanging down straight as a nail, my feet still touching nothing but air. I had miscalculated the drop to the cellar floor. How far down was it? I might have been hanging over a pit as dark and deep as a mine shaft. If I let go, I could plunge to my death. I tried to pull myself up and out of the darkness, but I was too weak. I worked my feet to try to find a rock for a toehold in the cellar's stone wall. What little edges I found proved slimy, and my sneakers slipped, unable to find purchase.

There was no way back up through the window. Juliette was not strong enough to pull me up. I could see her face as I glanced up. She seemed distant and faded, her pale skin a blurry smudge.

My forearms burned and trembled. I could not hold on. I closed my eyes and drew a deep breath and let go.

I fell perhaps five feet. My sneakers landed in a glop of unknown muck. I looked up. The window was far out of reach. The gray light from it did nothing to illuminate the inky black around me.

"You okay?" Juliette whispered.

"It's dark. I need a light."

I tried finding fingerholds in the masonry, believing I could climb out with a fresh start from the bottom, but this proved fruitless. The wall seemed slimed with grease.

"I'm going to have to find some stairs out of here. I can't get back through the window."

Somewhere behind me in the blackness of the cellar, water dripped. A small creature scurried away, claws clicking over rock.

I turned and saw nothing but the darkness of a tomb. "Keep a lookout," I whispered.

"I want to come down too. You talked me into coming all this way."

"It's nasty down here," I said. "Let me check it out first. If I can, I'll find a door upstairs and open it from inside. Let you in."

"You can't just leave me here."

"We can't both be trapped down here."

"Trapped?"

"Just keep a lookout."

I put my hand out and started walking the perimeter of the cellar, in search of stairs to the mansion above me.

My hand touched cold, slimed stone. I inched away from the window, using the wall as my guide. Something with many sticky legs scuttled over my hand, leaving a grit behind on my skin. Despite the cool of the cellar, my skin felt damp and hot.

"Come back," Juliette said.

My face pushed through spiderwebs. I moved farther from the broken window. My sneakers squelched in mud that smelled like a jellyfish left to putrefy in the sun. I willed myself not to retch as I lurched onward in the dark, peering up in the hope that I might spy a crack of light seeping through a floorboard above. There had to be stairs somewhere in the blackness.

I worked along the cellar's edge, palm to its wet stone wall, for what seemed an hour, until the window came into view again—a dim gray rectangle on a black field.

"Hey," I said. "I need you to find a stump or a . . . I don't know. I need something to step on, to get out of here."

Juliette did not respond.

"Juliette?" I called. "Juliette?"

She was no longer at the window.

I'd found no stairs or doorway by following the wall, so I headed away from it, hands outstretched before me in search of stairs or any object I could step on to escape. My shin banged against a hard edge. A stair. And another.

I climbed up into the blackness.

The stairs sagged beneath me. I must have climbed twenty-five steps when a pale rind of light began to hover above me in the darkness. It might have been miles away or at the end of my nose. I counted twenty more steps before my knuckles *thocked* against wood. A door. I felt for the knob, found it.

The door swung open easily with a faint creak of hinges. Though the light that washed over me was a smoky gray, I shrank from it like Nosferatu from the bright noonday sun.

The room I entered was palatial. A pair of elaborate gilt candelabra chandeliers hung suspended from a high ceiling of ornate pressed tin. The chandeliers were veiled in cobwebs, as if their crystal baubles were fantastic gold beetles trapped by a monstrous spider.

The windows' dark velvet drapes, luxurious as stage curtains, fell from ceiling to floor. They were drawn tight against the outside world, keeping the room in shadow. I pulled back the curtain. Far across the lake, in the western sky, the clouds had parted, and the sun slouched toward the Spectral Mountains.

A cavernous stone fireplace hulked against the far wall, black tongues of soot crawling up from its stone maw to lick at the underside of its ancient dark-wood mantel.

In the cold, barren room, my sneakers squeaked on parquet floor whose intricate design in blond and dark woods was obscured by a film of dust.

There was nothing in this room for me. I needed to be two stories above it to investigate before the last vestige of light leaked from the world and left me in darkness.

I started down a corridor so narrow and tall, it felt like an alley between two towering buildings, but instead of cobblestones beneath my feet, there was decorative marble tile.

I came to an immense foyer of white marble and dark wood. A marble staircase as wide as my house reached up to the second floor.

I thought about going out the door and calling for Juliette from the carport, but she was probably back at her house by now. Or with Clay. Where she wanted to be.

I climbed the stairs. They proved steep and treacherous, their white marble slick as wet ice beneath my sneakers. I clutched the balustrade for support.

On the second-floor landing, I heard a noise and stopped. Footfalls? Above me? And another sound. Was that . . . weeping? I strained to hear, but no other sound came. Whatever I'd heard, if anything, had quieted.

I made my slow ascent up the next flight, treading lightly in case there was indeed someone making the sounds I thought I had heard.

At the top of the stairs, I stood in front of a door whose glossy black paint shone as if it were wet. Behind this door, I imagined, was the room that had served as Silva's infirmary.

I stepped toward it and could have sworn I detected the smell of paint, as if a fresh coat had been brushed on just minutes before I arrived. I touched my palm to the surface, half expecting the paint to be sticky. It wasn't. I tried the doorknob. It felt cemented in place. I pushed my shoulder against the door. It did not move.

Stepping back to assess, I swore I saw a shadow pass by the crack underneath it. I jumped back and lost my balance at the edge of the landing. I grabbed the balustrade to keep from pitching backward down the steep stairs whose marble was surely harder than my skull.

As I righted myself, I saw the shadow from under the door shift and disappear. And I believed I heard a muted, mumbling voice come from the room, as if a woman were trying to speak with a hand covering her mouth. I reached back, gripped the butt of the revolver, and put my ear to the door. A part of me needed to know who was behind the door; another part urged me to flee this grim place and never return.

I pressed my ear tighter to the door and heard the sound of a slippered foot taking a careful step backward.

"Hello?" I whispered, afraid to speak to loudly.

The mansion had sunk into shadow.

An orange light glowed from under the door, as if the room behind it were in flames.

Someone, or something, lurked behind that door.

I tried the knob again. It remained locked.

I hadn't come here just to turn tail at the last second. I shoved my shoulder into the door. I might as well have thrown myself against a mountain.

I looked up and down the hall, at the doors on either side of the one before me. Perhaps, one of them was unlocked, and just perhaps, the rooms behind them adjoined this one.

I tried the one on the left first. The knob wiggled but would not turn. I thumped my shoulder hard against the door. It yielded with a sound of splintering wood. I shoved my weight into the door. It came unstuck, and I fell on my knees into a room drenched in an orange glow from the setting sun. The fiery radiance gave the room no warmth. The room was as cold as a morgue—so cold, my breath swirled. I shivered and rubbed my arms as the sun melted into the mountains and was gone. The room took on the purpled hue of the mountains, and the sheet-enshrouded humps of furniture became skulking beasts, waiting to spring at me. Halfway along the common wall with the adjacent room, I saw a door that I hoped might connect the two rooms.

I threw it open only to find a closet, barren save for a couple of garments draped on wire hangers, sagging like old hides and reeking of mothballs.

I went back into the corridor, to the door right of the center room. The knob turned, and I entered to find a room laid out in the mirror image of the one I had just abandoned. It even had yellowed sheets covering furniture that had been pushed into the middle of the room—and the same door in the common wall with the center room. I scrambled around the cloaked armchairs and couches and swung the door open to find another closet, all of four feet deep. A few bare wire hangers dangled from a metal rod. I stepped into the shadowed closet, coat hangers jangling as my shoulder brushed them, and heard it again: the somnambulant scuff and drag of slippers across the floor. I heard a weak *tap-tap* just on the other side of the wall. I rapped a knuckle against the wall, the sound dull and dead on the ancient horsehair plaster.

Another sound startled me. A noise from outside, below the triple Palladian window nearest me. The sound of a car engine. I sneaked to the window and eased the plush velvet drape aside, releasing a plume of dust that irritated my nose. Headlight beams sliced through the deepening darkness as a vehicle drove around from the woods in back and out of sight on the carport side.

A moment later, a vehicle door slammed shut. And another.

I darted out onto the landing. I took the stairs three at a time down toward the second floor. I was halfway there when I heard the foyer door shut.

I stopped, hand clutching the balustrade, and peeked down over the rail. Bright light bathed me from above and below as the chandeliers over the landings came on. A voice whispered far below. Voices. Male. Shadows shifted on the foyer's marble floor. Footfalls reverberated. The voices grew louder, still muddled by echoes but closer as the men climbed the stairs.

I ascended the stairs as quietly as I could and returned to the room I'd just left, the door creaking as footsteps fell on the marble staircase behind me.

Easing the door shut, I scrambled to find a place to hide. I doubted that the two men were coming to this room, unless they'd heard me. If they started to look for me, there was no place to hide—under the furniture shrouds or behind the drapes seemed comical, a five-year-old's hiding place. The closet was bare; I'd be discovered the moment the door opened. Voices came from the top of the stairs. As a last resort, I ducked into the closet and shut the door behind me, enveloped in darkness.

I eased the revolver out of my waistband, ready to spring and run. I could not calm my breathing, gasping as if I had just escaped drowning. I listened. *There*: the faint creak of hinges on the other side of the wall. I heard the hallway door snick shut. Heard male voices again. And a third voice, which was not really a voice at all. Muted. Fragile. Shattered. It might have muttered the word *no*, but it was impossible to tell. The sounds had a mournful singsong pattern—not words, yet a form of communication, nonetheless.

A male voice shouted, "Time to go!" startling me.

Another sound. A sob? I couldn't tell.

I waited.

A door closed.

The foyer door?

Was someone else entering the place? I had not heard another car drive up. A few moments later, an engine started, distant and muted. The visitors were departing.

I stood up, stiff and aching.

I raced out of the room and stood in the hallway. The chandeliers that had lit the corridor and stairs were now dark, and only the pewter light of the half-moon filtered in through the foyer windows. Bright headlight beams lit the dark foyer. I hurried down to the entrance and peered out to see a white van starting up. Just as its side door slid shut, I got a bare glimpse of a passenger's shadow in the back. The van roared away. When it was out of sight, I hurried back to the door to the center room. Had the men I heard taken someone from the room? I knocked on the door.

No one answered.

I tried the knob, knowing it would be locked, and was surprised when it turned in my hand.

I pushed the door open to darkness and reached around the wall beside me for a switch. When I found one, it was not a toggle switch, but a brass button. I pushed it. The room lit up in a dazzling white glow from a silver chandelier sparkling with crystal ornaments. The furniture was opulent and feminine, all slender curved white legs, royal blue cushions, and cut-glass knobs. Velvet drapes of the same deep blue fell from the high ceiling to the floor, concealing the imposing window. Next to the window stood a painter's easel and an upholstered Chesterfield chair on caster wheels. I found the source of the wet-paint smell I had detected out in the hallway: tubes of oil paints that sat perched on the easel's tray. Beside the easel sat an open can of turpentine, its astringent juniper reek bright in my nose. An unfinished painting, of what I supposed were the Spectral Mountains as seen from the window, reflected the work of a crude and amateur hand.

The centerpiece of the sumptuous room was a canopied four-poster bed, its white gossamer curtain concealing the mattress and whoever might be on it. A vanity with a pearlescent finish and a beveled and scalloped mirror stood against the left wall. A bedside table, ornate and whimsical in its design, stood to the left of the bed.

The canopy seemed to flutter the slightest, as if someone were breathing on it from inside on the bed. I sensed someone in the room with me, watching me. Listening.

I stepped closer to the bed. On the night table sat a hairbrush, fashioned of ivory or bone. Carved into the back of it were two detailed silhouettes of child faces, a boy and a girl. They faced away from each other. An eternity could pass, and neither child would ever know that the other existed.

I picked up the brush. I had expected it to have heft, but it weighed even more than I imagined, as if the bone or ivory were but a veneer over solid lead. I pushed my palm against the bristles. They barely gave. Badger bristles—the same hair that made up my father's shaving brushes. Stiff and coarse, at odds with the brush's decorative carvings. Long hairs twined in the bristles. I teased one out. Silver as Christmas tinsel.

I set the brush back on the table and stared at the canopy drawn tight around the bed. The sensation of someone hiding behind it intensified.

I took a corner of the canopy in my hand and cast it back.

The bed lay empty, with a slight depression at the center of the lofty mattress. A shallow, delicate depression, as if a fawn had lain on soft moss.

I touched the depression with my palm. The bedspread was hot, as if someone on the verge of spontaneous combustion had just been there. I yanked my hand away.

At the end of the bed lay what looked like a sheath of pale shed snakeskin.

I touched it. Picked it up. It was cold. A flimsy, filthy chiffon nightgown.

Disgust rippled through me. I dropped the nightgown, my eyes lighting on the nightstand. It appeared to have a single deep drawer.

I tugged on the handle. The drawer seemed warped, refusing to open. I pounded it with my fist, then pulled again. The drawer screeched open, and a smell of dank leather escaped.

In the dark well of the old drawer was a gilded frame with a photo of a teenage girl in the first flush of youth. She wore an ecstatic smile, a smile that had to exist still, somewhere in the heart and memory of a now-adult man. An ocean of curling red locks floated around the face of the young woman who, gauging from the 1940s-style scarf around her lustrous red hair, had to be in her fifties now. Also in the drawer was a book. I was about to pick it up when I heard what sounded like a shout from outside the room and down the hall.

I hurried out into the hall. No one was there. The noise seemed to have come from the far southern end of the long corridor.

I went to the door at the end. No light shone from underneath it. I put my ear to it and heard a low, steady *whoosh* followed by a muted *slap*, as if a breeze were coming through an open window and flapping a shade against the frame.

"Hello?" I whispered.

The knob was locked fast. I strained to hear. There was only the faint *whoosh, slap.* I knocked several times. "Hello? Hello?" I stood outside the door for a long time, knocking and saying hello to no avail.

Fatigued and bewildered, I descended the stairs back down to the foyer and made my way to the side entry I'd seen when coming up from the cellar. I hurried from the mansion as the door shut with a dead *thunk.*

The air outside was bracing with a strong breeze, and the moon sat low in the new night sky, its glow so bright now that my exaggerated shadow stretched far in front of me.

I battled my way back through the wild fields. Briar tore at my bare arms, leaving little runnels of blood on the soft insides of my wrists. I came to the overgrown drive and tramped along to the wrought-iron entrance gate. I scaled it, pricking my palms on spurs of rusted metal. At the top I squeezed over the bars and dropped down on the other side. I hit the ground, pain lighting up my injured ankle. I trudged up the hill. At its crest I hid in the dead sumac and looked back at the mansion.

A hand grabbed my shoulder.

I yelped, startled, and reached for the revolver.

"It's me."

I spun around to find Juliette's face inches from mine.

"Where did you go?" I said.

"Where did *I* go? Right after you *left* me, I saw a van parked at the top of the dirt road that goes along the lake. I wanted to see if I could get a better look. I called for you, but you didn't answer. I didn't dare call out too loud, so—"

"Did you see the people in the van get out?"

She nodded, smiled, and for a moment I almost forgot about her and Clay at her locker. Almost.

"What did they look like?" I asked her.

"It was hard to see. The light was failing, so they were just . . . shadows. One guy stood out, though, because he was so tall. Really tall." She shivered. "I need to get home. My parents. My mom . . . "

I didn't want to leave. I wanted to go back inside the old mansion. I wanted to knock down that door behind which I'd heard the *whoosh* and *slap*, even if all I discovered was a window shade flapping in a breeze.

"Please," Juliette continued, "I need to go."

Reluctantly, I nodded, and we started down the hill back toward town.

At a corner halfway between my house and Juliette's, we stood beneath the streetlight, bathed in its blue halo.

Juliette shivered again as she looked up at me.

"Leave me alone like that again, and I won't go along with your other plan."

"You still want to be part of it?"

"Unless you plan to desert me again, why wouldn't I?"

"You've got other people you can hang out with."

"Are you mad at me?"

"What would I have to be mad at?" I said, testing her.

"Beats me," she said, unblinking, the lie coming so easily it alarmed me. If I'd never seen her with Clay in the hallway, I would never have doubted her. The natural ease with which she said it chilled and saddened me.

She wrapped her arms around herself and rocked on her tiptoes, raising her eyebrows at me.

I wanted to pull her close and warm her. She was cold and, I thought, a little afraid. I knew I was afraid. She seemed about to say something too, and I sensed again that she was going to tell me about Clay. Confess. I didn't want to hear it. I couldn't bear her telling me how she liked me as a friend, trying to convince me that Clay was my friend too, but that, well, she and Clay—they liked each other—in a different way.

I braced for it, but it never came. "So," she said, looking up at me, blinking. I took a slow, deep breath, gathering my confidence to draw her close to me when she elbowed me, exactly as she had elbowed Clay in the school hallway. "Are you going to tell me your next big plan before I head home?" she said. "Your plan that's too creepy for me."

"Maybe next time."

"Come *on*." She elbowed me again.

"Next time," I said.

"Tomorrow?"

"Maybe. If you want."

"Don't sound so eager."

"Okay. Tomorrow."

"Okay. But tease me too long, I'll get bored." She elbowed me again and turned on her toes and moseyed away, balancing herself along the curb edge like a high-wire performer until she disappeared from view around the corner.

DR. ZANTZ

"Wayland? Wayland, wake up."

My mother. She had come home from bowling and found me asleep on the couch, the room lit by the glow of the TV's sign-off test pattern.

She switched off the set, and the room fell dark as she sat on the edge of the couch. I felt feverish. My hair was plastered to my skull with sweat.

"You okay?" she asked me. "You were crying out in your sleep and clawing at the air."

"Fine," I lied. I had dreamed I was clawing up my father's grave with my bare hands, the flesh of my fingers torn and bloodied. In the dream I'd been digging for years, for centuries. I was an old man.

"You don't look fine, and you don't act fine. I don't like the way you've been hiding out in your room, bad ankle or not," my mom said. She brushed my bangs back from my forehead with her fingers, as she'd done when I was younger and would come down with a fever. "I've been thinking," she said. "I should have gotten you help. Years ago." She pulled a wadded tissue from her uniform pocket and wiped her nose. "What do they say? 'Better late than never'? Well, I found someone."

I propped myself up on my elbows. "Someone?"

"To help you. To talk to."

"I don't need anyone *now*," I said.

"I scheduled it. I don't care what it costs. You can't keep saying these things. Believing them."

"They're true. The no—" I almost said, *the note.*

"The what?" my mother asked.

"Nothing."

"Is there some other reason you believe this? I know that over the years, you've had a . . . a difficult time accepting it. Been troubled. I've worried that you want to believe, for many reasons, that he didn't do it. I worry about your thinking. That's why, if you spoke to someone who—"

"There's nothing wrong with my *thinking*."

"His name is Dr. Zantz. I'm taking you to see him after school tomorrow, between my shifts. I don't care if I have to drag you there."

In school the next day, I avoided my locker. During biology and history classes, I hid in the back of the school library. I managed to go the entire day without encountering either of my "friends." As much as I had enjoyed investigating the mansion with Juliette, I didn't want to see her and Clay together or hear their lies. I'd had enough of lies.

Dr. Zantz's office was in a cedar-shake, gambrel-roofed home perched on the crest of an immaculate sloping lawn that was such a bright green amid the dead, brown lawns of April, it struck me as artificial. The place was secreted away in the shadows of towering bare elm trees at the end of a cul-de-sac, in a section of town I had not known existed. I wondered how I could live in such a small town all my life and not know every street.

My mother parked the J2000 at the end of the driveway, not ascending its steep incline—likely for fear of trying to back down its severe grade and perhaps ruining her loose muffler, which rattled as she shut off the engine.

I didn't want to be there. I felt anxious and conspicuous— manipulated.

"If you don't like it, you don't have to come back," my mother told me, putting a hand on my shoulder. "Just try it once."

I took a deep breath, got out of the car, and looked back at my mother.

"I'll pick you up in an hour sharp. I have errands," she said. "Then, I've got to get to work." She glanced over my shoulder at the house behind me. "It's going to be okay," she assured me.

I shut the car door and trudged up the driveway, the J2000 backfiring behind me.

The door to the house opened before I finished knocking. A short, slight, mustached man greeted me. I at first mistook him for an assistant, until he nodded at me and said, "Wayland, I'm Dr. Zantz. Do come in."

I stepped inside.

"Please. If you would," the doctor said.

He guided me down a hallway of closed doors that prevented me from seeing into what I imagined were the more personal rooms of the home. His hand brushed my lower back as he led me through a door on the left at the end of the hall. The hems of his pants—white linen that matched that of his collarless buttoned shirt—swished as he walked, and his dock shoes squeaked on the wood floor.

The room was furnished with two facing wicker chairs, their seats and backs padded with bird-print cushions. The table between the chairs was also of wicker, oval with a glass top. It seemed the kind of furniture for an atrium.

The doctor sat in the chair facing the door and motioned with his boy hands for me to sit in the other chair with my back to the door.

"Tell me," he pressed a thumb along his black mustache, "what happened that day." So much for pleasantries, I thought.

I avoided his pale eyes and focused on his dark mustache. It was too black, as if he had used a permanent felt marker to color it and then forgotten to do his hair. I avoided his eyes and kept my mouth shut tight as a walnut shell.

"Just ease into it," he said. "No rush. We have plenty of time."

"You won't believe me. And I don't want to talk about it, so what's the point?"

"I will believe whatever you tell me, unless you're here to lie to me. And I'll know if you are lying. I'm trained in that skill. And I don't blame you for not wanting to talk about it. I sure wouldn't."

He leaned forward and reached for a crystal pitcher of water with ice and lemon slices floating in it. He hefted the pitcher and poured water into a glass tumbler. He set the pitcher down without asking me whether I'd like some water. In fact, I saw no glass except his. He set the glass down, made a sound like that of a clucking squirrel, and wiped at his mustache. "*Are* you here to lie to me?"

"No."

The padding of my seat gave no comfort. A nail head poked the back of my thigh.

"Then I'll believe you."

"Someone shot himself in front of me when I was eight," I said.

He did not respond, just sat perfectly still, as if waiting for clarification.

Finally, when my silence made clear that no clarification was forthcoming, he cleared his throat and said, "That must have been traumatic," though his face betrayed no opinion of my statement.

"I thought it was my father," I said.

He nodded.

"It wasn't," I said.

I shifted in my chair to ease the discomfort from the nail head jabbing my thigh.

"Who did this person turn out to be?" he said.

"I don't know."

"Did they never identify him?"

"Didn't my mom already fill you in on all this stuff?" I said.

"That's not how this works. I'm here to help you. No one else matters or has a say."

"I don't need help. I need someone to believe me."

"I believe you. And I'll help you make sense of it. Take whatever steps are necessary."

He sipped his water, ice cubes sloshing and clacking.

"Do you trust people?" he said.

I shrugged. "I never thought about it."

"Think about it."

I fidgeted. I didn't like his prying nature. "There's not a lot of people in my life to trust," I said. "There's not a lot of people in my life, period."

"Who is in your life?"

"My mom, my sister. My friend, Clay. Another, I guess. Juliette."

"A girlfriend?"

I gave no answer.

"Who else?" he asked.

"No one."

"There's no one else? Just those four people."

"There's Molly, my dog."

"Do you trust these four individuals?"

"No," I admitted, and felt a wave of relief rush over me. "I don't trust any one of them."

"Why not?"

"They're a bunch of liars. Not my sister, really. I mean, she lies, but it's more like stuff she doesn't share."

"So you think not sharing stuff is the same as lying?"

"Sometimes."

"Like what?"

"Like, I know she got an abortion. I don't know *how* she got one. I'd think you'd have to get permission if you were a minor. But she got one. And she's barely fifteen. Her boyfriend is a twenty-year-old scumbag. He must have helped her somehow. And she never told me."

"How do you know she got an abortion?"

"I found a prescription note for some pills she was given, specifically prescribed for post-abortion stuff."

Dr. Zantz nodded. "And you expected her to share this with you?"

"We used to share everything. Stay up late at night talking in our bunk beds. When we were little. The first few years after it happened—the Incident. But we're not little anymore."

"What did you two talk about?"

"Him."

"Your father?"

"Yes."

"And you don't talk at night anymore?"

"We don't talk at all. Not really. She moved into a different bedroom years ago, the room that used to be my father's old den."

"It makes you mad that she doesn't share?"

"It makes me mad that she gets pregnant by an imbecile and gets abortions instead of having fun like any normal kid."

"Like you?"

"I said *normal.*"

"You don't think you're normal? You don't just have fun?"

I shrugged. "She's hanging out with that loser, screwing him. She's fifteen, and I'm almost two years older and I haven't even . . . " I snapped my mouth shut.

"Haven't what?"

"Nothing."

"Are you jealous?"

"Why would I be jealous?"

"Does she have a lot of friends?"

"She has Dipshit. That's it. That's all."

"Not a lot of people in her life, either. Not a lot of support. And your mom—do you trust her?"

"She threw out everything of my dad's. Just hauled it all to the curb."

Anger heated my veins.

"What does her throwing out your father's stuff have to do with trusting her?" Dr. Zantz said.

"It's weird. And it's wrong. Suspicious, don't you think?"

"What do you think?"

"I used to think maybe she just didn't want reminders of him around. She was sad or angry at him for what he did, what she thought he did."

"And what do you think now?"

"I think she trashed his stuff for another reason."

"You don't trust her motives?"

"She wasn't home that day, because she met some man in town. Some *guy*. What's that say? And there's other stuff she's hiding."

"So she's lying, not to be trusted, too, because she doesn't share everything in her private life with you?"

"You're twisting my words. There's something weird going on. There always has been. It's like . . . it's like, my mom tossing out everything. *Everything*. Now I look at it and I wonder, why? It was like she was getting rid of evidence or something."

"Evidence?"

"And not getting me any help to deal with what happened, what I saw. That's bizarre. That's . . . " I tried to think of the word. "Cruel. I was eight. Now, when I press my mom for real answers, she suddenly thinks I need help. I don't need help *now*."

"Why not?'

"It's too late."

"Then why are you here?"

"She forced me."

"Did she?"

"Well, she wasn't going to let up until I caved."

"What about this friend, Clay? And your girlfriend. Do you trust them?"

"She's not my girlfriend."

"Do you trust them?"

"No."

"You think they lie to you?"

"I know they do."

"Yet you call them your friends."

"Maybe they're not my friends. Not anymore. Maybe they never were."

"What did they do?"

"It doesn't matter." My anger simmered.

"Tell me more about that day. The day that has brought you here."

I hesitated.

"You might be surprised," Dr. Zantz said, "how good it is just to speak our thoughts aloud to someone who won't judge or argue or refute. Walk me through what happened. Take your time. Remember."

I sat forward. I took a deep breath and told him about my coming home early, the idling truck, John Denver singing, my entering the bedroom. I told him all of it, just as it happened. Or just as I remembered it. I didn't tell him about the note or the adoption or the annulment.

I must have gone on a while. When I finished, I was winded, my voice raw. The doctor waited a minute to make certain I was done. He set his glass down on the table. The ice was mostly melted now. "I'm sorry you saw that." His tone and his countenance were quite grave. "You believe that the man who did this was not your father."

"I know it."

"Did you tell anyone?"

"Not at the time. I didn't realize it till just last week."

"What triggered this realization?"

I explained about my father's feet not reaching the floor.

The doctor nodded. It was not a dismissive nod, but a nod of acknowledgment, confirmation. A nod of empathy. He did not request clarification or counter with alternative possibilities—a different mattress, bed frame, or sitting position, or simply a hopeful yet false and desperate memory.

"What would you like to see happen?" he said.

I didn't know what he meant and said so.

"If the man who shot himself was not your father, it has to be beyond confusing and maddening, beyond your normal daily emotions. It must be painful. You must want answers. I don't mean to put words in your mouth, so, why don't you tell me. What do you want to come of all this?"

"Like you said, answers. The truth. And I want to know where my father is *now*. He would not have just left us. Left me. Done that. Someone did something to him."

"Do you want to go to the police with your theory?"

"It's not a theory."

"My apologies. Poor word choice."

"They wouldn't take me seriously. I need real *proof* for that."

"I suppose you do. I believe you. But, yes, for the law, you'd need concrete evidence. Do you have any?"

I considered telling him about the note.

"Don't you think your mother would have noticed that the man wasn't your father?" Dr. Zantz said.

"His face," I said. "It was. It must have been . . . gone. And. She must have been in shock. Why *wouldn't* she think it was him? I did, and I was there. I was a witness. The only witness. I told her it was him. His truck was parked outside. Who the hell else could it have been? I mean, who else could I have *thought* it was, since I never saw his face?"

"Wouldn't your mother have noticed he wasn't wearing his wedding ring?"

I hadn't thought about that. It seemed something she would have noticed, *if* she hadn't been in shock and grief.

"I don't know. I don't know if he even wore a ring." I could not recall now whether he did or didn't. "I'm not sure. I don't know."

"And the police—there must be a protocol for identifying the deceased. Something . . . scientific. Forensic."

I tried to recall the police being there. I remembered an ambulance. It had eased up to the house in no great hurry. No lights. No siren. I remembered Mr. Kane shielding me, keeping me in the backyard. "I don't know about the police," I said. "I don't know if she saw the body to identify him, or what there was, face-wise, *to* identify. Who wants to see that? The casket was closed. I told her it was him. Why would they do anything more to ID him when a blood relative, his own son, witnessed him doing that?"

The doctor nodded.

He was not humoring me, even if he didn't believe me entirely.

"When you get proof, perhaps I can help you proceed, legally," he said.

I slipped my hand in my pocket and felt the note.

"Everything I say here stays between us?" I said.

"Unless you plan to hurt someone, or yourself."

I didn't know why he said that. Did he think I was planning to hurt myself or someone else? Did he sense something about me that I didn't?

I produced the note from my pocket, held it up as a street preacher might hold up a leaflet.

"What's this?" the doctor said.

"I found it at the feet of the person who was in his room that day."

"May I see it?"

He put out an open palm.

I wanted to stuff the note back in my pocket and leave, but Dr. Zantz held my gaze with his look of compassion. I laid the note in his palm.

Dr. Zantz nodded, appreciative. Respectful. He pulled reading glasses from his shirt pocket and put them on.

He stared at the note, gazed over the top of it at me, stared at it again.

"Who wrote this?"

"My father."

"Why do you think he wrote it if you found it at the feet of the deceased, yet you don't think that person was your father?"

"I compared it to his handwriting. It's his."

"*I am not who you think I am,*" Dr. Zantz read aloud. "I have to be blunt. It reads like a suicide note, or a confession, a regret. That's speculation, but it makes the most sense and it supports the idea that the person, the deceased, was in fact your father. Doesn't it?"

"Forget it," I barked. "Give it back."

He handed the note to me. "Who else knows about the note?"

"No one." I didn't want to tell him about Juliette or Clay. I doubted he'd care, anyway.

"Your mom doesn't know?" he said.

"She asked back then if there was a note. It was the first thing she asked, even before she asked if I was all right."

"Why didn't you tell her about it? Or show it to her or anyone else?"

"I . . . " My hands trembled as I picked at a thumb cuticle. The spring sunshine at the window felt harsh on my face, accusatory and interrogative. I'd felt until recently that the reasons I'd kept the note were private, between my father and me. I was the one who had walked in on him. I was the one who had found the note. What happened in that room was between us. Except, of course, that he could not have intended the note for me, because he could not have known I would be the first to see him. He must have expected my mother to be home. I wondered about my mom going to town to meet a man. I wondered whether that someone had played a part in my dad's note or in what happened that day.

"How did you come to walk in on him?" Dr. Zantz said.

I had already told him. I didn't know why he wanted to hear it again. "Like I said, I came home early from school. I had a stomachache. His truck was in the driveway, and—"

"So whoever it was could not have known you would show up."

"There was no way to know. But my mom was always home at that time. Always. She didn't work then. And she had this soap opera she loved—never missed it. Never. Except that day."

"His truck was in your driveway? But he wasn't there?"

I nodded. He was doubting me now—I could feel it—punching holes in my story.

"But the door of the truck was open, the truck running," I said. "Which makes more sense: that he was in a hurry to get inside and do *that* to himself, when he had to be expecting my mom to be home? Or that he left the truck running because he planned to come right back out?"

"Where was he if he wasn't in the bedroom? Where is he now?"

"I don't know!" I shouted, my anger frightening me. "How am I supposed to know? I wouldn't be here if I fucking knew." I felt as wretched and bewildered as ever, doubting everything I'd convinced myself of the past few days, telling it all to a complete stranger.

"It's difficult to understand," Dr. Zantz said. "Painful."

A sob hitched in my throat. I swallowed my anguish and rage.

"Maybe you should give the note to the police," Dr. Zantz suggested. "If it is evidence of some sort, they're the best equipped to verify it and do something with it. I'm not sure what. It's been so long. They could find out for certain that it's his handwriting."

"It's his handwriting."

"Can I borrow it?" the doctor said.

"I . . . " The thought of the note being in anyone else's hands for more than a few moments terrified me.

"I'll make a copy, and with your permission, I can bring the original to the police as a professional who sees validity in your reasoning or, at least, in your need for clarity, for resolution."

"*I* verified it. It's *his*."

"Just for their records. And they'll probably be taken aback by the mysterious tone of the note. They may want to speak to you. It will give you credibility if I vouch for you. You can hold on to the copy. I have a Xerox machine here in another room."

I didn't want to let the note out of my hands again. But the doctor was right. On my own, I had reached a dead end. If he could get it to the police on my behalf, as a professional, an adult who wouldn't just be dismissed, maybe he could help get them to actually investigate, to search for the truth of what happened to my father, perhaps even find him.

"And you'll give me the original back as soon as the cops are done with it?" I said.

"It's your property."

I took the note from my pocket, worried it between my fingertips.

"I don't know," I hesitated.

"I understand. It's precious to you. It's solely your decision. Just know, I only want to help."

I opened the note and read it.

I AM NOT WHO YOU THINK I AM

"I'll get it back straightaway?" I said.

"As soon as they're done. You need to trust someone."

Did I? I wondered. Did I need to trust anyone besides myself?

I held the note out to him.

He took it between two fingertips, read it again. "'I am not who you think I am.' What do you think it means?"

"I don't know."

"And what's this on the back? Initials? SFL? Do you know who this is?"

"No idea," I said.

"Okay. Well. Now—" He slipped the note into his breast pocket. "Think about whether there is more to tell me about what transpired that day, or what you've learned these past few days, while I make a copy of this note." He got up and left the room, the spicy fragrance of aftershave trailing behind him.

I sat looking around the sparse room with its wicker furniture.

Dr. Zantz returned sooner than I'd expected, as if he had just stood outside in the hallway and counted to ten before coming back in. "Sorry," he said, "I'm out of copy paper. I'm afraid I've been making copies like a fiend with my new toy, and my office is in a bit of . . . disarray."

"I'll take the note back and you can try to copy it next meeting."

"The police station will have a copier. I can go there straight from here and make a copy, give them the original, and give you the copy at the start of our next meeting."

"I don't know," I said.

"Let's say . . . " He flipped through a black leather appointment book. "Two days from now? We can meet—"

"Can I just have the note back now?" I said.

"Of course you may. But it would be good to get it to the police and get started, don't you think? You're welcome to have your mother follow me to the station when she picks you up in a few minutes. I can make a copy at the station and run it right out to you. I don't want you to worry. I want you to trust me. Trust is key. Both ways. For me to go out on a limb like this, I have to trust that you are telling me the truth, but you need to trust me too. You want to follow me to the station?"

I wanted the damned note back, but the doctor made good points about getting started. I considered having my mother follow him to the police station so I could get the copy straightaway. But I didn't want her to know about the note.

"We'll meet again, two days from now?" I said.

"Same time, same place."

"And you'll have a copy?"

"I'll make it at the station, pronto. I apologize for being out of copy paper."

"Okay," I said, regretting it in the same instant.

"Do you want to go to the station? Wait for the copy?"

"I trust you," I said, even though I didn't, not deep down. I just didn't want my mom to know about the note and didn't know what story I could tell about Dr. Zantz going into the police station and coming out with a piece of paper for me.

"Good. This has been a good start today. Beneficial. Don't you think?"

On the car ride home, my mother said, "I hope it helped, talking about it."

"Some."

"Would you like to go again?"

"I'm going back in two days, same time."

"So soon? Good. I suppose that's good."

That night I lay awake in bed thinking of Juliette. *Tease me too long, I'll get bored.* However deep my feelings of bitterness and dejection at seeing her and Clay together, my desire to see her proved more potent. It was Clay I never wanted to see again. It was Clay who was to blame. He was a predator. He sought out every girl he was attracted to, which was almost any girl at all. He watched them, studied them. He decided which version of himself would give him the best odds of *scoring*. The humble jock who shrugs off his God-given athletic talents, treats it all as a bore, a burden. Poor, blessed Clay. Or perhaps the version that wore a loose shirt to hide his physique, the Clay who softened his eyes and gave an easy, welcoming smile. Or the aggressive Clay who wore a sleeveless wifebeater after pumping iron for a half hour to get his muscles jacked and who bragged about his prowess and flirted with unabashed bravado. Whose smile was a leer, a challenge. It was Clay who had betrayed me. He was my friend, my *only* friend, and he had promised to keep away from Juliette, just as he promised he would never hit me again. He'd deceived me. He wasn't my friend. He'd never been my friend.

I wondered how Juliette would see him if I told her how Clay had reacted when his dad laid into him that day on the roof, when he'd cried like a baby, like a pussy. I wondered what she would think if she saw him blubbering like that with her own eyes.

At school, I again avoided my locker and sequestered myself in the back periodicals of the library during biology and history. I wanted to see Juliette, to run my plan by her, but I did not want to suffer having Clay swagger up to us in the hall, inject himself into our conversation, puff up his chest and spin his bullshit charm. I wanted to get her alone, in private, not in school. Until then, I didn't want to see her.

THE TALL MAN

Early on the morning of my second appointment with Dr. Zantz, I said to my mother, "Should I just walk to Dr. Zantz's after school, or are you gonna be able to give me a ride?"

"He canceled," my mother said as she poured a glass of Tang for herself and dropped a slice of white bread into the toaster.

"What? When?"

"He called while you were in the shower. He's sick."

"He was fine two days ago."

"Well, he's not fine now."

"What day did he reschedule for me?"

"He didn't. He doesn't know how long he'll be sick. He came down with something really nasty, apparently, soon after I picked you up."

"He thinks he's going to be sick *forever*? Like he won't be okay in a few days? Or next week? He can't schedule for next damned week?"

My mother looked down into the toaster to check the bread. "He apologized. Said he'd be in touch."

"That's crap," I said. "That's bullshit. He's got something of mine. I have to get it back. He lied to me."

"No one lied to you. I'm sure he'll return whatever he has next time you see him." She popped the piece of bread up from the toaster, inspected it, and put it back in.

"Which is *when*?" I said. "Never? Sick? He's not sick. '*Trust me*,' he said. Trust him. That crook. Where'd you find him? What are you two up to?"

Lydia wandered into the kitchen, plucked a Pop-Tart from a box, and broke the edges off, leaving just the frosted part to eat. "You are *so* mental," she said.

"He's upset," my mother said. She tried to pop up her toast, but it was stuck in the toaster. "This thing," she said, jiggling the handle.

Lydia grabbed a butter knife from the counter and stuck it down into the slot to try to stab the bread.

"Don't do that," my mother said. "You're going to get a shock, shoving that knife down there like that."

"He's *always* upset," Lydia said, working the knife into the toaster. "*Always*. All day. Every day. About something. That's what makes him mental."

"He's upset because his appointment was canceled. His therapist is sick and has something Wayland wants back."

"Is he even a real therapist?" I said.

"Of course he's real," my mother said.

"First you have to be dragged kicking and screaming to see this quack," Lydia said to me, "and now you're throwing a tantrum because you *can't* see him? Mental." She jammed the knife down at the bread again.

"Stop being cruel," my mother said, unplugging the toaster. She looked at me. "You'll get back whatever the doctor has of yours, I'm sure."

"He better *pray* I get it back. And you and he both better pray he is who you say he is."

I stormed to my bedroom. I grabbed the revolver from my drawer, stuck it in the back of my pants, and stomped out the front door.

"Wayland . . . " my mother shouted after me as I charged out of the house.

I marched across town to the doctor's home, foaming with anger. I needed that goddamned note. I'd get it too. It was mine. If he actually had given it to the police as he said he would, I'd get it back from them.

They couldn't stop me. I'd been an idiot to trust the "doctor." A complete stranger. Quack. Con man. Why would he want my note? Who was he? Was my mother involved? Had he told her about the note? Were they working together against me? I wondered whether she'd used him to get information from me that she couldn't get for herself.

When I arrived, no vehicles were parked in the supposed doctor's driveway. I pounded on the front door to the house and put my hand on the butt of the revolver in my waistband. I pressed my face to the cool glass beside the door, seeing nothing but an empty foyer and hallway. I bashed on the door with my fist. The doctor did not answer.

I circled around the side of the house. There was a deck at the back of the house, a sliding glass door. I tried to peer inside, but a curtain blocked my view.

I knocked on the glass.

No response.

I crept around the house looking in the windows, but all the shades were shut. I came full circle to the front door.

I knocked again. When no one answered, I looked back at the empty cul-de-sac and took a breath, then smashed my elbow into a glass pane beside the door and reached inside. I unlocked the door and let myself in.

"Doctor?" I said. "Dr. Zantz?"

The house was quiet. I eased my way down the hall to a closed door on the left and pushed it open with my knuckles to avoid leaving fingerprints.

The door opened to a small kitchen with tall, clean white cupboards and a glossy white linoleum floor. Not just immaculate, the kitchen seemed antiseptic. I opened a cupboard door. Bare. Each cupboard. Bare. I opened the refrigerator. Dark and empty. A whiff of dead air that stank of rubber gaskets and sour milk wafted from it as if it were expelling a last, dying breath.

Mouse droppings littered the counter along the back of the white porcelain sink.

I returned to the hall. The room behind the next door proved bare too. Window shades drawn. Not a stick of furniture. Not a lamp. Not even a rug.

Every room was just as barren as the last. None had a copy machine. The place was vacant. No one lived here.

The office looked the same as when I had visited. Two chairs and an oval table. But now, the furniture and the spare decor seemed like props in a play with no production budget. I'd been suckered.

I charged out of the house, slamming the door behind me so hard, more glass fell from the broken window to shatter on the step.

I stormed across town to the police station, up its steps, to the front desk, where a woman with gray hair pinned in a bun sat behind a clear plastic barrier. I spoke to her through the perforations in the window. "I want to see a cop," I told her.

"Is this an emergency?" she asked me flatly, her blasé eyes barely registering my existence.

"It is to me." I squeezed my hands at my sides and felt the revolver pressing my spine beneath the tail of my T-shirt. I hoped it was hidden.

"Do you wish to see a detective, a patrol officer, or—"

"I don't know! What's the difference? Something of mine was stolen. Something *important*."

"There's no need to shout," the woman said, and pressed a button beside her.

"I'm not shouting," I said trying to calm my voice and keep from shaking.

"If you would just take a seat." She nodded at a row of identical plastic chairs pushed with their backs to the wall.

I sat erect on a hard chair to keep the revolver from gouging my spine.

A man strode from far down the hall, pushed through a pair of glass doors, and entered the reception area. He wasn't wearing a police uniform. No badge in sight. Khakis and a white button-down shirt that stretched over a bit of paunch kept in check by a black belt. I didn't see a gun on him. He stank of caustic aftershave.

As the man approached me, the woman behind the barrier nodded at him, and he nodded at her. Winked.

He turned his focus to me. Gray eyes squinting, he placed his hands on his thighs and stooped, as if about to address a child with a skinned knee.

I stood.

The man stepped back and fixed himself in the erect posture of a soldier, making his gut strain all the more against his shirt. "I'm told you're upset about a theft?"

"Did a doctor drop off a note here to a police officer?" I said, my voice cracking. "To a detective?"

"Why don't you tell me your name and address?"

"I'm not giving you my name; *I* didn't do anything."

"I'll need it so we can contact you if we find what you're missing."

"I want to see if it's here first. It's supposed to be. If it is, you can just give it to me. It's mine."

"I'm Detective Marsh," he said, as if that would convince me to tell him my name.

It didn't.

"What is the item?" he said. "Why would it be *here* if it was stolen?"

"It's a note. I gave it to my doctor. He was going to give it to someone here. He promised me he'd give me the original back after a copy was made. But now his office is closed, and he claims he's sick. And I don't know where the note is or where he is, and I need the note back. Now. I should have never given it to him in the first place. I knew he'd trick me."

"So your physician—"

"He's not my—never mind. His name is Dr. Zantz. He says a friend of his works here. A detective."

"We should be able to solve this quick enough," the detective said. "We only have one detective, and you're looking at him."

"Did he give you a note?"

"Not as of yet. But I'm sure if he said he would, he will. He's a trustworthy man. If he says he's under the weather, I'm certain he is."

"His entire house is empty. His office is a fake."

"I can't account for that. But Dr. Zantz has not been by yet. When he comes in with this note—"

"*If* he comes, tell him I don't want him to share it with you. Or make copies. I want it back!"

"Let's not yell," the detective said. "Please. If I could get your name and address so I can—"

"*He* knows who I am. *He* knows where to find me. And he better give me my note back. Soon." I stalked out and stopped at the corner, shaking, my mind skittering, wondering what to do next and who I could trust to help me.

I thought about what Mr. Kane had said as I fled his cabin: *"If you need help, I'll . . . I'll give it to you . . . "*

I hiked the damp woods toward the dismal cabin at the swamp's edge. As I made my way, I had the sense I was being followed. Several times, I peered back but saw no one among the trees.

Nearing the cabin, I heard a voice up ahead through the trees. It sounded like Mr. Kane's voice, only plaintive and distressed. I couldn't make out the words, but Mr. Kane was pleading with a man who now answered in a stern, commanding voice. My blood dried in my veins.

I peered out from behind a tree. Through a veil of dead vines, I saw Mr. Kane nodding dutifully, like a reprimanded child, to a man whose back was to me. The man looked down on Mr. Kane and spoke with a voice so resonant, it seemed to make the tree I hid behind vibrate.

The man gripped Mr. Kane's shoulder. Mr. Kane grimaced yet did nothing to defend himself. When the man released him, Mr. Kane went limp, like a robot whose power supply has shut down.

The man turned and disappeared down the path toward the road. I chased after him through the woods as fast as I could without making noise. As I neared the road, an engine growled, the sound swiftly diminishing. By the time I made it to the road, the vehicle was gone. The man had escaped without my seeing his face. But I knew who he was: the man in my father's barbershop all those years ago. The man who had been on my porch, talking to my mom, just a few nights earlier. The Tall Man.

I deliberated whether I could trust Mr. Kane, if I should approach him at all. I waited for my blood to stop knocking at my temples, and for enough time to pass so it would seem unlikely I had encountered the Tall Man on the path.

I knocked on the cabin door. From inside the back reaches of the cabin, as if he were standing as far from the door as possible, Mr. Kane moaned, "Leave me alone. You got your way. Just let me be."

"Mr. Kane," I cried out. "Mr. Kane, it's me, Wayland."

Silence persisted, as if the blue sky above might crack open to reveal another world behind it. The door opened, and Mr. Kane stood there, slack-jawed and unshaven, eyes focused on the woods behind me, in the direction the Tall Man had gone.

"What do you want?" he asked weakly, his voice raw, eyes trained on the woods.

"I came for the help you offered. But the Tall Man. He was here. You said you didn't know him."

I waited for Mr. Kane to invite me in.

"I *don't* know him," he said. "I don't know who he is. I don't know his name. I caught a glimpse of him once . . . many years ago."

"Then why was he here now?"

"He—knew—*knows*—your mother."

"How?"

"When you visited me the first time, you left me distraught. I was concerned for your well-being if you continued in your pursuit. And now I fear I've betrayed you. After your visit I stopped by your mother's work and told her you'd been here, that you were very upset, that I was concerned. Not just about you, but about all of it. Everything about that day. All of it was such a . . . mess, and—"

"Why were you even at my house that day? Why did you take me into the backyard?"

"Because . . . " He scratched at the inside of his wrist. "Your mom called me and asked me to come over. She didn't tell me what had happened, just . . . I could hear it in her voice. Something monstrous had taken place. So I went. It was . . . such a . . . She asked me to comfort and distract you while she took care of things. The horror of it all, the absurdity."

"You had doubts, didn't you? That it was him in the room."

"I never doubted it was him. Like you, what I doubted was that he would *want* to do it. Even if he were depressed or wounded, under financial duress. And never with you in the room. Never. He adored you. And your sister. That's why . . . " He straightened, as if awakening and just now realizing where he was, what he was saying.

"Why what?"

"That's why I became so troubled about it all. We *were* friends. You were right."

I slapped at voracious mosquitoes biting my neck. They were lighting on Mr. Kane's forehead, too, but he paid them no mind, as if his flesh were numb.

"Your father would never have done that to you unless there were extreme circumstances," he said. "Some sort of . . . outside influence. My gut kept asking, *why* would he do it? I obsessed about it. I lost sleep. I lost weight. I lost my wife. I knew. If your father had done what he did, he'd been pushed to it. Forced. Whoever or whatever he was afraid of, he felt that doing that was the only and last option, that it would be better for you and your sister. But I could think of no other reason until—"

"Until you realized it wasn't him at all," I said. "Until that was the only thing that made sense."

"No. That's not it."

"Why was he here—the Tall Man? Who is he? How does he know my mom? What are they hiding?"

Mr. Kane scraped at a rash high on his cheek, just under his wet eye. I wondered why a rash would bother him, but not the mosquitoes. "He came here to tell me to . . . stop."

"Stop what?"

He gave a sad smile. "Bothering your mother. In the months after what happened with your father, I often met with her, and I'd inevitably end up telling her how I literally could not believe your father did what he did. I started to push: '*Why* did he do it?' There had to be a *why*. One day I asked her if there was something she'd done, perhaps. It was not my place to ask. And I didn't mean that I thought she'd done something intentionally. I certainly didn't mean to blame or hurt her. I . . . liked your mother. It was just that in the weeks before, I'd sensed a . . . space that hadn't existed before. The warmth they shared had cooled. That's why my wife stopped coming for dinner at your house. She said your parents seemed as if they were not even there in the room. Your mom got furious with me when I asked if she'd done something. She insisted *she'd* done nothing to hurt him. She would have done anything to keep him alive and safe. She had loved him more than ever. More than anything or anyone else. Still, I pressed. I told her I found that odd, that I'd sensed a strangeness between them. She slapped me and told me never to return."

Mr. Kane's fingernail dug at the rash on his cheek until the pink, dry skin turned into an aggravated red sore. "Then, you came here asking questions and making claims. So I went and saw your mother again. I hadn't seen her in years. She looked . . . I voiced my concern for you, for your state of mind."

"You shouldn't have done that."

"Probably not. I cared about her. And your dad. Your family. I look at you and worry."

"She sent me to a doctor because of you," I said. "Some quack who . . . " I didn't want to get into how Dr. Zantz was a fraud and stole the note. I didn't want to tell anyone else about the note. "The Tall Man. How does he know her?"

"I don't know. All I know is, he showed up and told me to stop. And I didn't appreciate his threatening tone."

"My mom wouldn't threaten you."

"Wayland. Listen to me. Don't wreck your future trying to understand the past. Knowing won't change what happened. People always want the truth. I did once and now, I wonder why. The truth is often ugly and mean. That's why we lie to one another, after all, isn't it? Whoever this man is who visited me today, he's serious. Dangerous. He's helping to hide something you don't want to know."

"You said you glimpsed him once, years ago. The Tall Man. Where did you see him?"

"At your house that day. I glimpsed him speaking to your mother at the curb in front of your house, just before the ambulance arrived." Mr. Kane put a hand on my shoulder. "Stop searching in the past. It's gone. Enjoy your childhood. There is so little of it left for you, you have no idea."

UNCLE

As I approached my house, I spotted my mother in our driveway, getting into the Pontiac to head to her lunch shift after a break. I sprinted and threw myself against the driver's window, startling her.

"Roll down the window!" I shouted, motioning for her to crank it down.

My mother looked alarmed as she cranked down the window.

"Who is he?" I shouted. "This 'doctor'? Where does he *actually* live? Who is this Tall Man? Who are they? What are you up to?"

Her alarm morphed to horror, terror. "I don't know what you're talking about. Why aren't you in school?"

"The house. The office. It's empty. It's a shell, a front. Sick. He's not sick. He's *gone*. And he has my property. And I have to get it back. And I was at Mr. Kane's and—"

"Don't ever visit him again, you understand me?" My mother looked stricken. "He's trouble. He . . . interferes where he shouldn't. Has strange ideas."

"Tell me what's going on," I demanded. "You tell me, or I swear." I thrust a finger at her so close, her eyelash tickled my fingertip as my spittle flecked her pale forehead. My mother shrank from me, her eyes bright with panic.

"I need to get back to work. Let me go. I need to *go*."

I leaned toward her. The image of my fierce grimace in the car's side-view mirror frightened me. I looked deranged. "What are you two up to!" I roared. "You and the Tall—"

A hand grabbed my shoulder and wheeled me around to face Mr. Dietrich, our neighbor.

"What's going on here?" he asked. "I heard your mother yelling, and . . . " He glanced behind me at my mother in the car. "Are you okay, El?"

My mother cringed at Mr. Dietrich using her nickname in such a familiar way. She had righted herself and brushed her hair back from her face and smiled a thin-lipped smile, looking as if she was trying to keep from being sick.

"I'm fine," she said.

Mr. Dietrich considered me. His beefy hand clenched my shoulder. He was massive, with the build of a guy who caught cannonballs with his abs when he was not busy crushing steel cans against his forehead. Bald, oiled scalp gleaming.

"You sure?" he said, peering in at my mom.

My mom nodded.

Mr. Dietrich torqued my shoulder, cranking me around to glare at me. "You shouldn't disrespect your mother." I could see the blackheads pushing up from the flaky pink skin at the side of his pulpy nose. "Apologize," he demanded, deepening his voice to impart authority.

He sickened me. He wasn't interested in my mom's well-being. He was grandstanding, leveraging our altercation as a way to insinuate himself into our lives, to come on to my mom in some pathetic attempt at chivalry. He had probably dreamed of riding to her rescue for the past decade while he watered his lawn in his Bermuda shorts and Hawaiian shirts for longer than necessary, pretending he wasn't ogling my mom and sister from behind his dime-store aviator sunglasses. "Go ahead, apologize."

"*I* was the one yelling at him," my mother broke in. "I get stressed and get on him too much."

I twisted my shoulder free of Mr. Dietrich's clutch.

"You sure?" Mr. Dietrich said, not out of concern for my mother, but because he sensed he was losing his reason for being in our driveway, for being near my mother. His voice couldn't conceal his disappointment that his window had closed.

"I'm sure," my mother replied. "Now, I have to get to work."

She backed the car down the driveway. Mr. Dietrich backpedaled so she wouldn't run over his foot.

My mother eyed me through the windshield just as she accelerated down the street. It was a look of fear, not just of what I'd done, but of something else, something I did not understand—not yet.

I sat on the front steps, furious and confused. Alone. Never more alone.

Tease me too long, I'll get bored.

I had avoided Juliette for days. I wondered how bored she was of me by now. Whether she would ever speak to me again. I shouldn't have cared, but I did.

I walked to school, arriving five minutes early for biology class.

When Juliette showed, gossiping with two girlfriends, she noticed me and offered a strained smile just as she looked away. She joined her friends at the back of the room and opened her notebook, unzipped a small plastic polka-dot purse, and took a pencil out from it. She did not look my way again for the rest of class.

I faced the chalkboard as Mr. Bouchard ventured to the front of the room and droned on about evolution and how we are all made up of the same matter, the same atoms, the same star dust, and had all morphed from the single-cell organisms known as prokaryotes.

At the bell I waited until the scuff of chairs and the slapping-shut of notebooks subsided, and the voices and footfalls faded away, before I closed my notebook and got up to depart.

Juliette startled me as I turned to leave. She had waited. She slung her backpack over one shoulder. "Where you been? Are you all right? You look really . . . " She cringed. "What's happened?"

"I've been laying low. Thinking."

"You were supposed to tell me your creepy plan and we were going to *execute* it. Days ago."

"Something happened." I studied her face for a sign of guilt, a recognition that I was, in part, talking about her and Clay. That her face betrayed no such guilt upset me all the more. "And my mom had me *see* someone, and he stole the note."

"Stole it? Who stole it?"

"Some doctor. Except he isn't a doctor. He's . . . I don't know what he is, but he said he was going to make a copy and give the original to the cops and . . . Forget it. He stole the note and now he's gone. *It's* gone. I think the appointment was all a ruse to get it. Set up by my mom. To get information, get what I knew out of me. His house, his so-called *office,* is totally empty."

Students shuffled into the classroom.

"But why ignore *me*? What'd I do?" Juliette said. "You avoided going to our classes, and I haven't even seen you in the halls. I know you were upset when we went to the mansion, and even Clay was saying—"

"*Clay?*" My guts curdled. "What's the mighty Clay saying about me?"

"Why are you so mad?"

"Am I?"

"Clay and I crossed paths. He asked if I'd seen you. He was worried about you."

"Imagine that."

"I'm worried too. You don't look like yourself. You look . . . "

"If you're both so worried, why didn't either of you stop by my house or call me the last few days? Why do I have to always be the one to stop by or call? To get punched, stood up, humiliated. Why should I—"

"I *did* call," she said. "Like, a million times. A few times no one picked up your phone. And the other times, the line was always busy. Do you leave the phone off the hook, or what? You need to get an answering machine."

She had called me? Multiple times? "My mom can't afford an answering machine," I said. "My sister's the only one who uses the phone, anyway. No one calls my mom or me."

"*I* called you. To see if we were still on for your plan. And to see if you were okay. Like I said, Clay and I were—"

Students gawked as they pushed past us to settle into chairs.

We walked out into the hallway, into the flow of straggling kids late for class.

I dreaded seeing Clay saunter down the hallway. "What else did Clay say?" I said.

Juliette adjusted her backpack, glanced down the hallway. "Nothing."

The bell for the next class rang.

"I've gotta get to trig," Juliette said. "You want to meet after school and execute your plan together, or not?"

"We can't do it in the daytime. It has to be at night, in the dark, after everyone is asleep."

"Mysterious. Where do we meet?"

"The cemetery gates."

"The cemetery," she said, eyes glinting.

"If you're going to blow me off—"

"I won't. I swear. What time?"

"Midnight."

"I'll wear black."

I went into the boys' bathroom to splash cold water on my face. The image looking back at me in the mirror was wretched. I hardly recognized myself, my hair greasy and flat, face gray as spoiled meat, my bleary eyes bloodshot and unfocused. I filled the sink up with cold water and pushed my face down into it to cool off.

The bathroom door creaked open behind me.

A hand smacked me on my back. Hard.

I choked and spit up water, wheeled around. "What the hell!" I huffed. "Stop hitting me. You promised—"

"That didn't count," Clay said. "That was a pat on the back." He leaned against the wall, arms crossed over his chest, and jutted his chin at me. "Did you catch the plague, or what? You look like death. Seriously. I don't know how Juliette still digs you. I saw you two in the hall earlier and—"

"What do you know about it?" I spat. I tried to get past him to leave, but he stepped in front of me, blocking me. He poked a finger against my chest.

"I know she digs you to even talk to you in public in the state you're in. You're a fucking mess. Where you been hiding, a sewer pipe?"

"I got other stuff to do than to hang out with you."

"No, you don't, unless it's hanging with her. And I *know* you haven't been doing that. You can't be wasting time. You have to move in or she's going to think you're a fruitcake."

"Not everyone is you. Not everyone *moves in.*"

"I'm telling you—"

"Well, *don't.* Don't fucking tell me. And don't lump her in with your conquests. Leave me alone. And leave *her* alone."

"All I'm saying is, if you don't do something, she's going to think you don't dig her. You dig her, right?"

"It's more than that."

"Whatever you call it, *act* on it. If she flips the switch to friends mode, you're DOA. That switch flips one way. And locks. You might as well be her brother after that. She's not hanging with you for your Nancy Drew bullshit. Kiss her before she flips that switch, or another guy catches her eye. Because another will. And it'll happen fast." Clay snapped his fingers. "Poof, she'll be gone. I'll give you tips. Write 'em down, steps to take before some other dude does. Before *I* do."

"Don't *say* that shit," I snarled.

He draped his arm around my shoulder, mocking me. "It's easy. First, you want to—"

I yanked away, swung at him, and missed.

He hauled back his fist as if to punch me. Instead, he roughed up my hair as if I were a lost puppy. I wished he had hit me instead.

That night as I opened the garage door to get the backpack with the foxhole shovel and crowbar in it, a buzz saw of speed-metal music assailed my ears.

Dipshit's truck rocketed up the street toward my house, swung into the driveway, and nearly hit me. It jerked to a stop before me, rocking on its springs as it idled. Greasy black smoke oozed from dual upright chrome exhaust pipes jutting up behind the cab.

The music stopped. A voice from inside the truck shouted, "Stop it! What the hell is wrong with you!"

It was Lydia, her voice carrying out her open window.

The truck's passenger door flew open, but Dipshit's hairy arm, polluted with ugly blue tattoos, shot out and grabbed the handle and slammed the door shut.

I charged toward my sister's side of the truck. "Let her out!" I yelled.

Lydia spun her head to look at me out her open window, startled to see me. Wet eyeliner and mascara streaked her cheeks, and her breath reeked of wine coolers.

"Let her out," I shouted at Dipshit.

"Piss off," he grunted.

I grabbed the truck's door handle as Dipshit smacked his fist down on the lock and started to crank up the window.

I shoved an arm inside the cab to try to unlock the door. Dipshit hauled on the window crank. "Don't!" Lydia shouted.

The window pinned my wrist to the door frame, sank into my flesh to gnaw at the bone beneath. I cried out, pounded the glass, wanting to shatter it, wanting to shatter Dipshit's face.

"Stop," Lydia shouted. "Please! Stop."

A horizontal crack appeared near the bottom of the window.

"Say 'uncle.'" Dipshit laughed. "Say it, punk."

I would die first.

The window cut deeper. Blood dripped from my wrist.

"Say it, you pansy!" Dipshit roared, laughing.

"Uncle," I croaked.

"I can't *hear* you," Dipshit taunted. Laughing.

"*Uncle*. Uncle, uncle, uncle, uncle."

Dipshit rolled the window down a crack. When I tried to free my hand, he cranked it up again, laughing louder as I howled in pain. He rolled the window back down, and I jerked my throbbing hand away, blood surging up my arm. My fingers hummed with pain.

The window rolled up tight again, and Dipshit gave me the finger from inside the truck.

I smashed my uninjured hand against the hairline crack in the window. I didn't care if I broke my hand. I needed to break the window to get at the lock and free Lydia. Her face was fiery with anger and shame. As Dipshit trapped her against the door, slobbering all over her neck, I pounded on the window. "*Stop!*" Lydia shouted.

I punched the window, imagining it was Dipshit's face. The glass splintered. Dipshit lifted his face from Lydia's neck, like a vampire coming up for breath after sucking blood. His eyes gleamed with lurid gratification.

As Dipshit lowered to my sister's neck again, I reached in my back waistband and pulled out the revolver, smacking its barrel against the window. The window shattered. Pieces of glass rained on Dipshit and Lydia. I hid the revolver behind my back. Dipshit pushed off of Lydia.

"My truck! Fucker!" he roared. "You fucker!"

"Fuck you," I hollered. I wanted to do something, for once. Not to be a pussy. To act. The revolver was as cold as ice and as real as death in my hand. "You fucking pedophile loser."

Dipshit sprang from his side of the truck and charged toward me.

I planned to aim the revolver square at his fat gut and make him kneel and grovel for his life, but Dipshit was quick, and in the darkness, he never saw the gun, never slowed. He was on me fast. He shoved me hard, and I fell backward on my ass. The revolver jarred loose, pinned beneath me.

Dipshit straddled my chest, his crotch an inch from my mouth as he slapped my face. Hard. One cheek, then the other. Harder. Over and over again, harder each time as he brayed like a donkey. My face stung, and my eyes burned with hot tears.

He slapped my face again. Softly this time. An insult. A baby slap for a baby.

I tried to worm my hand behind my back to get at the revolver, but Dipshit's weight on my chest and forearms made it impossible.

"Lydia!" I shouted. "Get in the house while you can."

Dipshit cried with laughter. "Who do you think you are? Her *father*?"

"When a girl tells you to stop, you *stop!*" I shrieked.

"You don't *get* it," Dipshit whispered, squeezing my face in his hand. He leaned all his weight onto my chest, crushing the breath out of me, keeping my arms pinned tight beneath his knees. His thin lips peeled back like those of a rabid mutt.

I struggled to free myself. He bellowed with laughter.

"*Stop!*" Lydia pleaded. She squatted near my head. "You're embarrassing yourself." She wasn't speaking to Dipshit. She was speaking to me.

"Let's go," she said to Dipshit.

"You're going?" I said. "With *him?*"

"Duh," Lydia said.

"Idiot little brother," Dipshit said.

"I'm her big brother," I said. I looked at Lydia. "You were telling him to stop when you pulled in."

"And now I'm telling *you* to stop. Stop whining; stop embarrassing yourself. Cut. The. Crap."

"But . . . " I tried to squirm free.

"Couples fight," Lydia said. "Then make up. If you ever get a girlfriend, you'll see. Even Mom and Dad fought."

"Mom and Dad *never* fought!" I shouted.

"What planet are you from? What galaxy?" Lydia leaned over me to look me in the face, genuinely bewildered. "Did you live in a completely different house with a different family? You make up your own reality."

"Not true!" I screamed.

I tried to knee Dipshit, but he just smiled. "Don't make me *really* hurt you," he said.

Lydia slapped the back of his head. "Let's *go.*"

Dipshit swatted at my sister as he slid forward on my chest. He clutched my jaw in his hand and forced me to stare up at his face. He leaned forward and let a long string of drool stretch from his mouth.

I fought to turn my face away, but he had me pinned in place.

He forced my jaw open and his spit dripped into my mouth. I bucked and grimaced. I spat it back up at him only to have it splatter back down on my face.

Lydia kicked his ribs. "Let's *go*."

"Take it easy." Dipshit finally got up. As Lydia huffed back into the truck, her back to us, Dipshit smiled at me and drove his steel-toed boot square into my crotch.

My breath left my lungs in a wheeze, and my guts shriveled as I groaned and an ancient, deadening pain flooded my body. Puke rose in my throat.

Dipshit swaggered to the truck. I reached for the revolver but withered with pain and curled up on my side. The truck's tires squealed as it backed up then shot out of sight.

I remained curled on the ground as the world swam around me. The pain eventually ebbed to a nauseating pulse, and I staggered to my hands and knees, taking slow, deep, deliberate breaths.

I managed to stand, my body weak and watery, my mind afire with images of revenge.

The night air chilled me as I stared into the dark woods behind my house. I didn't know where to go or what to do before I went to meet Juliette in the cemetery. I limped into the house and put on a black hooded sweatshirt. From the garage, I took the backpack with the foxhole shovel and crowbar.

I tramped along the sidewalk until I found myself on the street outside Clay's house. The windows were dark. Clay was likely hiding out in his room with his black light on, staring at his lava lamp while he smoked a joint. As I traipsed past the end of the driveway, I caught a silvery glimpse of chrome beneath the tree in front of the porch.

I sneaked up the edge of the driveway to get a closer look. A ten-speed Schwinn Varsity. Sky blue. A yellow smiley-face sticker on the handlebar post grinned at me in the dark.

A light rain began to fall. I pulled up the hood of my sweatshirt and stole along the side of the house. The purple glow of a black light bled from Clay's bedroom window. The window was cracked open, and the pungent odor of marijuana smoke escaped from it. A familiar laugh floated to me. I stepped on the bucket and pressed my face to the glass.

Juliette leaned with her shoulder against the doorjamb to Clay's room, thumbs hooked in the belt loops of cutoff jeans whose white tasseled fringes glowed in the black light. Her Sprite T-shirt rode up just enough to reveal a hint of smooth, pale belly. So much for her wearing black. Her hair was tousled, as if mussed by crawling fingers.

She gave a nervous laugh and glanced at a spot beneath the window.

I looked down. Clay lounged in a beanbag chair, his chest bare, white boxers glowing, one hand behind his head as the other hand held a joint to his lips.

He shoved himself up from his beanbag chair, picked up a piece of paper from the floor, and strode over to stand beside Juliette. She was tiny beside him. His blond fuzz of chest hair, which narrowed to a strip as it traveled down his muscled abdomen and disappeared into his boxers, was purple in the black light. He folded the piece of paper and tucked it into the back pocket of Juliette's shorts, then planted a palm against the jamb, just above her head, and leaned in over her, looking down at her.

I took the revolver in my hand and squeezed its grip so hard, I thought my bones might crack. Clay took Juliette's hand in his and touched her fingers to his face. Juliette whispered something I couldn't hear.

"Like this?" Clay said and took her other wrist and placed her palm on his bare chest.

I jumped off the bucket and ran.

FACE TO FACE

I arrived at the cemetery with my mind wild with foul thoughts and images. I shoved open the iron entrance gate, its hinges screeching. Crouching in the dark beneath an oak tree, I pounded my fists against my temples, unable to rid my head of what I'd seen. I never wanted to set eyes on Juliette or Clay again, yet here I was, my irrational heart still hoping Juliette would show, my dignity be damned.

The overcast night sky was as black as the grave I planned to excavate. I stuffed my hands in the pockets of my sweatshirt. The foxhole shovel and crowbar clanked in the backpack, and the revolver pressed against my spine.

Juliette was not going to show. I would perform the task alone while my mind tortured me with scenarios of the two of them. Rain pattered the dead grass as I prepared to set out alone into the back reaches of the cemetery.

The sound of the gate's hinges creaking and a shoe crunching on the cemetery's crushed-stone road stopped me.

I peered out from under a tree but could not see anyone or anything in the blackness, even as the sound of crunching gravel grew louder.

"Hello," a voice whispered.

Juliette.

I whistled from where I stood, just feet from her.

The rain started to fall harder.

"Wayland?" Juliette called out quietly.

I stepped out from the tree. I pulled the flashlight from the backpack and shone it at Juliette for an instant, then clicked it off.

Juliette stepped toward me in the dark.

I could barely make out her dark silhouette, but her briny, earthy sweat scent quickened my pulse. I should have told her to leave, told her I knew where she'd been, and to go back.

"What are we doing?" she whispered. She wore a black raincoat, unzipped, over shorts and T-shirt.

"Getting proof," I said. It seemed impossible that she could still not know what we were up to, there in a graveyard. "We're going to dig it up. My father's *supposed* grave."

"You're not serious." She zipped up her coat and blinked the rain from her eyes.

"All you need to do is hold a flashlight. We have six hours until dawn."

"This has to be illegal," she said.

"So was trespassing on the estate and in the mansion. Except this is my father's plot. My mom bought it. We own it. Why can't I dig it up?"

"There must be some law against it."

"If you don't have the stomach for it, just go back to—"

"Gimme the flashlight."

I handed it to her and said, "If we have to split up, get seen, or whatever, meet at the marble bench in the lilac bushes behind the library."

I took her to the back reaches of the cemetery, to my father's supposed plot.

In the pale halo of the flashlight's beam, I drove the foxhole shovel's sharp edge into the earth and began to cut a rectangular perimeter in the ground. Within the rectangle, I cut a grid of one-foot-square slabs of sod.

The rain fell steadily as I set each square of turf in a pattern mirroring the grave, to make it easy to put them back in place, just where they had been. I was methodical. I would leave no trace of my presence. Even though no one ever visited that backwater reach of the cemetery, I would make certain that when I was done, the earth there would look as smooth and unmarred as a golf course fairway.

With the earth's skin now peeled back, I dug into its flesh.

Beneath the grass, the springtime earth was a viscous muck. After an hour of toil, my effort seemed Sisyphean—for each shovelful of mud I slopped out of the hole, more mud collapsed back into it. Still, I kept at it and found myself submerged to the shin in a sludge that sucked at my sneakers as if it were wet concrete.

I redoubled my efforts. I had to be done before dawn's light exposed me. All the while Juliette stood as fixed in place as the headstones around her, the flashlight steady in her hand.

The rain fell harder and turned colder, saturating my sweatshirt, sneakers, and jeans. My flesh grew cold and rubbery as the rain pounded down, blurring my vision.

I dug until my bones ached and my fingers buzzed with fatigue. Sweat poured from me and cooled in the night air to mix with the cold rain, until I was left feeling sheathed in ice water.

Caked in mud, my breathing sharp and painful, I pulled my sweatshirt hood up tighter around me. One spadeful of muck at a time, slaving in a numbed trance, I edged closer to my destiny. Back knotted, I found myself standing thigh-deep in the grave. I checked my wristwatch: 3:00 a.m. The rain was a downpour now. With each shovel of mud, the walls threatened to collapse. Above me, Juliette coughed and mumbled to herself. I could hear her teeth chattering. "You must be close," she said once, her voice scarcely audible above the rain's onslaught.

By 5:24 a.m. I had dug a pit up to my neck. Soon, dawn's filthy gray light would render us visible.

Exhaustion racked my bones as I drove the shovel's blade into the earth.

I struck a hard object. I fell back in the sludge.

I heard Juliette say, "You *did* it."

I clawed at the last inches of earth with my hands, frenzied, a wild dog after carrion.

"Crowbar!" I shouted. "Crowbar!"

Juliette said something I could not make out over the din of rain.

I reached up and grabbed the crowbar at her feet and struck it against the coffin lid.

Juliette spoke again, sharper this time. "Someone's coming!"

I was too close now to be concerned with getting caught by a cemetery worker. Once I had the lid open and proved what needed proving, I didn't care what happened to me. I slid the bar's sharp edge along the seam at the head section of the coffin lid, just as Mr. Kane had once slid his fingertips along it at my father's memorial. I jammed the edge in and knelt on the bar with all my weight.

With a violent crack of splintering wood, the bar jumped free and smacked my forehead. Bright silver sparks erupted in my vision.

"Hurry!" Juliette urged, her voice jagged with panic. "*Please.*"

I licked at blood leaking down my face as I stabbed the bar into the casket's edge. Chunks of wet earth calved from the wall onto the coffin. I kicked the clods away, grabbed the coffin's handles, and yanked. The lid felt welded shut.

"We need to *go*," Juliette said.

I drove the bar's beveled edge into the seam again and again until it broke through the wood. I pried, and the lid gave a monstrous *crack*. I stumbled back as mud splashed in my eyes to mix with my blood. I couldn't get out. I needed to *see*. I pried at the lid. It cracked open an inch. I leaned all my weight down on the bar.

"Get out!" Juliette hissed. "*Now!*"

I heaved on the crowbar. The coffin lid cracked open wider. I tried to see in through the few inches the lid was ajar. I shrank away from what I saw.

The flashlight beam went dark. Juliette screamed.

I scrambled up out of the hole, crowbar in hand.

Juliette was on her belly in the mud and blinding rain, writhing to free herself from the hooded attacker who had knocked her down and lay sprawled on the ground behind her, grasping her ankles.

I brought the crowbar down and it glanced off the top of his skull. He grunted, and his grip slackened enough for Juliette to slip from his grasp.

"Run!" I screamed.

Juliette sprinted across the graveyard.

The attacker clawed at the back of his head, moaning as he rose and stumbled toward me like Frankenstein's creature, arms reaching out, face a blur in the darkness of his hood and the biblical rain.

As he lurched toward me, I stepped aside and he pitched into the grave, striking the coffin with a sick, wet thud.

I picked up the flashlight, flicked it on, and peered over the grave's edge.

The hood had fallen back, and I saw now who it was at the bottom of the grave. Clay. Groaning, he managed to get to his knees. He looked up at me, eyes wide yet ominously blank as blood poured down his face. He tried to lift an arm up for me to pull him out. Rage cooked in my veins, yet I was prepared to help him, alarmed as I was by the blood.

"I wanted . . . " He took a ragged breath. "You deserved to hear it . . . face to face. I confess I—"

I didn't want to hear it. If I never heard it, it would never be true. I struck his forehead with the crowbar. I felt the skull crack and recoiled at the spout of blood. Clay grunted and slumped back against the dirt wall of the grave. He blinked up at me and I brought the crowbar down on his face then fell backward. I remained there for some time, the rain pelting me.

Finally, I crawled to the edged peered over into the grave. Clay lay at the bottom. Blood pooled from his cracked skull and broken face onto the coffin's lid. He was still. And quiet.

I vomited into the grave.

I wanted to get back down there and open the coffin lid wider, to give myself greater certainty of what I thought I'd seen. But I could not move Clay's body without being sopped with his blood.

I went back to work with the shovel. My mind was in a state of agitation, but my body was calm and assured in its efforts, the two parts of me functioning independently of each other. In this way, I got the job done in an efficient manner.

Dawn's grimy gray light was nearly upon me. I replaced the sod and tamped it down with the back of the shovel as well as I could. The downpour, I hoped, would help conceal any disruption I'd made, by muddying the earth.

I shoved the crowbar and shovel into the backpack and ran.

As I approached the lilac bushes behind the library, a sob rose. I pulled the branches back to find Juliette trembling on the marble bench, her knees wrapped in her arms, her chin resting upon them. I crawled in to join her, and the branches fell back in place, concealing us. The rain had slackened to nothing more than a mist, though water dripped all around us.

"What did you *do* to him?" Her voice was fraught. Panic reared up in me. Did she know it was Clay?

"Nothing," I said.

"You *hit* him. Hard."

"Only to free you. He's . . . gone now. He took off. Why do you care about someone who attacked you, anyway?"

"He didn't attack me. He slipped in the mud and knocked me down." She shivered and her voice quavered as if she'd just been plucked from an icy river. "He scared me. But *you* scared me even more. The look on your face. You hit him so hard. It sounded—"

"I hit his shoulder blade," I said. "You heard the crowbar hit bone. He deserved it."

"Who was he?"

She didn't know that it was Clay. I nearly cried with relief.

"I don't know." I forced a smile, but my face felt plastic and numb. Juliette rested a palm on my knee and let out a long, hitching sob followed by a deep sigh.

"What took you so long?"

"I had to fill in the hole. And replace the sod so it looked normal."

"Right." She shuddered, then leaned against me, pressed her cheek to my shoulder. Her lips were close to mine. I breathed her warm breath into my cold lungs. I tried not to think of Clay—not of what had happened at the grave, but of he with Juliette, his hands on her cheek, saying, "*Like this.*"

"What did you see?" she said.

"See?"

"In the coffin."

"Nothing."

She squeezed my knee. "I'm sorry. After all that, you didn't get to see what was inside."

She misunderstood. I had meant I'd seen nothing in the coffin. From what I'd glimpsed, the coffin had been empty, or appeared to be empty, in the moment. Yet now I wasn't so certain. I wondered whether the dark void I'd seen through a crack of only a few inches had been the blackness of the night and my father's black suit. Had I mistaken it for emptiness? Either way, I let Juliette believe I had not had a chance to see into the coffin. If she believed that it was empty, she would have expected me to report it to the police, to have them dig it up and see for themselves. And, of course, I could not have that.

A noise nearby alarmed me.

"Get down." I slung my arm around Juliette, covering her body with my own.

She was so small, even compared to the bony likes of me.

I heard the jingle of a dog collar.

"Easy, boy," a soft voice said.

A woman in a rain coat was trying to get her shaggy dog to pee. The dog yanked the woman along, and they vanished into the thickening fog.

"Let me up," Juliette said.

I took my arm off her. Her cheek brushed mine. Her face and hair were wet and muddied. She smelled of wet earth.

"What if he can identify us? The person from the cemetery," she said.

"He can't."

"How do we *know*?"

I almost confessed. If anyone would understand, I thought in one moment of insanity, it was her. I'd believed she was being attacked and had defended her. I hadn't known it was Clay when I hit him—the first time.

"Because if it was too dark and rainy for me to see his face, he couldn't see ours, either," I said. "Not to identify us. It happened too fast. And anyway, everyone thinks we're asleep. No one will ever know we've been out here . . . "

"Together." She squeezed my hand and looked at me, our faces close. Even then, the two of us hidden in the lilacs and bound by our dark secret, I feared the turn of her cheek if I tried to kiss her. She smiled and touched her fingers to my face, placed her palm to my chest, exactly as she had touched Clay in his bedroom.

I tensed with anger. Juliette took her hands away and pulled her raincoat hood up. "We should go," she said. "Make a break for our houses before anyone knows we're gone. We've got just a few minutes before it's broad daylight."

"I . . . " I began to say, but no other words came.

"On three," she said. "*One . . . two . . . three.*"

She pushed through the lilac bushes and was gone.

I stumbled along the railroad tracks toward home and fell to my knees. When I tried to stand, I couldn't. Terror seized me. What I had done in the cemetery could not be undone, yet my terror was not borne of this fact; it was borne of the possibility of being caught. I realized I had no idea how well or poorly I'd filled in the grave and replaced the sod. I had acted in haste, in the dark, in the cascading rain. I worried that I had left the grave in a disturbed condition that might raise the suspicions of the rare visitor or worker who happened by. It would call attention to me eventually. My inquiries, my visit to the police station. My being the son. My deepest terror was that Juliette would find out what I'd done and think ill of me. I could not bear that.

I considered going back to check my work, but I couldn't risk it in the daylight.

I sat there for along time, afraid and unable to move.

Finally, fear relaxed its grip enough for me to find my feet again.

LONELY IS THE HOUSE ON THE HILL

My mother's car was not in the driveway. She had already left for the busy Friday breakfast shift. I sneaked into the house and clicked the door shut behind me.

Inside, I jumped back, startled to see Lydia jerk upright from the stool where she sat at the kitchen counter. She appeared to have been sleeping with her head on the countertop. She stared at me. I was caked in mud. I expected her to crack wise about me looking as if I had fallen into an outhouse.

No remark came.

She didn't even seem to notice that I was walking in the house so early, in a frantic, muddied state.

She turned away, trying to hide her face, her eyes.

"What's wrong?" I asked, though I knew. Dipshit.

"It's too boring to bother," she sulked, then continued anyway. "He was supposed to pick me up for school, so I don't have to ride the bus like a loser, but he's a no-show." Her voice was drained of its verve. She shuffled to the sink and slurped water from the faucet. All the drinking glasses were strewn around the kitchen, filmed with dried milk and juice. "If he doesn't show, I'm going back to bed. He's probably pissed I didn't stay at his place. I hate his bed. His stupid dogs. The damned bed is crawling with fleas."

My hands twitched, and I couldn't focus my vision. I could feel each squeeze of my heart. I wanted to escape to my bedroom to collect myself, try to think what I was going to do. I couldn't just go to school after what I'd done, could I? "I don't know why you bother with him," I said, straining to keep my voice normal. "He's old."

"*Boys* bore me."

"You'd rather be used than bored?"

"Where do you get this crap? If anyone uses anyone, it's *me* using *him*. For his wheels and his cash. He's not what's bothering me, anyway. It's my head. My thoughts. I hate the thoughts I have when I'm bored. I can't stand it." She pressed her thumbs against her temples. "My brain won't shut up when it's not occupied with *him*. His loud crap music and stupid truck, his obnoxious barking-seal laugh, his big mouth, his moron friends, the way he always needs to be *doing* something or *doing* me, doing something loud. He's so *loud.* He drowns out the crap in my head with all his noise. That's the real reason I bother with him, at all. The *only* reason. Without his noise, I feel like I could—"

"Drowns out what crap?" I asked.

"Are you *serious? This.* Us. This crap house. Poor, pathetic Molly. She should be put down or given to someone who cares."

"I care."

"Me too. But she needs someone who can care *for* her. She reeks. And then there's Mom. Slaving. I don't make it easy for her. I'm not stupid. I'm not heartless. I know I'm lousy. I'm a lousy daughter and a lousy sister and just . . . a lousy person."

"That's so not true," I said. "Don't say that; that's not true at all, you're—"

"I just can't seem to . . . help it. And then there's you. Poor you." She pressed her palms flat to her ears as if to block out a noise only she could hear.

"Me?" I said.

"You lock yourself in your room more than I do. But you lock yourself in *alone.* At least I have company. You've got zero friends."

"I've got Clay and . . . " I suddenly felt sure I was going to puke as the reality of what I'd done slammed through me. At the same time, it didn't seem real. I wondered, if I returned to the cemetery, whether I'd find the grave disturbed. I wondered if I'd ever been there at all.

"Clay? *Clay?*" Lydia scoffed. "He's no friend. He treats you worse than Loudmouth would ever treat me."

"Then why were you hollering for Dipshit to let go of you in the truck?"

"That was nothing. He's always pushing buttons. It's how he is. With everybody."

"Like how he kicked me in the balls."

"What? Since when did he *kick* you?"

"When I was on the ground and you were getting back in his stupid truck. He drove a boot square into my nuts. I was laying there for a half hour."

"Even he wouldn't stoop that low. You shouldn't make stuff up, even if . . ."

I yanked my jeans down to show her my naked inner thigh. Dipshit had kicked me so hard his boot print was visible as a purple bruise on my flesh.

Lydia stared at the bruise, aghast. "He did that?"

"He's a loser," I said.

"I know. And I *know* what everyone calls me for hanging out with him. At least I admit reality. *You* live in some other reality. Not that I blame you. What you saw. It *so* fucked you up."

"I'm not fucked up."

"Jesus. Every year, you concoct a new reason why it couldn't possibly have been Dad. You live in a dream world where he's alive or was forced to do it or . . . It's always some new theory, with no proof. It's so . . . *sad*."

"I don't make stuff up every year."

"Often enough."

"And I didn't make this up. I *have* proof."

"Mom's out of her mind with how far you're taking it." Lydia looked at me, really looked. "Why do you look like you just crawled out of gutter?"

"It's nothing."

"You lie for crap. I don't care what you were doing or about any of this. I'm in a mood because Loudmouth is a no-show and now I gotta listen to my own brain."

She grabbed the phone's receiver from its cradle, dialed a number, and stomped to her room, stretching the cord under her door as she slammed it.

I chased after her, but her bedroom door was locked.

"I'm sorry," I said through the door, even though I wasn't sure just what I was sorry about. Everything, I supposed. Everything except Clay. I wasn't sorry about that. Not yet. I was still numb and I hadn't yet learned what I soon would.

I knocked on Lydia's door. "Open up," I insisted, but she wouldn't.

I walked away as she sobbed, "Pick up the phone. Pick up, pick up, pick up. Where are you? Where are you, you idiot?"

I wandered into my room and shut the door.

I didn't want to go to school. I *couldn't* go to school. I didn't know what to do or how to act. I could barely breathe. My lungs felt filled with air that held no oxygen, as if I were continually breathing my own expelled breath.

I lay down on my bed, exhausted. Some time later I awoke with a start to the image of dirt falling on Clay's face. The house was quiet. I had slept the day away. It was late afternoon. My mom would be home soon from work to change clothes for bowling night.

I sat on the floor and dug through the crates of my dad's old books. I thought of reading one to get a sense of what my father had read in the days leading up to the Incident. I needed to distract myself from Clay's voice and image, which were starting to crowd my mind. I needed to find focus on something to distract me, to calm my brain.

I opened up a hardcover novel titled *Lonely Is the House on the Hill*. It had a clear plastic cover slip. It was a library book.

I read the jacket copy. It was about a wealthy, senile widow who referred to herself as "the Queen" in her ranting lunatic diary entries. She lived in the grandest home in a small, remote New England town, a Victorian home built at the crest of the highest hill, from which she planned to keep an eye on the town, if only she had not gone blind during the construction of her dream home.

It was not the type of book my father had usually read. It was not about World War II, or spies, or astronauts, or expeditions into remote tracts of wilderness. On the inside of the front cover, stamped in faded blue ink, was a watery image of the library's facade and name. There was no due-date slip glued to the circulation card sleeve.

I flipped through each page of the book, searching for any clue as to why my father checked out this strange book, and I found several underlined passages with notes in the margins.

Page 12:

They did not want the townsfolk to know the secret the Queen knew. They would do anything to prevent it.

SO WHY RISK TELLING HIM THE SECRET?

Page 39:

The truth had to be told. It was for the good, even when it caused pain.

GOOD FOR WHOM?

Page 119:

The babies she bore could never be prince or princess.

WHY?

Page 147:

They were a son and a daughter of sin.

WHAT DOES THIS MEAN?

Page 293:

She wondered whether he believed the messenger.

DON'T KNOW WHAT TO BELIEVE.

Page 341:

What would convince him? the Queen wondered.

STOP. WE WON'T DO IT. WE CHANGED OUR MINDS. DON'T EVER SEND HIM TO THE SHOP AGAIN. I DON'T CARE IF YOU EVICT ME. MY SON WAS THERE. HE WAS SCARED. NEVER DO THAT AGAIN. UNDERSTAND? NEVER. LEAVE IT ALONE. LEAVE US ALONE. OR I SWEAR.

My mind turned to glass.

These were not notes my father had written to himself about sentences he had underlined. These were his responses to sentences someone else had underlined.

I flipped through the book again, this time to discover on the lower inside of the back cover, nearly concealed by the flap, something written in a minuscule and precise hand:

FIC EDG.

Was this the next book my father was to have checked out of the library to continue the conversation? Why was the book still here, why hadn't he given it to the person who was supposed to read his response?

I searched the crate but found no other library books.

With the book in hand, I reeled out of the house and headed toward the library.

I was in such a hurry, I slipped on the library steps and lurched through the arched entrance and inside to the circulation desk.

The chair behind the desk sat empty. I hurried toward the fiction stacks, working my way through the periodicals section, where the sad old man dozed in a chair, his chin sagging to his chest and drool leaking from the corner of his mouth.

Trailing my fingertips along book spines, I searched among the stacks for "FIC EDG." The book wasn't there. I searched the spine of every book on the surrounding shelves. I did not find a book with that label. I returned to the circulation desk to find it unoccupied. A tiny silver bell sat atop it. I did not like to tap bells. Doing so made me feel conspicuous, impatient, and rude. A handwritten note propped against the bell read:

Please ring bell for help

I tapped the bell.

A door behind the desk opened, and the librarian appeared, tucking a pencil nub into the thicket of gray hair above her ear. She looked at me with alarm, and I realized I had never washed up or changed clothes since

being in the cemetery. I was grimed with mud. When I looked down, I
saw that my jeans were spattered with blood, though the mud and the
damp denim helped mask what it was.

I set *Lonely Is the House on the Hill* down on the circulation desk. The
librarian arched an eyebrow and flipped the book open with her thumb-
nail. She squinted at the slip pasted inside the front cover, looked up at
me, and looked back at the book. From a top drawer of the desk, she took
a pair of reading glasses and set them on her nose, picked up the book, and
opened its cover to see there was no due-date slip.

She peered at me. "What is this?"

"A library book."

"Yes, but where did you get it?"

"I'm returning it," I said, hoping she had the circulation card. I wanted
to know the exact day my father had signed it out, how close it was to the
day of the Incident.

The woman stared at me.

"It's from here," I said. To support my obvious claim, I pointed at the
faded blue stamped image of the Shireburne Free Library's facade.

"Did you get it at a tag sale or garage sale or something? Because it's
old and there's no—"

"It was my father's," I said. "He checked it out." I rested my palm on
the book, as if about to pledge an oath in court. "He never had a chance
to return it." I hung my head. "I found it in an old box of his belongings."

"Oh, I see. I'm sorry."

"I thought I'd return it. I don't know how much I owe for it being so
overdue."

"I think we can forgive whatever was once owed. I'm not sure we even
have the old circulation card for it. Perhaps . . . " She held up a finger
gnarled with arthritis. "One second." She stepped back into the room
behind the desk. I heard her say, "Dolores, do we . . . " before she shut the
door.

A moment later the librarian returned, waggling a circulation card
above her head as if brandishing a winning lottery ticket. "Dolores files
everything. She's a Godsend. Let me see, now." The librarian set the card

down on the desk, beside the book. She stamped it with a return date and I saw its original due date was for a day that had fallen a week after the Incident. I looked to see if my father had signed his name on the card in cursive or print.

My father's name was not on the card. Instead, there was another man's name.

I picked up the book in my trembling hands.

"Is something wrong?" the librarian sounded worried. "You look like you're going to be sick. Are you going to be sick?"

Yes, I was going to be sick. I was already sick. "I need to go," I whispered.

I wandered out of the library, dizzy.

At the corner phone booth, I looked up the name on the library circulation card. I found a single match: one Quentin Fredericks, Esquire, at 217 Overlook Drive. The address of the man who had signed out the book.

I had never heard of Overlook Drive.

I dashed back to the library, where the librarian was stamping a fresh stack of returned books with the efficiency of a Dickensian clerk, *stamp, stamp, stamp.* She aligned the books on a wheeled cart, then glanced up at me.

"Do you happen to know where Overlook Drive is?" I asked her.

She scratched the side of her nose with a pinkie nail. "Never heard of it. It's in Shireburne?" *Stamp.*

I nodded.

"Sorry."

Stamp. Stamp.

"You might ask at the town clerk's office," she said. "Do you know where it is?"

At the town clerk's office I was greeted by another shiny round bell perched on an unoccupied desk. I slapped my palm on it.

The woman who had helped me before with the records appeared from a long, dark corridor I had not previously noticed. She startled me. She stared at the bell, then at my disheveled and muddied state. "How is your *report* going?"

I'd nearly forgotten my lie from my first visit. It was hard to keep track. "Good," I managed.

"What was it about, again?" she quizzed me as she walked behind the desk.

I didn't answer. She slipped one hand into the pocket of her smock and stared at me as if waiting for me to confess.

"Do you know where Overlook Drive is?"

She looked at me askance. "Why?"

I hesitated. I could not tell her I'd seen a name on a library book circulation card from eight years earlier. A name that should have been my father's, who was supposed to be dead of a self-inflicted gunshot but, I believed, wasn't.

"For another school report," I said. "Town history as world history."

"Why Overlook Drive?"

"I'm picking names of places that sound mysterious."

She picked up a stapler from the desk, loaded a stick of staples into it, and snapped it shut. "It's on the estate." Her words were as bitter as an old copper penny.

I tried to conceal my astonishment.

She worked the stapler, *click, click, click,* until it jammed. Flattened staples rained onto the desktop. "It's not part of the estate, per se," she said. "It's a road just off the estate, along the lake, where the servants used to live. Maybe you'd rather write about a nicer place in town, something more communal—the bowling lanes or the drive-in theater."

"Who lives there now?"

"I've no idea. I was a girl last time I was out that way. Not sure anyone lives there now."

"How do I get there?"

"I just recall it's in the woods and fields along the cliffs at the lake's edge, north of the estate. You can't go there, anyway. It's gated. Private."

"Oh," I said, wanting now to tamp down my enthusiasm. "Maybe the bowling lanes would be better."

"Probably a wise decision."

RETURN TO SENDER

I left the town offices knowing that I could find Overlook Drive by way of the old mansion. The stone drive that led from the cliffside woods to the mansion had to be a spur that came off of Overlook.

I crept once again through the weeds and vines behind the mansion until I came to the stand of oak trees that stood sentinel for a good mile along the cliffs running to the north.

I stole among the trees, keeping the gravel drive in sight. On the other side of me, the ragged rock escarpment dropped some two hundred feet to the lake. After a spell, I saw through the branches, in the distance, the green of spring fields. I crept to the edge of the woods and looked out onto the fields.

A low stone house squatted on the side of a hill a few hundred yards away. It looked as if it had been built into the side of the hill. Its slate roof bowed in the center like the back of an old horse. It reminded me of huts I'd seen in pictures of remote, windswept Iceland or of mythical lands of dwarves and giants, sea serpents and mermaids.

Two ancient maple trees framed the house. Each tree leaned southward in a dramatic sweep of branches, their scoliotic trunks forever bent by the eternal north winds blowing off the lake.

Other stone houses crouched in the fields above the road. I crept along in the roadside ditch. The other homes looked in disrepair, with no vehicles parked in driveways rampant with weeds. As I picked my way along the ditch, I searched the rusted, lopsided mailboxes for the addresses or names.

Finally, on a black mailbox, I saw 217.

There was no way to approach the house without being conspicuous. The fields were green with shoots of wild grasses no higher than the soles of my sneakers. Except for the maple trees that guarded each house, no trees grew. There was no place to hide, so I hurried across the road and up the drive to the stone house. There was no car parked in the drive, nor any garage to conceal one. The gravel drive simply ended by a side door.

This home appeared maintained in a way the others did not. The black paint on the door seemed fresh. The windows of the other houses were dingy with dust, but the windows of 217 were clean and bright. The door was outsized in proportion to the home, and nearly as wide as it was tall.

I didn't know what else to do, so I knocked.

No one came to the door.

I glanced back at the road below me. It was as desolate as the broad expanse of lake that was now kicked up into frothy waves.

I peered into the window beside the door. I saw only a small, dark foyer with a brick floor, the wallpaper a dark maroon bedecked with gilded and flocked filigrees. A mirror hung on the entrance wall. As I pulled my face from the window, I glimpsed, in a lower corner of the mirror, a reflection of light from down the hall. I gauged by the island crafted of dark barn board and Formica that the room at the end of the hall was a kitchen.

In the distance, I heard an engine rev. I wheeled around. I saw no vehicle and could no longer hear an engine. Had a car stopped? Was a vehicle idling just out of sight and out of hearing range?

I stepped down the drive and took in more of the road.

I heard the muffled sound of an engine starting up again, sputtering and stalling.

Out on the lake, maybe a hundred yards from shore, a boat rocked in the whitecaps. It looked like any old V-hull an angler would use trolling for salmon or lake trout. I could just make out two figures, men, standing near the bow, behind the low windscreen. If I was not mistaken, one of the men was looking my way. Not at me necessarily, but toward the hills.

The engine fired up again, and the boat cut through the chop as it swung sharply and headed out for the broad of the lake.

I put my face to the window once again and thought I caught movement in the kitchen at the end of the hall.

I walked around to the back, to a slate patio. It was bare of furniture or any sign of use at all except for wind chimes so twisted together they clacked a discordant and strangled tune as they swayed in the breeze.

A set of French doors led from the patio into the kitchen.

I peered inside.

A quick movement on the floor at a corner of the island caught my eye.

A black cat. Or, more precisely, a black cat's tail, flicking as the creature licked its one white paw and then set to licking the floor.

I knocked on a windowpane.

I expected the cat to dart away, but it only arched its back and peered over its shoulder at me before again busying its tongue on whatever morsel it had found stuck to the kitchen floor.

I tried the handle to the door. It swung. I eased the door open and stepped inside the kitchen.

"Hello?" I called out.

A sudden hum made me jump. The refrigerator rattled to life.

A fruit bowl sat in the center of the kitchen island. The bananas and oranges in it looked fresh, though a small cloud of fruit flies hovered above.

"Hello?" I called again as I walked around the island.

I peeked back over my shoulder, expecting someone to be standing there. No one was.

I wanted to flee. Yet part of me needed to know more about this man who had signed out the book that my father had read—who had conducted a secretive communication with my father. I walked down the hallway off the kitchen, toward the opposite end of the house.

On the hallway wall hung an old color photograph of a man. The image stopped me dead. It was of the Tall Man. In it, he was many years younger than when I'd seen him in the barbershop. Perhaps thirty. Judging by the hair and clothes, I would have guessed the photo was from the late forties, maybe a little earlier. A woman was also in the photo. A young woman with skin pale as milk, long red hair shining like hammered copper in the bright sun. She was a good deal younger than the Tall Man—ten years younger, at least. As I peered closer, I saw she was much younger. Perhaps sixteen. The Tall Man had one arm around her slender waist as she stood beside him, leaned into, *pressed* into him, both of them grinning, beaming, champagne flutes hoisted toward the photographer with such glee that champagne sloshed at the lips of the glasses. Their eyes were glossed. I didn't know who the girl was, but I knew that red hair. It was the hair I had seen through the widow's-watch window. It was the hair, and the girl, from the photo I'd found in the bedside table in the old mansion. In the background, regal and imposing, stood the old mansion.

I ventured farther down the hall.

I came to a door and knocked on it. I don't know why. I knew that the house was empty, and as expected, nobody answered my knock. I opened the door to a cramped office with a low ceiling and exposed beams whose dark rough-hewn wood was marked and pitted with the borings of ancestral worms and insects.

Behind a wooden desk, a modest bay window overlooked the lake.

The walls were built-in bookshelves painted a glowing pearlescent white. On one shelf sat a framed diploma, a law degree from Yale. Quentin Fredericks.

A Smith Corona typewriter sat square in the center of the desk, on a green ink blotter. Beside it was a stack of letterhead for Quentin Fredericks, Esquire.

A piece of paper wilted forward in the typewriter, curling on itself. I came around the desk, took a corner of the sheet between my fingertips, and bent it backward so I could read it.

`My Dearest Silva,`
`    It is with`

Silva.
Other than those six words, the page was blank.
It is with . . . what?

The Tall Man, Quentin Fredericks, was an attorney. I stepped over to the shelf nearest me. Each book possessed a dry professional or academic title. *Family Law: Its Applications. Estate Management. Laws of Inheritance. Trusts and Will.*

I slid open the center desk drawer and found nothing but a few blank envelopes, a roll of twenty-cent stamps, and a letter opener.

The desk's left cabinet door was locked. It had a brass keyhole just above a brass pull. I searched the desktop for a key but couldn't find one.

I heard an engine and looked out the bay window at the lake. The boat was back, very near shore, bobbing in place as if anchored. Both figures were looking toward the house. One of them had his arms up, elbows cocked, looking through binoculars.

I backed away from the window.

I studied the desk's side cabinet. I didn't want to force it open.

I heard the clatter of a vehicle on the dirt road outside. I pinned myself to the bookcase and peeked out the window. I saw the blue truck. It eased along in low gear. I thought it was going to pull into the driveway, but it crawled onward, along the edge of the cliff and into the trees, where it disappeared on its way to the only destination possible: the mansion.

I knew that I needed to leave, just as I knew that the Tall Man, this Quentin Fredericks, Esquire, had been the one to underline the sentences in the library book and then deliver the book in his black bag to my father at the shop, and that my father had been the one to write the notes to him in return.

I opened the top center drawer again, hoping that the key was in there, hidden in one of the envelopes, perhaps.

I fished through the refuse of staples and rubber bands, then took out the blank letterhead and envelopes and scattered them on the desktop, feeling inside each envelope. I found no key. What I did find was an empty envelope with an address on it. My address. It was handwritten in block print, along with my mother's name. The envelope was postmarked. It had been through the mail. It had been opened very carefully with a letter opener, but there was another mark, too, in red: "Return to Sender." The return address was 217 Overlook, but without a name of the sender.

The postmark was dated April 6, 1984. So, just a few days earlier, my mother had received a letter from the Tall Man and sent it back to him without opening it. But the letter was missing. I searched through the drawers again but found no letter. There was a small metal waste-basket beneath the desk. I dumped out the trash and fished through the wadded-up papers. One sheet of paper bore the attorney's letterhead. It was not blank. In the same handwritten print, it was addressed to . . . Laura.

> IF HE DOESN'T KNOW BY NOW, HE WILL SOON. I SPOKE WITH HENRY ON THE PHONE. I INSISTED HE BACK OFF AND DENY. BUT I FEAR HE'S CLOSE TO <u>CONFESSING</u> TO WAYLAND WHAT WE DID. I MAY HAVE TO PAY HIM A PERSONAL VISIT.

I shivered upon reading my name. And Mr. Kane's first name, Henry.

> WE SHOULD NEVER HAVE DONE WHAT WE DID. I SHOULD NEVER HAVE EXACERBATED ONE PROBLEM, ONE WRONGDOING, BY ENGAGING IN OTHERS. I SHOULD NEVER HAVE TAKEN PART IN ANY OF IT, START TO FINISH. I SHOULD HAVE OWNED UP TO MY RESPONSIBILITY LONG AGO. IT WAS A MISTAKE. I MISJUDGED THE RAMIFICATIONS. <u>ALL OF THEM.</u> WE <u>ALL</u> DID, I DARESAY.

I heard the truck out on the road again. I heard brakes squeak as it stopped and idled.

I grabbed the letter and envelope and fled.

GO

I ran through the woods toward the mansion. The sun was starting to sink behind the Spectral Mountains on the far side of Forbidden Lake, leaving the sky bruised.

In the darkening woods, I leaned against a tree and stared out at the old mansion. I felt exhausted and afraid as the irrevocability of what I had done in the cemetery began to squirm inside me, infesting my mind's eye with one parasitical image after another of Clay in the grave.

A light blinked on in a third-story window—a window no one could see unless they were positioned where I was among the trees.

I threaded my way through the brambles to the cellar window. Lowering myself into the blackness, once again I breathed in the fetid air of the cellar. I found the stairs, climbed them, and hurried to the foyer, where I paused, listening. Hearing nothing but the sound of my beating, guilty heart, I climbed the hard marble stairs to the third floor.

From the landing I saw a yellow light bleeding from under the center hall door. I pressed my ear to the door. I believed I could hear shallow rasps of breath, but they may have been my own.

I listened more intently and caught the same sound I had heard at the widow's watch. A moan. Not of pleasure—I knew for certain now—but of pain. I couldn't sit back hiding anymore.

I grasped the doorknob. Its porcelain felt cold against my palm. Another moan rose, mournful.

I peered through the keyhole. In the room, a woman stood with her back to me. Her long red hair spilled down her back, almost entirely veiling the sleeveless black dress she wore. She swayed as if in a trance, the dress's hem whisking the floor, her moan, unbroken and morose, coming from deep down within her. I saw now that her skin—at least that of her narrow shoulders—was not pale and smooth as I had believed when looking with binoculars through the widow's-watch window. It seemed to be coated in a thick white cream like the stuff my mother used at night. When I saw the woman the first time, she had appeared to be in a contorted position. Now I saw that her spine was as crooked as a snake run over by a car. What I had seen as obscene perhaps erotic contortions just a couple of weeks ago—how could it have been such a short time and not years?—was only my juvenile mind leaping to a prurient assumption. The woman was severely deformed.

Though her back was to me, I could see the masquerade mask's elastic band, tight against her red hair. Downy golden plumage of exotic birds fanned out from the mask.

I froze at the sound of a cough from somewhere to the left of my keyhole view. I couldn't see who had coughed without entering the room and revealing my presence.

The woman's swaying took on a slow rhythm as she made inhuman sounds in a language made up entirely of vowels, as if she were trying to cry out from the depths of a dark nightmare, unable to shape words in her deep and haunted slumber. Perhaps she was drunk, drugged, or otherwise entranced or fevered. Perhaps she was ill beyond recovery.

I strained to decipher her nightmare language. The way her body was angled and the way her arms and hands gestured, she was, without a doubt, speaking to someone—someone who knew her well enough to understand her alien sounds. Someone I could not see.

I needed to open the door.

I needed to see.

I needed to help her.

I sneaked the door open, just a whisker.

"Come," said a sonorous voice. "Let me see you."

I knew that voice from Mr. Kane's cabin and from the barbershop, where I had heard it half my young life ago.

The woman hung her head, turned a shoulder to him. I feared she might glimpse me through the crack in the door, but she didn't.

"Allow me, then," the Tall Man, Quentin Fredericks, said.

Though he remained just out of my sight, his fingers, pale and long, reached into view. He lifted the straps of her dress and lowered it off her shoulders, letting it pool at her feet. She remained with her back to me. She was naked, yet her long hair concealed her from any immodesty.

His hands disappeared from view then appeared again, holding a lamp with a tubular bulb. He flipped a switch, and a bright blue light sparked and flashed like a strobe. It was the light I had seen through the widow's-watch window the night I was chased. The hand moved over the woman's pale skin, working the light in slow arcs as if it were a magic wand. The light seemed to be some sort of treatment. It blinked out. The hand disappeared, then reappeared without the light. With tenderness, as if the woman were made of blown glass and would shatter at their touch, the fingertips of one hand removed her mask. The other hand held a tiny and ornate glass jar. Three fingers dipped into the jar and came out with a glop of white cream. The hands began to apply the cream to her front as she moaned in her odd, indecipherable tongue.

"Let me see you."

Finished with the cream, the Tall Man stepped into view. If he so much as glanced my way, he would spot me. His hands moved to her hair, as if he intended to entwine his fingers in it. Instead, he lifted the luxuriant red mane from her scalp and let it flop to the floor. The woman tripped the switch on the lamp beside her bed, and the room fell dark.

I ducked into the adjoining room, horrified by what I had seen. It had happened so fast, I could not be sure whether what I'd seen was a trick of the light, my imagination, or real. The head beneath the wig was a misshapen gourd, noduled and barnacled, the skin so thin and pale and shiny that it was like a membrane stretched too tight and too thin. It looked as if, had I pressed a finger to it, I would have broken straight through the fragile skull to touch her brain.

The woman's scalp, and the flesh at the base of her head and her neck, looked *melted,* with just a few errant sprouting strands of long silver hair. I could not imagine what her face looked like.

I knew who the woman was, of course. Silva. My father's mother. I knew who the Tall Man was too. I wondered whose choice it had been to give my father up for adoption, that of the thirty-year-old family attorney, or the fifteen-year-old girl from the town's most prestigious family, whom he had impregnated. Yet, all these years later, Quentin Fredericks still touched her disfigured and broken body with tenderness, longing and adoration. Perhaps they did love one another in their way. My grandfather and grandmother.

I heard the door to the next room click open, then footfalls making their way toward the landing, fading as they descended the stairs. When all seemed quiet, I opened the door and peered out into the hallway, feeling for the revolver's grip in the small of my back. I went to her door and leaned a shoulder into it. It yawned open on stiff hinges.

In the shadows at the far end of the grand room, she sat in the Chesterfield chair, facing away from me, the long red tresses back in place. She faced the window that overlooked the cliffs and lake and mountains, though none of these were visible to her. Darkness had fallen, and the curtains were drawn. The room smelled of turpentine and the tubes of oil paints on the easel in front of her.

A tortured, hacking racket escaped her throat. She eased the chair around on its casters. A veil concealed her features. She clutched a black journal to her chest, fingers so tightly intertwined around it that they seemed fused together. She did not seem alarmed to see me. In fact, I wondered at first whether she saw me at all. Perhaps she was blind as well as mute. I stepped closer to her.

She opened the journal and smoothed her palms over a clean blank page. Taking a pencil wedged in the back of the book, she began to write in a patient and, apparently, painful manner. She held the page out to me, inches from my face, as if she couldn't judge distance. I read what she had labored to write:

60.

"I won't go," I said. "I know about the library books. I know you underlined sentences and he . . . " I nodded toward the door to indicate Quentin, who had just departed. " . . . delivered the books to the barbershop. You underlined sentences to communicate secretly with my father. And he replied by writing notes. I want to know what it was about. I'm not leaving until I know."

She thrust the journal at me again:

60.

"I know who you are," I said.
She worked the pencil on the journal's page:

BuT You DON'T KNOW WHO You ARE.

"I do," I said. "I know everything now."

You KNOW NOTHING.

She lifted her veil.

What I stared at was not a face, but a melted devastation of larval-pale flesh that sagged and slouched—warm wax lumped together by numb fingers. The lower jaw hung crooked, as if broken by an ax handle, the mouth slung open in an eternal howl, neither ecstasy nor agony. No lips, just the approximation of them painted with a garish oily pink lipstick. The eyes, however, amid the ruin of flesh, shone bright, not with the spark of life, but with what seemed acute pain. The wig sat pitifully crooked on her forehead. I forced myself not to look away.

The veil fluttered down to mercifully conceal her face once more. Her pencil scratched in the journal:

I KNEW YOU'D COME ONE DAY. BUT YOU CAN'T BE HERE. GO.

"I *am* here. And I want to know—"
She shook her head so hard, I thought she might break that delicate neck. She wrote:

DON'T BLAME YOURSELF. GO.

"Blame myself?" I said.
She blinked, confused.

YOU DON'T KNOW.

"I—"

I SAW YOU. I SAW IT ALL.

"When? Where?"

THAT DAY. YOUR PARENTS' ROOM.

"You weren't there," I said, bewildered and enraged by her lie. "I would have known. You could have helped us, all this time. Helped *her*. My mom. Instead, you let her struggle and suffer. Let us *all* suffer, just a mile away. We're family."
She snorted.
The window curtain lit up from outside. As I went to the window, Silva clutched at me, wrapped her arms around my waist, and pressed her face to my spine with a groan. I freed myself of her clawing hands, fending her off so I could peel back the curtain.
Headlights shone down at the mansion from the road along the

darkening cliffside woods, then drifted out of sight toward the carport.

I let the curtain fall and turned back to her. She held out her journal:

I WAS THERE.

Was she mad? She had never been in our house that day. It wasn't possible.

I heard the faraway yet unmistakable sound of the foyer door slamming shut.

She scribbled quickly, trembling.

DON'T LET HIM FIND YOU HERE.

"I want to see him," I insisted. "I want to know what message he delivered in the barbershop that night, what he told my father. What he did to my father, his own son. What you *had* him do."

She wrote again, frantic:

NOT HIM.

"Who?"

MY BROTHER. HE WON'T LET YOU TELL—

The pencil tip broke off.

Her eyes went wide. Her mouth moved as if to speak, yet all that came forth was a wretched gagging sound. She jabbed a finger at the bedside table, motioned as if writing. She wanted a fresh pencil. Out in the hall, footfalls drew closer to the door.

Silva tapped her finger on the journal:

GO.

It was too late for that.

She jabbed her finger at the closet.

The doorknob turned.

I dashed into the closet and peered through the keyhole just as the door to the room opened.

"Time," a man said as he advanced on her. Not the Tall Man, but a man I knew from the *Gazette*, and from the evening I fell out of the tree beside the widow's watch and got chased. Buell Vanders III. Silva's brother.

Silva shrank against the back of her chair as he closed in on her, holding a small black velvet box in his hand.

"Dear sister, must you always object—"

I heard a *click*. Silva's brother stopped, stared at her, at the revolver, my revolver, my *father's* revolver, clutched in her trembling hand. She had swiped it when she wrapped her arms around me as I'd tried to look out the window.

"What's this?" her brother said, his voice placid, as if having a revolver pointed at him was a common occurrence. "Poor, dear Silva." He stepped toward her. The revolver wavered in her weak hands. Buell's eyes searched the room, settling, for a moment, on the closet where I hid. I dare not move or breathe. Buell smirked, dismissive and imperious. He took a step, within reach of her now, and stared at the gun. "It's not even loaded." He laughed a high, shrill woman's laugh. Silva glanced at the revolver.

Buell wrested the revolver from her grip. Silva screeched. I thought for a moment that she might speak. Instead, she spat in her brother's face. He wiped the spittle from his cheek as if wiping away a crumb. Setting the revolver on the easel's tray, he opened the velvet box and produced a syringe and a brown vial.

Silva moaned. It sounded to me as if she were struggling to speak without a tongue. She kept at it until I believed she was actually trying to form a single word. "Poison."

Buell pushed the syringe into the vial and took hold of her wrist as she thrashed.

I sprang from the closet and slammed the crown of my head square into Buell's lower back. He lost the syringe and crashed into the easel. The revolver clattered to the floor. Buell regained his feet and gaped at me.

"You," he spat. "I warned her, years ago, not to open this nasty box of snakes."

He glanced at the revolver in the corner. Apparently satisfied that I could not reach it before he could, he picked up the syringe from the floor.

"Don't poison her!" I shouted.

He held the syringe aloft. "*This* is the opposite of poison. This is Haldol, the only thing that keeps her halfway . . . reasonable. After the trouble she's caused this family since the day you were born, the least we can expect from her is to be reasonable."

Since the day I was born?

He tried to take hold of her wrists, but she kicked out at him. As he struggled with her, I rushed for the revolver. I grabbed the gun as Buell stomped down hard on my hand. I howled in pain. Buell picked up the revolver and pointed it at my face. He knew it was loaded. "Go, while I let you," he said. He watched as I edged toward the door and put my good hand on the knob.

He tucked the revolver in his pants and addressed his sister, the syringe clenched sideways in his teeth. He clasped a hand around her throat and yanked up her dress sleeve with the other hand to expose her withered arm, bruised yellow from needle marks. She bucked. "Easy," he said. She kicked, her feet striking the easel, making it teeter. That's when I saw it. The can of turpentine.

I grabbed it and sloshed turpentine all over Buell, soaking his head and back with it. He screamed and wheeled around. I doused his face and eyes. He clawed at his face, spitting, and dropped to his knees. Again, the syringe fell to the floor. I snatched up the revolver and dropped the can of turpentine. The reek of the turpentine burned my nostrils.

Buell blinked up at me, his face a raw hamburger pink from the turpentine, his squinting eyes red as blood and weeping.

"Get in the chair," I commanded as I dragged a chair from a corner, having no clue what I would do next.

Buell's hair was dripping wet with turpentine, his shirt dark with it. He blinked at his sister. "He doesn't have a clue," he said. "He doesn't know."

"Get in the chair," I repeated, the revolver aimed at his forehead.

He gave me a savage look, but he got into the chair, rubbing the heels of his palms into his eyes. My mind hummed. I kept the revolver trained on him and glanced about the room. I grabbed at the white braided draw cord of the curtain, yanking hard to free it. I tossed it to him, told him to tie his ankles to the chair legs.

"You don't know what you're doing," he said as he bound his ankles tight to the chair.

"I know that you are the cause—this *family* is the cause—for whatever happened to my father. Who was on his bed that day? It wasn't him. You did something to him and then let us all suffer. For appearances. To keep him from revealing who he was. You should have helped us."

I tied his wrists to the chair's arms, one hand tight, the other with a bit of slack. I stood behind him. The long dressing mirror on the far wall reflected his image, seated in the chair, and me, standing behind him.

"Look at me in the mirror," I said.

He looked up at my image.

"Look me in the eye," I demanded.

I placed the revolver in his hand and stepped back.

He tried to contort his arm to aim the revolver over his shoulder at me, but the short tether did not allow him the angle. It permitted only enough motion for him to point the revolver at his chest or face. From my pocket, I took out the box of matches I kept on me. I plucked three matches from the box, prepared to strike them.

"Put the gun barrel in your mouth. Or I light the matches."

"You'll burn too," he laughed. He was right. Enough turpentine had splashed on me that if I lit the match, it was possible I'd catch fire.

"I don't care," I said. And I didn't. Not about anything. Not any longer. And I saw in his eyes that he understood this.

I scraped the three matches along the side of the box, away from me, and held them out as they sizzled and popped into flame. Buell shut his eyes tight. No explosion came. I held the matches out above his head. "If you don't do it the quick way, the matches will land on you for what you've done and what you've hidden, for never helping us. For keeping her imprisoned here all this time."

He laughed harder. "Is that what you think? I've imprisoned her? That she can't move around with that twisted body of hers? Oh, she can move, all right. You think she can't leave here? I take her to and from that damned carriage house anytime she likes so she can watch the tourists at the inn, and feel almost a part of the community over there. You think she can't speak. She can speak! I've heard her in her nightmares. Did she say I kept her here against her will—some poor burned, disfigured, crippled Rapunzel? Is that what she told you?"

She had told me no such thing, of course, but I had inferred enough. The disgraceful, disgraced, ill younger sister who had seduced the helpless older family attorney, had gotten *herself* pregnant, carried my father to term, and then given him up. The shame *she* had brought on the sacred family name. The need for the older brother to silence her, keep her under control and away from the world. Silent. Never mind the old lawyer's hand in it all. Never mind she had been younger than I was then; a *child*.

"*Tell him.*" Buell kept his eyes on Silva. "Tell the boy the truth."

The three match flames joined to become a single hot blaze that twisted and jigged, searing the hair of my knuckles as it crawled toward my fingertips.

The flame guttered, died.

I dropped the matches to the floor and took three more from the box.

"Tell him!" Buell shouted. "You can speak! You spoke that day and have chosen not to ever since! Tell him, or I—"

A noise escaped from Silva's throat, a high screech like that of the rusted cemetery gate. "*Eeeeasse-oooooh.*"

I struck the matches. Flames snapped to life. "Put it in your mouth." I nodded at the revolver.

Buell stared at me. Hands shaking, he pressed the revolver muzzle under his chin.

"*Eeeeasse-oohhh.*"

"Do it," I demanded.

He didn't do it—couldn't, perhaps.

He shouted, "You're . . ."

I cocked my arm behind me and swung it forward to throw the matches on him.

His eyes went wide, and the revolver fired—a small snap like a fire-cracker.

His head lolled to the side. He looked as if he had nodded off, except for the blood spurting from his throat.

"No-o-o-o!" Silva moaned.

The revolver fell to the floor.

Buell did not catch fire. I had flung the lit matches backward over my shoulder and brought my empty hand forward in a feint. The match flames had gone out before the matches hit the floor behind me. Buell had not waited to discover how it felt to burn alive. I let the box of matches fall to the floor. When the blood stopped spurting from Buell's wound, I untied his body. It sagged forward and thumped onto the floor. I didn't touch the revolver. I wanted no part of it.

Silva seemed in a fugue, eyes blank, her body slack. I feared she was dead.

"What was he talking about?" I asked her, still needing, desperately, to know the truth. "What did he want you to tell me?"

Her crooked finger pointed toward the bedside table. She wanted a pencil.

I went to the table and flung the drawer open and dug around for another pencil. I found one and turned back to Silva.

I stopped, stricken. She was lying on the floor beside the body of her brother. She held the turpentine can over her and was pouring the last of it onto the length of her ruined body. She dropped the can and picked up the box of matches beside her, grabbed some matches from it, and struck them against the box.

I staggered backward from the flames and tripped, falling against the window so hard it shattered. It was only the velvet drapery that saved me from pitching out into the darkness as Silva had done all those years ago.

The flames devoured her.

I KNOW THIS ROOM

The heat was monstrous. For a moment, I stood as paralyzed with horror as I had eight years before in my father's bedroom. Then, I fled.

As I hurried toward the landing, I saw a door shut at the far end of the hall. Had Quentin returned? Or someone else? If someone else was in the mansion, they needed to leave before the fire spread.

I ran to the door and opened it onto an empty room. I stood there, confused. The person *had* to be there. The only exit was the window, and no one could have escaped through it without being crippled or killed. I checked the window. Locked. A moan rose from inside the closet. I checked it.

Except for a few moth-eaten wool coats draped on wire hangers, the closet lay bare. I swept the coats aside to see, deep in the rear of the vast closet, another door, which had to lead to the room where I had heard the *whoosh* and *slap* on my previous visit.

I peered through the keyhole—and gasped. My bones turned to dust.

I knew this room. I knew the chair. I knew the bureau. Knew the trunk, the nightstand. I knew the drinking glass and the lamp and the stacked photo albums on the nightstand.

I knew the faded photos of me and Lydia displayed in their finger-painted Popsicle-stick frames.

It was my parents' bedroom—or a replica of it, set up in the center of a room so cavernous, the furniture could have been a set on a sound stage. Yet it was not just a replica. The furniture and all the other belongings were not props. They were the originals that I had thought my mother threw out years ago.

This diorama broke from the faithful reproduction of my parents' original bedroom in two aspects. One was the medical equipment, monitors and machines set up next to the bed to maintain the vital functions of the body lying on the bed. For it was just that: a body, not a living human being in any real sense. The body lay on its side, its bony back to me, the knuckles of its spine pressed against skin so pale as to be nearly translucent. The head was bald as an egg. The second difference from the original room: the walls were pasted with scores of photos of Lydia and me over the years. School photos and other pictures. Artwork too.

One of the machines, a pump in a tube, made a rhythmic *whoosh, slap.*

I became aware that I was feverish, my skin too hot, bathed in sweat. I smelled smoke.

When I again put my eye to the keyhole, a woman stood with her back to me as she climbed into the bed and lay down beside its occupant. Even with her back to me, there was no mistaking who the woman was. Did she know I was here? Did she know that the mansion was on fire? She wrapped her arms around him, and he shifted, rolled over, so that I saw what should have been his face. It looked as if it had been blown apart with a stick of dynamite and stitched back together by a blind man using butcher's twine and a fishhook. Tubes fed into the toothless wound where a mouth had once been. Another tube snaked into two dark holes where once there had been a nose, in its place a flap of flesh, pink and smooth as putty. One eye was gone, the lid fused shut to the cheek as if it had melted there. The remaining eye had no lid and stared out, unblinking. I knew that eye. My father's eye.

My father had been on the bed that day. He had shot himself. He just hadn't died.

Had he been in this room ever since that day, with his birth mother just a few doors down?

I eased open the closet door and stood in the room.

"Dad," I said.

My mother jerked up from the bed, gaping at me as if I were an apparition. It was Friday night. A bowling night. A night she always came home happy.

My voice came out weak and cracked. "Why didn't you tell me?"

She swallowed a sob. "She wouldn't let me."

"What does she have to—"

"She was at the house that day."

"No," I insisted. "She wasn't. She's a liar, she—"

"She said she *saw* you pick up a note. That's why I asked if you had found one. She swore you picked it up off the floor and read it. But you said you didn't, and I believed you, because I knew even then there was no way he would ever need to write such a . . . " She glanced at my father. "If you did find a note, whatever it was, then you know she's telling the truth. You know she was there, behind you in the doorway."

I winced at the smoke that leaked into the room and stung my eyes. "Why would she have been at our house?"

"To confront *me.* She'd read your birth notice years before and wanted to confront your dad and me then. Her brother stopped her, said it would ruin *the family.* Then she had that horrible . . . accident, if that's what it was. Locked away here most of her days, no connection to the world except library books signed out by Quentin."

The air in the room rippled with heat.

"That's how she found out I gave birth to your sister," my mother continued. "Your sister had scrawled her full name in crayon in a library book your father had signed out. When Quentin took out the same book and Silva saw Lydia's name in it, she realized we'd had *another* child. It triggered her to contact your father, no matter what her brother threatened.

"She underlined sentences in a book that spoke for her and had Quentin take the book to the shop. Your father refused to believe her claims, until Quentin showed him papers that proved it."

"What papers?" I said. "What claims? Adoption? So what if she's his mother? If she is, why didn't she help us? Why did Dad—"

"She's not just . . . She made demands of your father and me. We caved. At first. But we love each other. We refused to sign."

"We need to go."

"She went mad," my mother continued, so absorbed in her confession, she seemed oblivious of the heat and the smoke now in the room. She seemed only to want to unburden herself of a story she had kept secret for so long. "She escaped from her room one day and sneaked through the woods to confront me at home. Broken as her body looks, she can move like a snake. Quentin called your father at the shop and told him to get home, that he thought Silva was heading to the house. He told your father to call me, get me out of there. I left so fast, I didn't even turn off the record player. I met Quentin in town, at the diner. That's who I met. That's the man I met. Your father rushed into the house to tell Silva to leave us alone, that what she'd told us didn't matter to us. That he would no longer answer to her."

"What did she *tell* you?"

"She refused to leave," my mother continued. "Said if we didn't keep our promise, she'd reveal who we were—shame us, even if it ruined the entire family."

The heat in the room was now so intense, I thought my shirt might melt to my skin.

"But why would he shoot himself?"

"He didn't shoot himself," my mother said.

"But I saw him. I . . . " I stared at the man in the bed. Was it my father? It had to be. Why else would the room be made up like the room where he had known such happiness and love?

"We never wanted you to know. He never wanted you to know. To remember."

"Remember what?"

"I feared all these years that getting you help would worsen things for you. Make you remember. And I couldn't bear that. Your father, over months, learned to communicate by tapping a finger. He told me. He tried to drag Silva from the house, but she fought with those claws of hers. She was like a wild animal. He got the shotgun from the closet and . . . He

just wanted to scare her. He chased her into your room and called Quentin
at the diner from our room, to come collect her. He thought the gun was
empty. He would never have been so careless if he'd thought it was loaded.
He was sitting on the edge of the bed with the gun resting against his
knees, waiting for Quentin. He never heard you, he was so consumed by
his anger. You . . . *startled* him."

No, I thought. *No*. But it was true.

I reached out for him. And the gun went off.

"But—" I said. "His feet. They dangled. How—"

"I told you. Tried to. The old mattress was thicker. That's all it ever was."

The world was teetering and fading. I was sick from the heat and
smoke. If we didn't leave now, the mansion would be our crematorium.
"How could you—how could *she*—fake his death? An empty coffin, get
doctors to cover—"

My mother gave a sad shrug. "Money," she said. "That's all anything
ever takes."

"Why did you agree to it? Hide him from me? From Lydia? Poor Lydia."

My mother's voice was dreamy, her eyes lost. "So I could be with him.
She promised she'd pay for the best of care—care I could never afford—
to keep him alive, if I never told anyone he had lived. I made a choice,
a . . . sacrifice. If he had died, we would have ended up the same or worse,
you and Lydia and I. Don't you see?"

I coughed so hard at the smoke, I thought my lungs would bleed.

"I'll get him out," I wheezed. "Go. Now." I pointed to the door to the
corridor.

"That door is nailed shut."

"Through there." I waved my hand at the closet and the room beyond
it, its wallpaper bubbling as tiny blue flames licked the walls.

I tried to lift my father, but he gave a bestial groan and gripped the
bed rails. I could not pry his fingers free; it was if they were clamped with
rigor mortis.

My mother sat on the edge of the bed and sobbed.

I yanked her to her feet and shoved through the closet, dragged her
into the next room, the walls ablaze, the air choked with smoke. I held

my breath and squeezed my eyes to slits. I found the doorknob. I had no idea what I might encounter on the other side of that door. If the corridor was on fire, I would have to push my mother out the window and leap out after her.

The hallway just outside had not yet caught fire, but the far end of it was a cyclone of flames. I forced my mother down the stairs as she fought to go back to the room. In the foyer she stopped and gawked up at the flames raging on the third-floor landing. I yanked open the door and forced her out into the cold night, where she collapsed.

I looked back at the place. Except for a weak orange glow in the third-floor windows, one would never know that an inferno had begun to rage inside the old place. The mansion was so well concealed from town, it might burn to the ground and its ashes go cold before anyone knew there was so much as a candle lit inside.

I knelt beside my sobbing mother. I tried not to think of my father, but it was impossible.

I needed to get my mother away from there. It occurred to me that her car must be parked nearby. I walked away from the house, to see the carport. Her car was there.

When I turned back to get my mother, she was opening the front door of the mansion. A fiery orange light roared from inside. I could feel a rush of foundry heat blast out from it.

I bolted for my mother, screaming for her to stop.

She walked into the mansion and shut the door behind her.

I threw open the door, the heat ferocious, knocking me back. The floors above were engulfed in flames. I watched as my mother climbed the stairs and vanished into the flames. I stood in that feral heat, certain I would catch fire, yet as cold as I ever would be in my life.

I turned and ran along the overgrown drive, climbed up and over the old locked gate, and scurried up the hill. At the crest I plowed into something, knocking it to the ground.

Juliette.

My mind was not working. She could not be here. She could not be real. I stood over her, hyperventilating, wracked with grief.

As she stood, her outline quavered and doubled before me as if she were a hologram. I could not tell which was the real Juliette and which was the mirage. Her face and bare arms were begrimed and scratched from pushing through the woods and fields in the dark.

"What's wrong?" she said. Her voice sounded remote, as if I were in a dream and hearing someone speaking to me, trying to bring me back to the wakeful world. I tried to block her view of the mansion. Far below, it blazed and spewed black smoke. Still, no one would know for some time that it was on fire.

"What happened?" Juliette said as I hurried away from the inferno, down the other side of the hill, yanking her along with me through the woods toward town.

"I looked everywhere for you," Juliette shouted, panicked. "What happened? What's happening?"

We stopped at the edge of the town green, hidden in trees. I was trying to catch my breath when Juliette took a piece of paper from her pocket. "Clay wanted me to give this to you."

How had Clay given her *anything*? When? For a moment, I let myself believe that the events at the cemetery had been no more than a nightmare. "When did he give it to you?"

"Before I went to the cemetery. It was raining, and I didn't want it to get ruined, so I held on to it. Then, with what happened, I forgot to give it to you."

"I don't want it."

"What happened at the mansion? Is it . . . on fire? What's wrong with you? There's something wrong, I—"

"I saw you. And Clay. In his room," I said, but only to distract her.

Her faced morphed to an expression of shock and confusion. "*That*. That was . . . He was *helping* me." She touched the fingertips of one hand to my cheek, pressed the palm of the other to my chest. Just as she'd done with Clay. Just as she'd done in the lilac bushes. "He was showing *me* what to do, because you're so shy. He wasn't coming on to me. He's your *friend*. He told me to do it 'like this.' He believes your dad didn't shoot himself. He felt awful for punching you. Teasing you in the bathroom.

He wanted to apologize in person, face to face. But he was afraid you wouldn't forgive him." She held the note out to me again. "So he wrote you this note. Take it."

"What's it say?"

I remembered the piece of paper Clark had picked up from his bedroom floor and handed it to Juliette.

"I don't know. I promised not to read it."

I took it and read it. And I understood, believed I understood, everything.

When I finished reading it, I said, "Tell the police or whoever that I fell from the cliff into the lake. Tell them you saw me fall."

"What?" she said and backed away. "What do you mean, *fell*? You're scaring me. I don't understand."

"I know you don't." All that mattered was that *I* understood—understood that, as my father had done, I needed to be dead to the world. "Just tell them I fell into the lake. That's all you know. Promise me. Clay and I . . . " Out of a need to protect myself, and to shield Juliette from the truth, I lied to her. "We went out to the mansion together, to look into things. He came to my house. He apologized already. And he did something in the mansion. Something bad. It was an accident. He didn't mean it. He was defending me."

"What did he do?"

"It's better I don't say. The Vanders family, if they ever find out we know the truth. They'll do anything to protect their image." I paused to let her mind fill in the blanks with whatever terror she could imagine. "I *know* Clay was just helping you in his bedroom. When he came to my house to apologize, I told him I'd seen you two, and he explained what happened. Still, it made me *so* jealous, and I wasn't *sure* he was telling me the truth. But after hearing you tell me the exact same story . . . "

"You believe me?"

I nodded. She smiled with such relief, I knew she'd told me the truth. There had been nothing between her and Clay. And there was something between us.

"Tell them I fell," I said. "If you can't, then go home and forget you were ever at the mansion."

"I don't get this. What's happened? Where is Clay? Why are you acting like I'll never—"

"He's . . . waiting for me. Tell them."

"I don't—"

"I have to go. I have to meet him." With that, I left her there, running from her as fast as I could.

When I was out of Juliette's sight, I slunk through backyards and along shadowed hedgerows.

From my pocket, I took out the note from Clay and read it again.

I'm so fucking sorry I hit you, man. I really am. I really, really fucking am. I don't know why I do that shit. Actually, I do. I'm a bigger fuckup than you are. A bigger pussy. I should be telling you this face to face. Instead, I'm writing a note. That's what a pussy I am. I really pissed you off and I don't know if you'll ever talk to me again, but I am sorry. And I do believe you about your dad, man. I even went to the library to dig around and try to help you out, and I found this shit in the microfilm and printed it. I also tried to help you out with Juliette. Don't get crazy. I didn't do anything like that. And I'm sorry I teased you as if I would. She's a cool chick, though, and she really, really does dig you and I tried to give her some of the kinds of pointers that you wouldn't take from me. I hope she uses them on you in the cemetery. I hope you take this note and my help as a truce. I should probably tell you all this face to face, in person. You deserve it. But I'm afraid you won't accept it. Like I said. I'm a pussy. But if you do accept, I won't ever hit you again. Ever, man. Not fucking ever again. I promise.

Folded up in Clay's note was a photocopy of my birth announcement, from the microfilm archives of the *Shireburne Gazette*. Clay had underlined a specific part. I needed to see the original announcement on the microfilm at library, with my own eyes.

I made my way to the bushes across the street from my destination. The night was quiet, the street empty. I stared across the street at the library entrance, "Shireburne Free Library" carved into its stone arch. I stared at those three words for a long time. I thought I might be ill.

I dashed across the street to the lilac bushes in back and found a basement window. I didn't know whether the library had an alarm system, and I didn't care. I kicked in the window. No lights came on, and no alarm sounded.

I shimmied backward through the window and into the library basement. It was dark as the bottom of the ocean, but as my eyes slowly adjusted, I saw dim light above.

I went up the stairs. At the top I opened a door to an office. Light sifted through the window from the streetlamps outside. I opened the door on the other side of the office to find myself behind the circulation desk. In the distance, I heard the fire station's siren, howling like an injured wolf.

In the semidark, I found my way to the microfilm room.

I slid open a drawer and searched for the *Shireburne Gazette*. I found the reel I wanted and wound the film onto the machine. The bright white light that leaped from the blank screen startled me. I searched the film until I came to the issue from the day after my birth. I found my birth announcement: "Wayland Henry Maynard, 8 lb. 4 oz. boy, born to Roland Maynard and Laura Maynard (née Smith)."

I brought out Clay's photocopy. Compared it with the screen image. The section he'd underlined was "née Smith." My mother's maiden name.

I sat looking at her name on the screen, trying to make sense of what it meant in the context of my parents, of Silva's "accident," and me.

At the mansion, my mother had told me: *When Silva had seen Lydia's name, she knew we'd had another child, and it triggered her to contact your father.*

Silva had known that my father, the son she gave up as a baby, had moved back to Shireburne as a young husband, with my mother. But she hadn't known *who* he'd married, until she saw my mother's maiden name in my birth announcement. And she knew that name and knew what that name meant.

When I'd searched for my father's birth certificate at the town clerk, I had fleetingly seen my mother's name on a birth certificate. But I hadn't recognized it as hers. While her given name was Laura, since childhood she had always gone by El, her pet nickname. Her maiden name was so common, I'd made no connection to her when I'd skimmed it, obsessed as I was with finding my father's birth certificate.

I felt dazed and weak. My mother's birthday was the day before my father's, but he'd been born at 12:38 am. It was possible she was born only minutes before him, yet on a different day; possible for them to be who I now knew they were, what they were. Silva knew it, too. She knew the names of the adoptive parents she had given up both her two children to, even though one of the children, her daughter, had never known she was adopted.

I looked at my stump pinkies and thought about being born with my fingers fused together, why that might be.

I doubt that my mother even knew she was adopted, until Silva told my father, and he had to tell my mother what they really were to each other.

She made demands of your father and me. We caved at first. But we love each other. We refused to sign.

Annulment papers.

I recalled my mother telling me in the kitchen, days earlier, when I attacked her once again for throwing my father's belongings away: *He was more than just your father, you know. He was my husband. More than just my husband. He was . . .*

I walked out of the room, dazed.

In the dim, empty library, the normal noises seemed louder. In the basement below me, the furnace groaned, and all around me, concealed in the shadows, radiators ticked and pinged. Water burbled from the broken water fountain. A cricket chirped from some corner of the history stacks.

I had one last task to endure. One last book to check out.

At the card catalogue, I found the drawer I needed, and slid it out. I hoped I was wrong, hoped I would not find what I feared I would find.

I thumbed through the cards as fast as I could. My breath caught when I saw the one I had been afraid to see. I tore it from the drawer and headed for the fiction stacks, searching along the spines of books, following their labels.

There it was.

I grabbed the book, paralyzed by all the horrid truths that had descended on me.

It was a thin book, a novel of 217 pages. The author: S. K. Edwin.

I read the jacket copy. The novel was about a boy who fell down a well on the town green, and no matter how loudly he screamed for someone to come and get him out, no one came, even as he saw their shadows above him and they tossed their pennies down onto him. No one came.

I flipped from one page to the next, wetting my thumb to turn the pages at the upper corner, careful to check every single one. Each page was unmarred by pen or pencil. I didn't find so much as a smudge, let alone an underlined sentence or a note.

I flipped the last page to find the library circulation card tucked in its pocket.

I took the card out.

There it was: my father's name, in my father's hand. Roland Maynard.

It had been signed out a week before the Incident. No one had checked it out in the years since. Unlike those books that Quentin Fredericks had brought to the shop, it was a book that my father had never written in. It was the last book my father ever read for leisure.

I stared at the faded blue stamped image of the Shireburne Free Library.

I felt a desperate need to go home, to see Lydia. Yet I couldn't. I didn't know how to face her, what I could ever tell her. I wanted to see Molly too—hug her and tell her she would be all right without me. But I didn't dare go home. Lydia was better off never seeing me again, never having me further muddle her mind with half-truths and lies I would tell her to cover what I'd done and to protect her and ease her mind. She was better off inventing a scenario she could live with.

I wilted against the bookshelf and considered turning myself in to the police.

I looked at my father's name on the library circulation card again. His neat, hand-printed name. It matched the handwriting of the note that had led to this moment in a closed, dark town library while the mansion burned, and my parents burned with it. The note that had led me through a labyrinth of lies to finally reach the truth.

I sobbed, only beginning to comprehend what I'd done and what I had become in pursuit of a truth I no longer wanted to know. A truth crueler than any doubt I had ever suffered.

I tucked the book in my hip pocket.

Out on the dark street, I pushed along the sidewalk, head down and hood up, passing by the hardware store and the Grotto Arcade. I didn't know where I was going except away from town. As I rushed along the front of the Whipple Pharmacy, I bumped into someone, mumbled apologies. A weak voice cracked, "Wayland?"

Dr. Zantz. He stood there holding a red-and-white-striped prescription bag.

He looked deathly ill, his face pale as suet, eyes wet and pink. I tried not to meet his eyes, as if this would render me invisible, our exchange unmemorable.

"I want to apologize," he said. He hacked up phlegm and spat a quivering lump of it onto the sidewalk. "I've been trying to kick this bug. This is the first time I've even had the energy to get out of bed to get my prescription. I'd planned to drop off the note next." He took the note from the pocket of his trousers and glanced toward the police station.

Though I could ill afford a conversation, I couldn't help asking, "Why is your house empty?"

He eyed me with confusion.

"I stopped by to get my note back, and the place was empty."

"Oh. That's not my house." He coughed, his chest rattling like a dried gourd. "Well, it *is*, technically. You caught me on my last days using that office in the back. My new office will be on Elm Street, in my new home, a much smaller place to accommodate the stage of life in which I find myself. I had to empty the old house to have it ready to show."

"I don't want the cops to have the note. Everything's been . . . resolved."

He stared at me with his rheumy eyes, as if expecting an explanation. I didn't give one. "Are you certain?" he said.

I nodded.

He handed me the note. "Sorry for the trouble." He shambled away, coughing and hacking, raising my hopes that his illness might cloud his mind enough that he wouldn't remember the exact time he encountered me, if he remembered our exchange at all.

I took out my father's book from my back pocket and compared the handwriting on the circulation card to that on the note.

A perfect match.

The note had never been a message to me or to anyone else. It had never been a confession. It had never been a mystery to solve.

It was simply a jotted reminder from my father to himself, to sign out a book from the Shireburne Free Library. *SFL*.

I tore up the note and let the scraps of paper float away on a breeze as I stared at the book in my hand: *I Am Not Who You Think I Am*.

Then, with the scent of smoke on the air, and the April night sky glowing orange in the west, I ran.

AFTER

I didn't go far. I didn't have to. It didn't take much to disappear in those ancient days before cameras recorded every corner of our lives, and the unholy internet created the mythology that your business was every stranger's business, and every stranger's business was yours.

I found a job pumping gas for cash in a small New Hampshire town just ninety miles from home. I slept in a tent in the woods. I washed in the gas station restroom. I ate candy bars from vending machines and steamed hot dogs from the store next door. When I wasn't numbed by what I had done, I was plagued with regret and shame, my mind besieged by fractured images and thoughts.

As far as I knew, no one was looking for me. There was no way for me to keep up on the news about the fire, about my mother. The police must have identified her, but there was no way to know whether they had identified my father as the other male victim. There was no reason for them ever to suppose the man in that bed was my father. I doubted anyone held suspicions about me or Clay being involved, but wondered if Juliette had been compelled to tell my story about falling from the cliff.

I thought about Lydia, about calling her. Every day for the first few months, I took a pocketful of quarters to the pay phone outside the gas station and started to dial the number to our house, but I never finished. What would

I say? I didn't even know whether she was at the house any longer. At night I drifted into a sleep as thin and fragile as the first skim of autumn ice on a puddle and awoke to wonder what would become of my sister.

I thought about calling Juliette, too, but never dared.

My life became nomadic and insular as I drifted across the country. I never returned to high school. I never made another friend. Never married. Never had children. I never shared my life with anyone.

I became the unmemorable name-tagged stranger who rings you up at the video store, movie theater, or bowling alley.

I found myself in the Rockies and tried but failed to forget what I had done, to forgive myself or start anew amid the mountains' moody grandeur and the blue skies that, in a moment, could boil black with storm clouds and drive shadows across the land. I could neither forget nor forgive.

Each year when autumn bowed to winter, I migrated to the Southwest to avoid being buried in a dark grave of despair. Come spring, I meandered north again.

I grew older. Then old.

Now, I am the old man dozing in the library periodicals.

And now, I am dying.

I am the old man hunched at the computer station, his chair angled to block his internet browser from passersby in a furtive way that makes you wonder what he's up to.

Ten years ago, twenty-six years after I fled, in one quick search, I found this old article:

THE SHIREBURNE GAZETTE

INFERNO CLAIMS FOUR LIVES AS HISTORIC MANSION IS
GUTTED BY MYSTERIOUS FIRE

A raging fire lit the night sky for miles late last night and early into the morning as it claimed the lives of two members of one of Vermont's most prominent families, and left one of the most historic mansions in New England a shell of smoking stone ruins.

Siblings, Buell Vanders III, 55, and Silva Vanders, 53, perished in the fire whose origins remain unknown at the time of publication, though police are calling it a murder-suicide. It is believed that the sister, Silva Vanders, shot and killed her brother, then lit herself and her brother's body on fire. The motive is unclear, though there is speculation that the brother, perhaps with help from the longtime family attorney, Quentin Fredericks, who seems to have fled town, may have been keeping Silva in the mansion since 1968, when she suffered severe burns and injuries in a tragic and mysterious accident that now appears even more mysterious.

The remains of a third victim, since identified as Laura Maynard, were found on a marble staircase that had partially collapsed. What she was doing there is not known. Her son, Wayland, appears to be missing and is rumored to have fallen from a cliff into Forbidden Lake. A search for his body is ongoing. A friend of Wayland Maynard, one Clay Baxter, is also missing.

The remains of a fourth victim were found amid the melted and charred remnants of medical equipment. That victim has yet to be identified.

None of the follow-up stories ever identified my father. My body, of course, was never found. Neither was Clay's.

With another fingertip search online, I found information about my sister. At age twenty-three, she married an accountant. At age twenty-five she divorced him. She never remarried, but she did have a daughter. Laura. Lydia still lives in Shireburne, where, as some of you might know, she works as the high school guidance counselor.

I found Juliette online too. She married in 1989, to a man whose name I don't recognize. They've been together thirty-one years. They live in Pennsylvania. She works in sales for a national florist chain. He is a state college administrator. They have two daughters, twenty-eight and twenty-six years old—both girls at least a decade older than Juliette and I were that long-ago April. The older daughter has a two-year-old son. Juliette is a grandmother. In the pictures I've seen, she looks happy.

Both of Clay's parents are dead now, each passing within a year of each other in just these past two years without ever knowing what happened to their son.

I am a fifty-two-year-old man now, far older than either of my parents ever lived to be, nearly as old as Silva Vanders was the night the mansion burned.

I've written this over and over and over the past several years, in part to clear my conscience, I suppose, though I know now from the act of writing it that I have not succeeded in that measure in the least. With the passage of time and perspective, my regret and guilt only deepen, my sorrow and shame only sharpen.

But perhaps, you can at least exhume the boy who was once my friend and bury him in his own grave. And you can exhume my father's remains from whatever unmarked grave he was buried in following the fire and put him to rest in the plot where he belongs. Perhaps, there is no one even left who cares. If there is, you now know the full story and, in knowing, perhaps you can put it all behind you.

Or perhaps not.

POLICE DEPARTMENT
To Protect and To Serve

April 19, 2020

Dear Shireburne citizens:

I wish to update you with facts regarding the matter of Wayland Maynard, who sent the town the manuscript and notes.

We have since determined that the body of Clay Baxter was indeed found in a cemetery plot marked for Roland Maynard. He was the victim of homicide. No other remains were found in the grave. Based on the information provided in the manuscript, we exhumed the remains of the unidentified fourth victim claimed by the fire of April 1984. Using DNA evidence from his daughter, we have concluded that the remains are those of Roland Maynard. They have been interred in the grave site originally intended for him. Attorney Quentin Fredericks was located in a hospice ward in Bethel, Maryland; while infirm and aged, he managed to confess that he and Silva Vanders, parents of both Laura and Roland Maynard, had acted with Laura Maynard, to propagate the story of Roland Maynard's suicide and had subsequently kept him in their care at the Vanders mansion, located on the estate that went bankrupt and fell into decline in 1985. As most citizens know, the mansion was never rebuilt, and in subsequent years, the inn, carriage house, dairy barns, and all other structures fell into disrepair, and were finally razed in 2002, then sold off in subplots for Deer Run Shopping Plaza and the Box Store venture.

Using the postage meter stamp on the envelope in which the manuscript was sent to the town, we finally located Wayland Maynard in a cabin outside Santa Fe, New Mexico. We found him deceased from a self-inflicted gunshot wound. His sister wished that we keep this information private until she was able to transport her brother's remains back home, where he now rests after a private burial, between his mother and father.

If more information comes to light, we will share it with you as and if we can.

Serving you,

James Kirkpatrick

James Kirkpatrick
Chief of Police
Shireburne Police Department
Shireburne, Vermont

ACKNOWLEDGMENTS

Thanks to everyone who has encouraged my writing over the years, particularly my lovely and loving wife, Meridith, and my daughter, Samantha, and son, Ethan, for their smiles, hugs, and joy, and for their love of books and stories. Many friends, teachers, and extended family have supported me over many years; my thanks to all of you.

A very special thanks to everyone at Blackstone Publishing, especially to Josh Stanton, not only for believing in this book, but for having enough faith in my writing to take on the next three books. It is an immense relief and pleasure to know my books have a true home and the backing of a committed and gifted team. Thank you to Editorial Director Josie Woodbridge for leading the way and shepherding this book through the editing process.

There were so many details and challenges along the way that my savvy editor Michael Carr caught to help shape and improve this book in ways I never could alone. We went back and forth many times, honing it down to get it right. He approached it with the utmost professionalism, knowledge, and good humor. It was a lot of work but a lot of fun too. I hope to do it again.

Many thanks to Ciera Cox and Courtney Vatis, who fine-tuned the book with a keen eye that proved irreplaceable.

Special thanks must go to Ryan C. Coleman at the Story Factory, who worked with me for countless hours on the phone and by email, often late on weeknights or over the weekend. Your direction and support are invaluable.

Of course, none of this would be possible without my agent Shane Salerno and the Story Factory. They are, simply, the best. Shane believed in me from the very first email I sent him when I was seeking a new direction for my work and my career. He fought for me and for this book, and for my future as an author. We spoke dozens of times along the way and left messages back and forth, often when it was as early as 4:00 a.m. in Los Angeles. The Story Factory put immense time and energy and dedication into championing my work, finding the perfect publisher, and putting up with my addled brain, of which very little is left after long days of writing and longer, though joyful, nights spent corralling two young kids. A sincere thank-you to Shane for all you've accomplished for me and for my family, and all the frustration you've endured along the way.